FRAMED AND FROSTED

Cupcake Catering Mystery Series Book 3

KIM DAVIS

Cinnamon & Sugar Press

Framed And Frosted

Kim Davis

Chapter 1

A gun-toting ex-NFL lineman lookalike wasn't who I'd expected to greet me when I'd agreed to deliver the catering tasting menu on behalf of my sister. I definitely wasn't on board with it. I inched backward.

"Whad'ya want?" His deep voice sounded menacing, and his non-welcoming manner ruled out his job being the butler. Perhaps he was a bodyguard. Or had I stumbled into a crime in progress?

"Is this the Jorgensens' residence?" My voice squeaked, and my arms, cradling the heavy ice chest that contained the food, quivered. I inched backward another step, prepared to drop everything and sprint for the safety of the catering van. I would give my sister a piece of my mind for not warning me about this guy if I got out of this place alive. If the job hadn't been so important to her, I'd have turned around and driven off just as fast as the van could take me.

"Tiny? Is that the caterer?" A sharp, high-pitched voice belonging to a woman filled the air as it crackled from the intercom speaker. "It's about time."

Tiny? I must've mouthed his name because a flicker of a smile appeared on his lips.

"I was a preemie, and the nickname stuck." The giant's voice didn't sound quite so menacing, but I couldn't help but notice that he kept his hand resting on the gun after he'd returned it to his holster.

He opened the door of the colossal three-story Spanish-style house just wide enough for me to step in. "Mr. and Mrs. Jorgensen are waiting for you on the patio."

I stepped inside and tried not to gape at the ornate interior of the house. A triple-story octagon entryway greeted me. Fifty people could've comfortably gathered in the space, which was empty, aside from a wrought-iron table, graced with a floral arrangement almost as tall as my five-two stature. A fili-gree wrought-iron chandelier cascaded halfway down the open space from the round skylight flooding in light overhead. On the second and third floors of the house, arched openings with wrought-iron railings dotted the interior octagon walls to overlook the entryway. The walls of the octagon appeared to be marble with inlays of mosaic tiles. A wrought-iron staircase curved directly across from the doorway I'd just entered. When the front door shut with a loud bang, I jumped.

"If you'll follow me, I'll take you to the patio." He jerked his shiny bald pate toward the back of the house.

"Perhaps I can put the food in the kitchen first?" I bobbed my head toward the ice chest I held. It was getting heavier by the minute.

"They want to see you immediately." He turned and strode at a brisk pace.

I tried to calm my racing heart as I followed the large man down the corridor lined with objets d'art and fresh floral arrangements that were works of art themselves. The corridor led into a great room dotted with inviting groups of sofas and cozy seats. A large stacked stone fireplace was featured at one end of the room, but that wasn't what grabbed my attention. Instead, I could barely pull my gaze away from the wall of glass doors that looked out onto an expansive patio, and beyond that, the sparkling blue expanse of the Pacific Ocean. Located on a premium lot in the prestigious Sapphire Bay gated community in Laguna Beach, the house sat on the edge of a cliff overlooking the water.

The doors were open, and I could feel a refreshing breeze blow through the room. It felt heavenly on my flushed skin after sitting in my sister's un-air-conditioned van, stuck in traffic, the day before the Jorgensens' *Dîner en Blanc*-themed Fourth of July party. Presenting a tasting menu one day before the party—that Mrs. Jorgensen had approved more than two weeks ago—because Mr. Jorgensen had demanded it added to my ire. My sister had already purchased all the ingredients and started preparations for the event. To say that this had been a nightmare event from the very first was an understatement. But my sister was in desperate need of both the money and potential catering contacts this job offered.

Beyond the doors, the patio gave the illusion of extending into space. Several delivery men in khaki uniforms arranged banquet tables and chairs, along with several patio heating towers. Even if the days were hot, evenings could turn chilly, thanks to the sea breezes and occasional fog that rolled in. I followed Tiny to the left side and around the corner of the house, where a small outdoor living space had been built. A snow-white tablecloth dressed the table. Fine china, crystal, and silver sat in a formally arranged array. Flutes, filled to the rim with bubbly champagne, sat in front of the Jorgensens, while a water-beaded silver bucket sat to the side, holding an upside-down empty bottle of champagne.

From the furrows above Mr. Jorgensen's shaggy gray brows, I surmised he wasn't happy about my tardiness. His cheeks were ruddy, and I couldn't tell whether the heat or drinking too much champagne on an empty stomach had caused it. Mrs. Jorgensen—only my sister was allowed to call her Lisette—had a smooth face that belied her mature years. I assumed Botox, or the miracle services of the best cosmetic surgeon in Orange County, kept her frown at bay.

"I apologize for being late." I longed to relieve my arms from the weight of the food. My limbs were quivering again. "An issue at the front gate delayed me."

"This is highly unprofessional. I'll be speaking with your employer about this." Mrs. Jorgensen sniffed. "She should have taken care of this herself."

Not sure how to tactfully explain that having a private menu tasting the day before your caterer was serving you and your thirty guests an elaborate dinner—on a holiday, no less— wasn't doable, I decided to bite my tongue and remain quiet. Besides, didn't she know that Carrie was my sister and I was the cupcake caterer? While we were almost identical twins, Carrie's gorgeous red hair leaned more toward auburn, while my shade of red was better suited on a clown. Her hair was always sleek, whereas mine was frizzy. Again, kind of like a clown's. Her eyes were deep green, and mine had muddy-brown flecks mixed with green. Despite her having recently given birth, she retained a girlish figure, whereas mine reflected my love for buttercream. And most of all, she didn't have a generous sprinkle of freckles dotting her peaches-and-cream skin.

The silence lingered in the air for a long moment while the couple looked me up and down with their matching arctic-blue eyes, which were obviously colored contacts. My chubby, overheated appearance surely didn't meet their perfectly coiffed and groomed standards.

Mrs. Jorgensen shook her head slightly then huffed. "Well, aren't you here to serve us lunch? Why are you just standing there?"

"I haven't been shown where the kitchen is."

"Tiny!" Mr. Jorgensen's voice boomed. "Show her to the kitchen."

The ice chest almost fell from my arms when Tiny tapped me on my shoulder, and I jumped. The way Mr. Jorgensen had yelled, I was certain the large man had been all the way at the front door. Instead, it appeared he had been right around the corner. "Uh, thank you. It shouldn't take me more than a few minutes for me to bring the hors d'oeuvres out."

Tiny must've noticed my quivering arms from the weight of the food because he plucked the ice chest from my hands and motioned for me to follow him. As he led me to the kitchen, I couldn't help but gawk at the stunning, unobstructed view of the sea from every room we passed through. In the distance, several sailboats tacked in the breeze, and I wondered if they were heading to Catalina Island, situated less than thirty miles off the coast. My mom and stepdad had taken us there for a Fourth of July celebration when we were in our teens, and the spectacular fireworks display wasn't one I'd ever forget.

Tiny led me into an industrial-sized kitchen that featured white marble counters, white cabinets, and stainless-steel appliances. He set the ice chest on the counter. "I'll be nearby if you need any assistance carrying out dishes."

I wondered if he had orders to keep a close eye on me to make sure I didn't pilfer any of the silver. "Thank you. I appreciate the help." I had to return to the van to retrieve food from the warming drawers, and I'd grab the serving tray then. I didn't need a gun-toting giant that close to me during meal service.

I quickly unpacked the chilled items and placed dainty wedges of Brie, aged white cheddar, Asiago, and Swiss cheeses on a white china plate that had been left on the counter for my use. I added spears of asparagus, slices of radishes, and petite florets of cauliflower to the plates along with a few water crackers for the hors d'oeuvres.

On a new plate, I carefully arranged two skewers of fresh buffalo mozzarella interspersed with ripe cherry tomatoes and fragrant basil leaves. A quick drizzle of olive oil, aged balsamic vinegar, and fresh cracked black pepper completed the presentation. I plated the last appetizer, consisting of shot glasses of herbed artichoke white bean dip with spears of red bell pepper strips, orange carrot sticks, and crispy pita chips. Mrs. Jorgensen had wanted the food to be completely *blanc*, but my sister had finally convinced her it would be more appetizing to have some colorful garnishes. At the actual party, this ensemble would be on a buffet table for guests to help themselves during the pre-dinner cocktail hour.

I juggled the three plates of hors d'oeuvres and managed to put them in front of the Jorgensens without dropping anything. I explained each item served then stepped to the side to wait for any questions or comments they might have. I noticed they had opened a new bottle of champagne.

Instead of sampling any of the food I had placed in front of him, Mr. Jorgensen waved his hand over the table. "What kind of crap is this? Why is everything white?"

My mouth fell open, and I waited for Mrs. Jorgensen to explain the *Dîner en Blanc* party concept to him. Instead, she lifted her champagne flute and took a sip.

His cheeks turned even redder, and a slight slur tinged his booming voice. "Answer me, young lady. What kind of crackpot caterer are you?"

Somehow, I managed to convince Mr. Jorgensen that the party theme was acceptable and we could proceed as planned. I ended up showing him—on my cell phone—that *Dîner en Blanc* had originated in Paris in the 1980s. While his party didn't stay true to the theme because the original used a secret location and guests brought their own food and wine, his would be a sophisticated and well-praised affair. Not once did Mrs. Jorgensen come to my rescue and defend the menu choices that she had signed off on. In fact, she seemed to be purposely directing his wrath at me. I hoped that Carrie never,

ever accepted another contract from this couple, but I'd wait until the Fourth of July event ended to tell her the angst I'd endured.

Chapter 2

As Carrie, her new employee, Salvador Cruz—or Sal, as he preferred to be called—and I hustled to set up the hors d'oeuvres buffet table and organize the food that would need to be plated, I surreptitiously watched Mr. Jorgensen. He'd made an early appearance to the patio, dressed in a white linen suit, and had beelined for the bartender. After a heated exchange, our client disappeared for a few minutes then reappeared carrying a bottle of amber liquor in one hand and a crystal glass filled with the same in his other. He shoved the bottle at the reluctant bartender then shook his finger in the employee's face.

"What was that all about?" Sal asked, keeping his voice low. "The *jefe* seems like kinda a jerk."

"You have no idea." I smoothed my hair away from my face and turned toward the young man. "My guess is Mrs. Jorgensen has only stocked the bar with white refreshments, which isn't to her husband's liking."

He shook his head, which sent his long black braid swaying across his shoulders. "This is kinda a *loco* theme anyway, if you ask me."

"Agreed, but it's a job that's paying well at least." I

studied the twenty-two-year-old as he bent back over the buffet table and deftly arranged flatware and napkins with nimble brown fingers. My sister had hired Sal shortly after the premature birth of her son at the recommendation of her friend, a local community college culinary instructor. I'd stepped in to help Sal with Carrie's existing catering contracts while she poured her attention onto her son, who'd spent the first six weeks of his life in the hospital, and her twin six-year-old daughters. Despite Sal's and my best efforts, several lucrative clients had still taken their business elsewhere. As a result, Carrie was in the process of rebuilding her company, which necessitated putting up with people like the Jorgensens.

According to the instructor, Sal had been shuffled back and forth between his large extended family after the death of his mother when he was a young boy. With a scholarship from a mentor he'd connected with in the Boys and Girls Club of America, he'd followed his passion of cooking by attending the culinary program but needed some hands-on experience. Carrie had been all too happy to hire him, and I was relieved to share some of the responsibilities I'd taken on to help her business out.

Between my cupcake catering business and Carrie's contracts, I hadn't had a chance to spend enough time with my boyfriend, Randall. Plus, his expanding security firm kept him traveling more than I liked. Maybe after the busy summer season, things would slow down and we could take a vacation together and reconnect.

Carrie handed me a stack of hors d'oeuvres plates. "Can you arrange these while I bring out more?"

Nodding, I set the plates on the table then winced. They were Bernardaud Louvre china with a distinctive leafy vine pattern circling the edges. I'd assumed rental ceramic dishes would be used, but no, only the best for the Jorgensens and friends would do. I cautiously moved the plates away from the edge of the table, since I couldn't afford to break even one of the plates.

I'd gone back to the kitchen to collect platters of cheese for the buffet table when Mr. Jorgensen bellowed in anger, "Just who do you think you are barging into my home?"

"I'm with Pacific Palates Catering." Sal's soft voice sounded calm. "I work for Mrs. Berger."

Carrie and I looked at each other, dropped the platters we held in our hands, and scrambled as we ran for the patio. When we reached the wide-open doors, we stopped in horror, trying to take in the scene in front of us.

"We don't want people like you here. Get out!" Mr. Jorgensen towered over the slight young man. He grabbed Sal by the collar of his white button-down shirt and pulled him toward the door. "Tiny, remove this intruder at once!"

Carrie moved first. "Wait! Salvador works for me."

Mr. Jorgensen turned his bloodshot gaze toward her. "I don't want him here. You can do without him today."

My sister placed her hands on her hips and stood straighter. "We're bonded and insured, so I don't see what the issue is."

"I said I don't want his kind here." The large man jabbed a finger toward Sal. "Tiny, get him out of here."

Tiny materialized from the shadows inside the house and out onto the patio, illuminated by the early-evening sun and bright globe lights crisscrossing the outdoor area. I glanced at Sal. His chocolate-brown eyes shimmered, and he held his lips so tightly together, nothing but a grim line could be seen. His hands, clenched tightly into fists, had almost turned white, but I could see his arms were trembling. Could it be anger, or was it fear?

"If you kick Sal out, then my entire team is leaving." Carrie stepped over to Sal and placed her hand on his shoulder then turned toward Tiny. "Don't you dare place a hand on him."

"I'll sue you." Mr. Jorgensen's face turned even redder. He looked like a prime candidate for a stroke or heart attack. "You'll never get another job in this town again."

"What is going on, Arthur?" Mrs. Jorgensen's voice was icy as she glared at her husband. "Tiny, how much has he had to drink today?"

Tiny shrugged, which made Mrs. Jorgensen huff. "Take him to the kitchen and get him some coffee. And for God's sake, keep him away from the Scotch."

"This is my house, and you won't be telling me what I can and can't do!" His shouting made me cringe, but it didn't seem to bother his wife.

"We have guests coming in twenty minutes, dear. Can you please have some coffee with Tiny and let me take care of the catering problem?"

Carrie and I exchanged a look. Catering problem? That was what she thought this situation was?

After what seemed a long time, Mr. Jorgensen threw his hands up in the air. "Fine. Have it your way, but don't ever use this company again."

Once the two men had left the patio, Mrs. Jorgensen circled her hand as if motioning us to get busy. "Carry on. Guests will be here shortly, and I want everything ready."

Without another word, she marched over to the bartender and snatched the bottle of Scotch from the counter. Since it was impossible to avoid hearing her berate the man for getting her husband drunk, we pretended not to listen.

"This is freaking unbelievable." Carrie's hand still rested on the young man's shoulder. "I am so sorry that happened to you, Sal. If you want to leave, I'll pay your full wage for the job."

"It's not your fault he's an *idiota*. I'll stay out of his way for the rest of the evening." Sal shrugged off Carrie's hand. "Karma has a way of catching up to people like that."

Chapter 3

By the time the white-garbed guests had arrived, with all the women wearing white fascinators, I'd seen Mr. Jorgensen sneak back to the bartender for another full glass of clear liquid on the rocks. It sure wasn't water, and Tiny hadn't kept his employer away from the bar, despite Mrs. Jorgensen's directives. In fact, I hadn't seen Tiny since he'd supposedly taken Mr. Jorgensen to get coffee from the kitchen.

The patio looked like a fairy-tale setting with the sun kissing the horizon and the sky a brilliant shade of red fading to pink, orange, and purple. Besides the overhead globe lights, white fairy lights, which had been wrapped around the wrought-iron fence separating the patio from the sheer drop to the beach below, twinkled on. The long table, where all thirty-two guests would dine al fresco, was covered with a crisp white tablecloth. Gleaming silver vases holding arrangements of white roses with accents of baby's breath glowed from the multitudes of candles that dotted the table. Classical music poured from hidden speakers, but from experience, I knew it would soon be impossible to hear over the chatter of the guests.

With cocktails and hors d'oeuvres consumed, everyone

took a seat, and Mrs. Jorgensen motioned for dinner service to start. Since Carrie had decided to keep Sal in the kitchen plating instead of serving and as far away from Mr. Jorgensen as possible, the two of us ran ragged. With seven courses to serve to thirty-two guests, there wasn't a moment to take a breath. When a guest waylaid me to ask for the recipe for the whipped goat cheese served with cranberry stars that we had just begun serving for the amuse-bouche course, Mrs. Jorgensen waved Carrie over.

In a loud whisper that only the far end of the long table could fail to hear, she said, "Get that other server out here. I expect everyone's food to be served immediately, or I'll reduce your pay."

Carrie's face and neck flushed as she placed the plate she held in front of Mr. Jorgensen. "Yes, Lisette."

"When's the real food coming out?" He pushed the goat cheese dish away from him and snatched up the bottle of Grgich Hills Fumé Blanc sitting on the table. A brief tug-of-war between Mr. and Mrs. Jorgensen over the bottle occurred, but in the end, he triumphed and filled his wine goblet to the brim.

I deposited my plates in front of guests and ran back to the kitchen, Carrie close on my heels. "We need your help in serving food."

He raised an eyebrow. "Now or for the main courses?"

"Mrs. Jorgensen says now."

Sal quickly removed his apron and rolled down his sleeves to cover the colorful tattoos sprinkling his forearms. He grabbed the large round tray and began loading plates onto it. With the heavy tray fully loaded, Sal easily hefted it while Carrie and I followed carrying small trays holding plates of amuse-bouche.

Once guests were eating, the three of us rushed back to the kitchen and started plating the soup course of white gazpacho with crusty slices of baguettes served with sweet creamy butter. I took a tray out and started clearing empty plates. Mr. Jorgensen hadn't touched his goat cheese bite and instead had poured himself another glass of wine.

He grabbed my wrist as I reached over to remove his plate. "Girl, where's dinner? I want some real food."

With the way he was slurring his words, I thought I'd better have Carrie prepare a plate of the garlic rosemary roasted pork tenderloin with the salads served alongside and skip the soup. "I'll bring something to you right away, Mr. Jorgensen."

He pinched my bottom then wrapped an arm around my waist and tried to pull me down into his lap. My cheeks flamed when a couple of men sitting close by chuckled. I wanted to throw the expensive china down and quit on the spot. Unfortunately, I knew how much my sister counted on the job, so I slapped his hand and pulled away. As I ran from the table toward the kitchen, I heard Mrs. Jorgensen chide her husband, but in his inebriated state, it wouldn't deter him from harassing me again.

"What's wrong now?" Carrie eyed my hot face.

"Mr. Jorgensen is so drunk he just manhandled me." I practically dropped the plates into the sink, not caring if they chipped or cracked.

Carrie whipped her apron off and stormed toward the door.

"Where are you going?" I grabbed her arm.

"We're quitting. They can withhold payment, and they can sue me, but I will not let you and Sal be harassed by that man anymore."

"It's okay. We can't let you take a hit like that," Sal said then looked at me to confirm my agreement.

"Sal's right. We'll get through it, and we'll stay out of his reach." I planned to hand his plate to Mrs. Jorgensen, and she could put it in front of him. My sister had enough financial hardship without not getting paid for this event.

14

"Emory, you can take over in the kitchen, and I'll serve."

"Oh no, I'm not going to do that. You and Sal are much better at making sure everything is perfectly presentable than I am." I'd catered enough with my sister that I could do it, but I much preferred casual, laid-back events in which a splash of sauce where it didn't belong wasn't an emergency. "I can handle the drunk now that we know what to expect."

"I'm not paying you to stand around talking all night. My guests are hungry." Mrs. Jorgensen glared at us. "And bring my husband a plate of pork with the pasta salad and bread. He needs something to eat."

Carrie inhaled a large breath as if she was preparing to go on a rant. I couldn't let her jeopardize her payment. "Yes, Mrs. Jorgensen. We're right behind you with the gazpacho."

I picked up a tray of the double shot glasses of soup with the plates of baguettes and headed for the patio. Before I reached the door, I overheard Carrie instruct Sal to plate the main course for Mr. Jorgensen and bring it to me. Sal muttered beneath his breath in Spanish and slammed his palm into the countertop.

Somehow, we made it through the salad course of jicama and apple salad served with a citrus-ginger dressing with no mishaps. Mr. Jorgensen ate the pork along with the hearty orzo salad with roasted red pepper, feta cheese, and Kalamata olives in silence. Perhaps the event would turn out all right. The guests seemed to be enjoying the food, although the majority of thin, overly Botoxed women only ate a smidgen of the portions served. However, they managed to consume and refill their wine goblets with every new wine presented by the bartender with each course we brought out. Polite chitchat prattled around the table, and every so often an overly loud chuckle would burst from an overserved guest.

As Sal and I brought out the swordfish with lemon wine sauce and roasted cherry tomatoes, a guest sitting at the farthest corner away from Mr. Jorgensen tapped my arm then motioned me over. He pointed at Sal. "Go serve our host and hostess. This young lady doesn't need to be subjected to him."

"No! I'm fine." Too late. Sal had already headed directly toward the Jorgensens.

"Psst." I tried to get Sal to stop so I could deliver their course. But he forged on ahead, ignoring me.

I carefully set down the small plate of tender, succulent fish in front of the guest who had detained me. "You didn't need to do that."

"My conscience wouldn't be clear if I didn't say something about how you were treated. Besides, there's no reason why that young man can't serve our hosts." The guest appeared to be in his mid-forties and had a smattering of gray in his thin, auburn hair. His amber eyes scarcely had any lashes, and his cheekbones were sunken in. The white of his button-down shirt made his skin look sallow and washed out, and I wondered if he'd been ill. He refilled his wine goblet with water and appeared to be the only sober one at the table.

I started setting a plate down at the empty place setting next to the man while keeping an eye on Sal. Again, the guest briefly touched my arm. "That space is empty. My aunt planned on attending, but she cancelled and guilt-tripped me into coming anyway."

"I'm sorry. I hope she's okay." My mind barely focused on the conversation as I watched Sal.

"Between you and me, she's fine." His low chuckle was the first real laugh I'd heard from anyone all evening. I tore my gaze from Sal to look into the man's amber eyes. "This isn't her scene, but our hostess wouldn't let her decline, so she came down with a sudden migraine this afternoon and sent me with her regrets."

I smiled then returned my gaze back to Sal. He'd reached Mrs. Jorgensen's side and carefully placed the warm plate in front of her. For a beat, Mr. Jorgensen ignored Sal, but just as the server released his hand from the plate, her husband wrenched Sal's arm and twisted it away from the table.

"I told you to get off my property." His voice slurred and sounded overly loud. All conversation came to a halt, and the only thing that could be heard was scratchy violin music coming from hidden speakers. "I know you murdered my son, and now I'm gonna make you pay for it."

Chapter 4

S al pulled away from the angry man. "I don't know what you're talking about. I never killed no one."

"That's what all you punks say. You pushed your filthy drugs, and he died. Now you deserve to die." Mr. Jorgensen stood, and his chair toppled over.

"I don't know what you're talking about." Sal backed up several steps as the larger man advanced toward him. "I don't even know who your son is."

"Tiny!" Mrs. Jorgensen's shrill voice cut through the silence. When he didn't show up, she muttered, "Where is that man? He's got a lot to answer for in letting this situation get out of control."

Sal kept his gaze on Mr. Jorgensen and continued to back away from the table. The guests were riveted to the drama going on, and not one peep could be heard.

A sigh of relief escaped from Mrs. Jorgensen's lips when Tiny stepped out onto the patio. "See that Arthur is taken care of. He's overly tired."

So that was what she called his drunken tirade. The entire table watched, seemingly mesmerized, as Tiny quietly led him away. I wondered why he turned so docile when, just moments before, it looked like he could have murdered Sal.

I motioned for Sal to return to the kitchen and gave his arm a quick squeeze when he passed by me.

"Oh dear. I had no idea I would create such a scene by switching servers." The auburn-haired man looked distraught, and he dabbed at his mouth with trembling hands.

"It's not your fault. You had no way of knowing there had been an issue."

He mopped his brow with the snowy-white napkin. "I apologize. I shouldn't have opened my big mouth. My aunt says my good intentions always get me in trouble."

I squeezed his shoulder then dropped my arm. "Truly, there's only one person here to blame, and it's not you."

Mrs. Jorgensen clinked her long, lacquered nails against her crystal goblet. "I hope you're all enjoying our delightful meal. I apologize for my husband. He hasn't been feeling well, and I'm afraid the wine didn't mix well with his medications."

The understatement of the year. Although he'd been pretty nasty even before he'd imbibed huge quantities of alcohol.

"Miss!" My attention snapped back to the hostess. "Can we have the fish served before it gets cold?"

"Yes, Mrs. Jorgensen."

By the time the guests had consumed their dinner and cleansed their palates with lemon sorbet, my feet were killing me. The auburn-haired gentleman had complimented me several times on the food we'd served and asked that I pass his praise on to my sister. His enthusiastic regard for both my safety and our food had started making me feel a little uncomfortable, although I couldn't pinpoint why.

Mrs. Jorgensen decided to wait until the fireworks on the beach started before we hand-passed lemon drop martini cupcakes and champagne cupcakes with flutes of Cristal champagne. With thirty minutes to clear the table and prepare trays of cupcakes to serve, I barely had time to gulp a glass of water and use the facilities.

"I'll be asking Mrs. Jorgensen for hazard pay, and I'll be splitting the tip money between you both." Carrie brushed her hair away from her face. If I hadn't been so tired, I might have enjoyed seeing her frazzled for once. "Neither of you deserve the treatment you've received. If you want to leave now, I fully understand and support your decision. They can pick up their own dang cupcakes from the trays for all I care."

"It's okay. We're almost done." Given the sense of entitlement that surrounded the Jorgensens, I didn't want to give them any reason to withhold even a penny from my sister. "Sal, you can leave if you want. I think Carrie and I can handle it from here."

"Naw. It's fine. I can stay." He rolled his shoulders and cracked his neck. "This is the craziest job I've ever done. My teacher will never believe something like this happened to me."

"You'll do no such thing, young man." Mrs. Jorgensen marched into the kitchen. "Before you leave tonight, you'll each sign a confidentiality waiver. In exchange, there will be a five-hundred-dollar bonus for each of you."

My eyes practically popped out. So this was how they contained any hint of Mr. Jorgensen's extremely erratic and depraved behavior. I wondered what she had to do to guarantee that their guests wouldn't talk.

When no one said a word, Mrs. Jorgensen turned red. "If you don't sign the agreement, you can kiss the entire catering fee goodbye, and you'll be served with a lawsuit. Do I make myself clear?"

"Yes, Mrs. Jorgensen," we said in unison. We waited until she walked out of earshot then clustered close together.

"I'm so sorry I got you in this mess. I should have known there was a reason she'd been willing to pay such a high premium for us to cater at such short notice." Carrie gave us each a hug. "There ought to be a website for companies to leave ratings on customers. Kind of a reverse Yelp."

"No *problemo*, Carrie. I really need the money." Sal rubbed the back of his neck. "My clunker needs new brakes."

"And you know I need the money too." My snake of an ex had left me deeply in debt. I put every extra penny I could make toward paying off the credit cards he had taken out in my name and paying off the money he'd borrowed from my mother and stepdad without my knowledge.

She nodded. "Okay, then. Let's get ready to serve cupcakes."

By the time patriotic music filled the air, we were staged with our trays of cupcakes. Despite the *Dîner en Blanc* theme, Mrs. Jorgensen had decided we could embrace the Fourth of July theme with red, white, and blue cupcake wrappers. The champagne cupcakes were topped with small, juicy strawberries while the lemon drop cupcakes were garnished with fresh blueberries.

The bartender had passed out the flutes of Cristal champagne, and from the looks of things, several guests had already drained their glasses and were going back for more. When the first whistle of fireworks shot into the air, the overhead lights turned off so that the only illumination to the patio came from the sky. Carrying a tray of buttercream-topped cupcakes in a crowd of people drinking and not paying attention to their surroundings seemed like a disaster in the making.

Mrs. Jorgensen stabbed her forefinger at us as a way of indicating she wanted us in the throng of people, passing out the dessert. I tried to weave amongst the clusters of guests, all who had their heads tilted back to the sky.

"Excuse me, would you care for a cupcake? I have champagne-flavored ones or lemon drop martini cupcakes."

None of the women accepted, but most of the men plucked one or even two from my tray. I came across the auburn-haired man, who bent his head low to say something.

His words were drowned out by the explosion of bursting fireworks overhead. I had no idea that a display of this magnitude would happen so close to the houses. It felt like bombs were going off, and I wanted to cover my ears.

When a lull in the explosions occurred, he practically yelled in my ear. "You'd better take care of your friend. Arthur is headed his way."

Being short, I had to stand on my tippy-toes to try to see where Sal stood. With the women all wearing stiletto high heels and the men all taller than the women, I couldn't see. The man who had warned me grabbed the tray from my hands and pointed me toward the fence that guarded the cliff drop-off. As I pushed myself through the clusters of guests, I finally glimpsed the back of Sal's head. He held the tray balanced on the palm of one hand, shoulder high, his head raised to the sky, watching the dazzling display of lights. Mr. Jorgensen lurched straight for him.

I yelled Sal's name, but my voice got drowned out in another string of explosions. Colorful bursts appeared overhead then disappeared into a smoky haze. More high-pitched whistling sounds came from the beach below, and then a shower of glittering drops fell from the sky. Booms immediately followed that shook the patio right before they melted away. I tried to reach Sal, but he was still too far away to hear me.

With Mr. Jorgensen's height and bulk, he cleared a path to the cupcake server with no hindrance. I frantically looked around for his wife or Tiny to see if they could control what I feared would happen. They were nowhere to be found. As if in slow motion, I watched Mr. Jorgensen snatch the cupcake tray from Sal's hand. The server turned to face the house to see what had happened to the cupcakes. He came face-to-face with a scowling, red-faced Mr. Jorgensen. The drunk host examined the cupcakes and carefully chose one then tilted the tray and smashed the cupcakes into Sal's face.

The force of the blow pushed him into the fence, and for one terrifying moment, I feared that the buttercream-frosted Sal would topple over backward and fall to his death. I screamed and pushed through a group of people who were still watching the overhead display of spiraling rainbow-colored lights. As Sal fought to regain his balance, Mr. Jorgensen calmly took a bite of the cupcake then turned away and walked toward the bar.

I managed to reach Sal, who bent over trying to wipe buttercream from his face. I rested my hand on his back and patted as I leaned down to yell in his ear in order to be heard. "Are you okay? Aside from almost falling, are you hurt?"

He shook his head then straightened. A few people finally noticed the frosted server. When they laughed, Sal's fists clenched, and he brushed my hand off when I grabbed his arm. He stomped toward the bar where Mr. Jorgensen stood laughing with the bartender. Nothing I could do would stop the confrontation, but I had to try.

"Sal! Stop! He's not worth it." As I ran after him, my voice disappeared into another cacophony of explosions. And then to my utter horror, Mr. Jorgensen teetered then fell, face-first, landing at the white-sneakered feet of Sal.

"You murderer. You killed him." Mrs. Jorgensen's shrill voice rang out loud and clear in the calm, quiet air, right before another round of detonations started.

Chapter 5

T he police led Sal away in handcuffs. There wasn't any proof that he had killed Mr. Jorgensen, but in this neighborhood, an accusation against someone like Sal would be enough for an arrest to be made. One of the guests, a doctor, had proclaimed that his host appeared to have been poisoned, probably from the cupcake he'd eaten. I thought all the alcohol he'd consumed, along with whatever medications he'd been on, had probably contributed to his death. I questioned the doctor's own sobriety in making his pronouncement without any tests administered.

The remaining cupcakes were confiscated by the crime scene investigating team while Carrie and I sat in the kitchen waiting to be interrogated. It seemed ridiculous that we were being treated like criminals when there was a very good chance that Mr. Jorgensen had died of natural causes. Well, as natural a cause as mixing alcohol and drugs that shouldn't have been combined. I couldn't stop yawning, so I poured a cup of coffee for myself and offered a cup to my sister.

"No thanks. I'm still drinking decaf." She yawned and stretched her arms over her head. "Tommy's still not sleeping through the night, and I'm afraid caffeine would disrupt what little sleep I can get."

"I hope Thomas will get up with him and let you sleep tonight." My brother-in-law proved himself to be a good husband and father, but sometimes I wondered why he got to sleep throughout the night and my sister had to get up with the baby.

"I forewarned him, so he's planning on sleeping on the trundle bed in the nursery." She rolled down the sleeves of her white blouse as a breeze blew in through the opened window. "I know he's had a long day taking care of the kids, but I'm ready to crash."

"I thought they were spending the afternoon and evening with Mother and Lars?" Lars, our stepdad, had taken us in and treated us like his own daughters ever since we were twelve.

"They did, but it's still a lot of work keeping the girls entertained. You know how they are."

I did know how my six-year-old twin nieces were. While they adored their baby brother, they'd gotten a little wild ever since his arrival. I suspected Kaylee and Sophie felt like they were being neglected whenever baby Tommy got the spotlight, so they upped their hijinks whenever possible.

Carrie looked at her watch again, sighed, and closed her eyes.

"Excuse me, I don't mean to barge in." The auburn-haired man stood in the doorway. "I wanted to see if you needed an attorney for your employee?"

I looked at Carrie then back at him. "I don't think we do, Mister..."

"Oh, I'm sorry. I didn't introduce myself at dinner." He pulled his wallet from the back pocket of his white slacks and extracted a business card. He held it out for me to take. "I'm William Trenton, but my friends call me Will. I'm a defense attorney, practicing in San Diego."

"Nice to meet you, Will." I stood and shook his hand then retrieved the card he held out. "I'm Emory, and that's my sister, Carrie."

Carrie gave a half wave but didn't get up. Sheer exhaustion lined her face, and she leaned her head back against the wall.

"Does your friend need legal assistance? I feel like it was my fault putting him in the path of Arthur. I'd like to help if I can."

"We're not sure what's happening." I shrugged and lifted my palms up. "My guess is Mr. Jorgensen over-imbibed and, with whatever medication he took, had a reaction. I know Sal will be grateful to know there's someone he can talk to if he's charged. Can I call you once we find out anything?"

"Absolutely. I'll touch base with the detective and let her know that I'll be talking to Sal as soon as charges are brought."

Her? This was a first for me. I just hoped she was more open-minded than the detective who'd wanted to arrest me in the past.

Once Will departed, I viewed the stacks of dirty china, fine crystal, and cutlery piled high on the kitchen counters. The clutter bothered me, and I fought the urge to start washing dishes. It was a sure sign the coffee had kicked in. "I wonder why Mrs. Jorgensen didn't have her housekeepers come in this evening to keep on top of all the dirty dishes. It'll be a nightmare to get all the dried food off of them tomorrow."

"I have a feeling Mrs. Jorgensen doesn't much care about creating extra work for people doing her bidding." Carrie rested her eyes. "At least she gave me the final check when the fireworks started, even though we hadn't signed her waiver."

"She did?" That was one worry I could check off my list.

"Yep. She came into the kitchen just after you and Sal left

with the cupcakes." Carrie patted her pants pocket. "She even included the promised tips."

So far, we'd avoided talking about the murder, aside from Will's conversation. It was like having an elephant in the room, and I couldn't stand it any longer. "How are we going to help Sal?"

Tears gathered beneath Carrie's lashes. "I don't know. Neither of us has enough money to hire an attorney, like Will, or even collateral to post bail."

"But it's all circumstantial based on a drunk doctor saying he'd been poisoned by my cupcakes." I gasped. "Oh no. They're going to think I poisoned him."

"Did you?" The soft-spoken voice of a woman jarred me, and I splashed coffee onto my slacks.

"No! Definitely no." I raised my eyes from the brown stain saturating my pants to see an Asian woman, perhaps in her early thirties, standing in the wide doorway. She was tiny, even shorter than I was, and wore black slacks and a short-sleeved T-shirt-style burgundy silk shirt. A black lanyard with a badge attached to the loop hung around her long, slender neck, which was made all the more prominent by her sleek short bob.

"Which one of you is the caterer, Carrie Berger?"

My sister roused herself and walked toward the woman. "I am. How can we help you, Ms...."

"I'm Detective Tran." She raised her chin in my direction. "You're obviously sisters. What's your name?"

"Emory Martinez. I'm the cupcake caterer." I thought I might as well dive right in, since everyone already knew it. "I made the cupcake that Mr. Jorgensen ate."

Detective Tran cocked her head the side while her black eyes studied me. "Don't tell me you're the Emory Martinez who killed her husband's girlfriend."

Chapter 6

"No! I didn't kill her." I scrunched my eyes together as the memories of getting arrested filled my head. "I just found her."

A wry smile twisted the detective's glossy, full lips, and I thought I heard her mutter beneath her breath, "Just my luck to be on call tonight."

But I'd probably misheard. I was innocent of murdering my ex-best friend just like I was blameless in the murder of a Bavarian barmaid at a Halloween party last October, despite being a suspect in both crimes. It was just my streak of bad luck that my cake pops were found with her body.

"All righty, then, who wants to go first? I'm sure you both know the drill by now?" She tucked a strand of her blue-black hair behind her ear.

"Talk to Carrie first. She has little ones at home, and it's already late."

My sister smiled at me, but I could tell she was exhausted. "Thanks. I'm ready to drop."

The detective led Carrie out of the kitchen. Once they were out of sight, I checked my cell phone again. No reply to my earlier text to Randall. He'd flown back to Tampa the previous week to be with his mom while his dad underwent heart bypass surgery. It had been successful, and his father was recuperating, but Randall had decided to stay an extra week. I desperately wanted to hear his voice, but given the time difference, I'd decided it was too late to call.

I smiled when Tillie's text and her photo of my Goldendoodle-mix rescue dog, Piper, sitting on her lap, popped up on my screen. My octogenarian friend spoiled my dog. Worried about the stress fireworks would cause for Piper, Tillie had offered to stay home and be with her. Tillie wasn't sacrificing much, despite being a social butterfly with several invites to parties. She let slip that her new beau was grilling dinner for them both and then they'd watch the several fireworks displays going off all over Newport Beach from her balcony... which just happened to be attached to her second-floor bedroom. In her text, Tillie assured me that Piper tolerated the fireworks and was safe and sound, sleeping on her bed.

While I waited for Carrie and the detective to return, I amused myself by snooping through a few drawers and then headed to the walk-in pantry to see what they kept on their shelves. When I opened the oversized door, a clipboard with a list of names with black check marks alongside sat on the pantry's marble counter. My eyes ran over the list, and I realized it was probably the guest list. I pulled my cell phone from my pocket and took a few pictures of the names. It might be helpful if I needed to help prove Sal's innocence.

"I smell coffee." The detective's voice made me jump. I hadn't wanted to be caught snooping. "Do you have any left?"

"Uh, sure. It's not decaf, though." I shoved my phone back in my pocket and closed the pantry door behind me. After retrieving one of the white Bernardaud china mugs, I poured a cup. I hoped my shaking hands didn't make me look guilty.

"Thank God. I'll be lucky to sneak in a nap tomorrow afternoon, but until then, I need all the caffeine I can get."

"Cream or sugar?" I held out the mug.

"Cream, if you have it." She took the mug, blew on it, then guzzled half of the contents down. "Can I top this off?"

"Sure, help yourself." I placed the container of cream next to several filled coffee carafes. "Are you hungry? There's plenty of leftovers from the party, just no cupcakes."

"Coffee is all I need." She poured a generous dollop of cream into her now-full mug then gestured at the small table Carrie and I had been sitting at. "Shall we talk here?"

I sat and folded my hands in my lap while I let the silence linger. I studied Detective Tran as she sipped her coffee, apparently more interested in caffeine than in grilling me. That might have been a promising sign. She didn't think I was guilty and wasn't rushing to arrest me. The blue circles of fatigue under her eyes were visible beneath the overhead pendent light. I wondered when she'd last slept.

The detective caught me staring at her, and a quirky smile lit up her face. She set her coffee down. "I must look a wreck. I have a toddler at home, so between this job and a kid who thinks sleep is only a suggestion, I'm running on caffeine."

"That must be tough. Help yourself to as much coffee as you'd like." The death of Mr. Jorgensen had seen to the end of the party. We hadn't had a chance to offer guests any of the gallons of coffee we'd prepared. Fortunately, the brew was in carafes that would keep it hot without overheating it and turning bitter. "You're more than welcome to take a sealed carafe as long as you return the container."

"That's very kind of you, but I'll be okay." She got up and refilled her mug. "Now, tell me everything you can about this party. Gabe says you've got a good eye for detail and somehow you get yourself in the middle of investigations."

"Gabe? Gabe O'Neill?" I narrowed my eyes at her. "You checked up on me."

Her tinkling laugh made my shoulders relax. "Of course, I did. I recognized your name and remembered that Gabe was the investigating detective from your last, ah, unfortunate incident. I called him after I sent your sister home."

Detective Gabe O'Neill was my best friend, Brad's, partner. They'd started dating right before I'd found the Bavarian barmaid dead, in my bathtub. I almost caused them to break up when the detective arrested me, but I eventually got over it, and now we were good friends.

"I hope he vouched for me so you know I didn't poison Mr. Jorgensen?"

"Well, technically, since he wasn't here, he can't vouch for your innocence." She paused for a moment. "That's why I'm investigating and will find out whether you're guilty or blameless."

And here I thought we were bonding and becoming friends over coffee. "Okay, I get it. But truly, I didn't kill him, and I'm sure Salvador is innocent too. Someone set him up. He was framed!"

"Let me do the investigating, Ms. Martinez. Until then, no one is in the clear." Detective Tran pulled her cell phone from her back pocket and tapped a few times. "Do I have permission to record our conversation?"

I nodded.

"Please give your verbal consent, Ms. Martinez." Her voice was brusque. Her detective mode had kicked in.

"Yes." And so, we began. Since the detective had spent little time with my sister, I had assumed I'd be out of there in mere minutes. Instead, over an hour crawled by while she took me forward and backward over timing, who was where, who said what, and how creepy, now that I talked about it, Mr. Jorgensen acted. This wasn't an information-seeking interview. It had turned into an interrogation to trip me up into confessing I'd murdered the host.

Chapter 7

Surprisingly, I hadn't been arrested, and I'd crawled into bed in the wee hours of the morning. A ding emanating from my cell phone pulled me awake, and I groaned when I saw it was only seven. Too early after such a horrific event the day before. It was from my BFF, Brad.

Call me.

I hit the connect button. Brad picked up before the phone even had a chance to ring.

"Hey, Cupcake. I heard you had another incident at the party yesterday." His voice sounded much too chipper for this early in the morning. Before Gabe had moved in, he'd been a night owl. Now, it seemed, Brad had turned into an early bird.

"Do you know what time it is?" I threw off the covers and sat on the edge of the bed.

"I waited a full two hours to call you." Now he sounded pouty. "Do you want me to bring over coffee and donuts?"

"Where's Gabe?"

"He had to fly out this morning for a conference in DC."

That explained the early-morning phone call and the offer of coffee and donuts. Brad was bored. "C'mon over. Just bring me the largest coffee they have, and I want an apple fritter and a chocolate-filled donut. Bring a glazed yeast donut for Tilly too."

"You feeling okay, Em?" Brad knew I limited myself to one donut. I had to save my calories for taste testing all the cupcakes I created. Which reminded me I had four dozen lemon drop martini cupcakes to bake for my mother's annual day-after-the-Fourth-of-July party for her bridge group and their spouses.

"Between running my tail off for the event, no dinner, and then being interrogated until one this morning, I'd say I deserved it. Especially since I didn't end up in jail this time."

"Ouch. That bad, huh?"

"You have no idea. Just bring coffee and the donuts, and I'll tell you all about it."

As soon as we disconnected, I shuffled to the kitchen and started a pot of coffee. Even though Brad would bring me a cup, I knew it wouldn't be enough to get me through the day. I suspected I'd be hearing from Detective Tran for further questioning. I fumed that she wouldn't tell me when they'd release Sal. I'd have to find out how we could let him know we were doing everything we could to set him free.

By the time I'd dressed in shorts and a Fourth of July T-shirt and ran a brush through my tangled, frizzy hair, Brad was at the security gate. He held the donut shop bag in one hand and a venti coffee in the other. When I opened the gate, he handed the coffee to me and brushed his lips across my cheek.

"You don't look too bad for no sleep last night." He grinned. "Detective Tran pumped Gabe for the goods on you. Hope she wasn't too hard on you."

"Ugh. She thinks I'm the one who poisoned the cupcake Mr. Jorgensen ate, or at least helped Sal poison him." I couldn't think of any other explanation for why the detective had treated me the way she did. When trying to gain my confidence didn't obtain a confession, she'd resorted to interrogation.

"That wasn't what Gabe thought." Brad followed me into the house. "Where's Piper?"

"She had a sleepover with Tillie last night." I looked pointedly at my friend. "It's too early to call her."

His face turned pink, and he tucked his chin to his chest. "Sorry about that. I guess I wasn't thinking about the late night you had under uncomfortable circumstances."

I took a sip of the latte then raised it toward him as if toasting. "You're forgiven."

"So…" He stroked his reddish-gold stubble that covered his cheek. "Tell me what happened last night. I want all the deets."

"I'll tell you, but first give me the scoop on Detective Tran. How does Gabe know her?" I was positive that Brad had questioned his detective closely after the phone call last night.

"For starters, they went to college together and graduated at the same time with a criminal justice degree. They've kept in contact off and on, but it's only been within the last year that they reconnected when Gabe moved to Newport Beach." Brad pursed his lips together while he collected his thoughts for a moment. "If I remember correctly, Natasha, that's her first name, has been in Laguna for a couple of years now. She has a reputation for being tough but fair. Guess as a woman in the field she'd have to develop a tough shell."

I could understand that. "Last night she mentioned something about having a toddler at home. I take it she's married?"

"Nope, she's a single mom. I'm not sure what the story is about the father, but Natasha's parents take care of the little girl when she works."

"That's got to be a doubly hard career to thrive in without having a spouse to care for your child." I narrowed my eyes at Brad. "How do you already know so much about her? You didn't grill Gabe in this great of detail last night, especially since I know you would have been more interested in my misadventure."

His musical laugh filled my kitchen. "See? You're observant about the details. No wonder you've solved a couple murders."

"It's not like I planned on getting involved, but if I didn't, I'd have ended up in jail, just like Sal." That thought sobered me. "We have to figure out how to get him out of there."

"Gabe said to tell you to let the police do their job and to keep your nose out of it."

I stuck my tongue out. "We'll see. I know Sal is innocent. Someone framed him, and because he's... well... not white, those people aren't going to care one bit if he's convicted of a crime he didn't commit. It makes me angry, and it makes me want to cry. I can't stand by and let it happen."

"Whoa! Calm down, Em. Natasha isn't going to let that happen. She'll be fair and open-minded, and trust me, she knows exactly what kind of prejudices you're talking about." Brad held out the donut shop bag to me. "Peace?"

"Sorry. I didn't mean to take it out on you." I dug into the sack and extracted the apple fritter before handing the bag back. "It seems so unfair, and those people at the party last night were atrocious."

Brad extracted a maple bar and set it on the napkin lying in front of him. "It is unfair. There's so much injustice, even where we live. But believe me when I say Natasha and Gabe are fair and only want to see the truth come out."

"You never answered my question. How do you know this Natasha so well?"

"She's brought her daughter over a couple times to swim in our pool, and we were invited to her little girl's third birthday party a few weeks ago. The little girl, Alyssa Mai, is the cutest kid you've ever seen." Brad appeared wistful, and I wondered if he was considering fatherhood.

Once we'd consumed our coffee and donuts, Brad

departed, and I immediately called my sister to see if she'd heard from Sal yet.

"No. I haven't heard a peep." Carrie paused to whisper something to her husband before continuing. "I tried calling his emergency phone number from his application, but it's been disconnected."

"Has he discussed family or close friends with you?"

"Nothing. Sal is a very private person. All I know is he was haphazardly raised by a bunch of relatives who shuffled him between their homes frequently. I've left a message for Betty to see if she knows someone we could reach out to on his behalf."

"Who's Betty?"

"She's the culinary program instructor over at Golden South College." Again, Carrie covered her phone and whispered something. "Sorry. I really need to go. Thomas broke his toe last night, and the girls decided they wanted to make pancakes all on their own this morning. They just spilled the entire sack of flour, and their father says he's in too much pain to help clean it up."

"Oops." My poor sister. This on top of the nightmare event she needed to recover from. "Hope he feels better, and I hope it's not as big of a mess as it sounds."

"Unfortunately, I can't even begin to describe how big a mess it is or I'll start crying."

"Leave it, and I'll be there in about twenty minutes to clean up. It sounds like you need to go take a nap."

"No, it'll be fine. I think right now might be the time I switch back to full-leaded coffee." Carrie heaved a huge sigh. "I'm worried sick about Sal. Can you call the jail and see if you can find out anything? I don't want that poor kid to think we've abandoned him."

"That's exactly what I'd planned to do but wanted to check with you first to see if you'd heard from him."

We disconnected but not before I heard Carrie yelling at

her hapless husband. I made a mental note to schedule a play-date and sleepover with my nieces later this week. It would give Carrie some downtime to catch up on rest, even with her infant son at home.

I tracked down the phone number to the Laguna Beach jail. The officer who answered was surprisingly pleasant and helpful. He confirmed that Salvador Cruz was jailed there but would be transferred to the Orange County jail in Santa Ana the following morning. When I asked what visiting hours were, the officer indicated no visitors were allowed unless I was the inmate's attorney. I also found out that Sal had not used his one phone call privilege, which meant he didn't have an attorney and had no one but my sister and me.

Chapter 8

Another text arrived on my phone. It was Tillie checking to see if I was up yet. I let her know I'd be right over. I grabbed the sack of donuts and the carafe of coffee I'd made for her, along with a bowl of juicy strawberries and plump blueberries. In addition to providing some accounting services for him, one of my terms of employment when Tillie's son had hired me the previous summer was preparing breakfast and dinners for his mother. At that time, she'd been recovering from a tumble down a staircase and had suffered a broken arm.

Besides myself, only two people knew what had really happened to cause the accident. Tillie knew, and the man she was sexting knew, as she walked down the stairs and missed a step. Her secret stayed safe with me, and she'd never blurted out a peep to her bridge group. She was anything but frail or bordering on dementia, as her son had claimed when she'd fallen. Once she'd healed, Tillie had been more than happy to have me continue preparing meals and living in her luxurious pool house. We'd become close while sharing stories and secrets over breakfast each morning and over gimlets several evenings each week.

Before I could step into the alleyway that separated her mammoth home sitting on the edge of Newport Bay, Tillie and my Goldendoodle mix, Piper, came through the security gate. She bounded straight for me then danced on her hind legs, begging to be picked up. Her happiness at seeing me came through her *rrowr—rrowr—rrowr* noises and the way her furry tail helicoptered behind her. I set the coffee carafe onto the blacktop and bent down to scratch beneath my dog's chin.

"Somebody missed you." Tillie scooped up the carafe. "I thought we could sit on the patio and let Piper get some of her energy out. I meant to take her for a walk, but I never got around to it."

"That sounds like a great idea." I'd been so busy with the Jorgensens' event I hadn't taken Piper for a walk in several days either.

Once we were settled on the turquoise-patterned cushions that made the wicker patio chairs extra-inviting, I handed Tillie the bag of donuts, poured cups of coffee for us both, and waggled my eyebrows. "How was your date last night? Ira, wasn't it?"

"*Phew.*" Tillie took a chomp of donut and ground her teeth together. "Men! I don't know why I bother."

I knew why she bothered. She liked a challenge, and she liked thinking she was getting away with something that she knew her son and grandsons would disapprove of. "I'm so sorry. What happened?"

"That harridan, Frances Allain, swooped in and stole him away." She harrumphed. "Her son just bought a yacht, and at the last minute, she invited Ira to motor over to Catalina for the fireworks. My balcony couldn't compete."

"Is that the same Frances I met at your club?"

"Yes. That hussy thinks she's one-upped me. I'll show her." Tillie chomped another bite of the donut.

I well-remembered the woman. Mean-spirited, the tiny, almost bird-like woman had a sharp tongue and blue hair. "I'll bet Ira comes crawling back to you. It probably took him all of fifteen minutes with her to realize he'd made a dreadful mistake."

"You're right, but he's lost his chance."

"Oh? Is there another silver fox waiting in the wings?"

"We'll see. Frances may have done me a favor." Tillie winked at me, and her cheeks colored a pretty pink. "But enough about my woes, tell me all about the party. Were the fireworks fantastic? I've heard they're some of the best in the county."

I grimaced.

"Uh-oh. I know that look." She reached over and gave my hand a quick pat. "What happened? No one died, did they?"

I gulped some coffee then squeezed my eyes together. "Sal's been arrested for murdering Mr. Jorgensen."

"That poor kid. What are we going to do to get him out of jail?" Tillie blew out a long breath of air. "I've heard stories about Arthur, even though we don't move in the same social circles. The only surprise is that he hasn't been murdered before now."

"I'm not sure it really was murder. Mr. Jorgensen sucked down alcohol the entire time we were there. I can't believe he hadn't passed out before the fireworks even started. Besides, his wife said he was on medication, so I'm hoping it was accidental and Sal will be released soon." This was exactly why I worried about telling my friend. I quickly explained what I'd found out from the officer I'd talked to that morning. "The bottom line is he doesn't have family, and he doesn't have money or collateral for bail. I don't know if they'll even let him post bail for a charge like this, so we'll probably have to wait and see what the cause of death is."

"Tomorrow we'll visit him, and I'll post bail if allowed." She took another chomp on the second donut she'd retrieved from the sack. "Then you and I will start investigating, and we'll find the real killer."

"I hope it isn't murder. Besides, I can't let you do that. If Mr. Skyler finds out you're spending money on bail for a murder suspect as well as investigating, he'll fire me for sure." I didn't want to voice the niggly thought I'd had all morning. What did we really know about Sal? If Mr. Jorgensen had been murdered, I couldn't be one hundred percent certain that Sal was innocent. Plus, there was that accusation hanging in the air that he had killed Mr. Jorgensen's son. Was it possible Sal had been responsible?

"I don't know why you're so formal with my son. He wouldn't care if you called him David, especially given his previous relationship with your mother." Tillie's conversations often ping-ponged around to other subjects, but I knew she wouldn't let the murder conversation go. Not by a long shot.

"That's exactly why I need to call him Mr. Skyler." I crossed my arms and hugged them tightly against my stomach. I couldn't admit that despite my support for the search in locating my half-sister given up for adoption at birth and whom I'd only found out about last fall, it made me uneasy. What if she'd had a life filled with tragedy with no one to love her like my mother would have done? What if she resented us or even hated us for having a life with her mother while she'd been discarded? I wouldn't blame her if she did.

My mother and my boss, Tillie's son, had had a relationship in college. They'd gone their separate ways, and my mother gave up my sister, Tillie's granddaughter, for adoption. Her grandson, Brian, had agreed to provide a DNA test and attempt to locate her via several ancestry sites online. So far there hadn't been a match. Given Carrie's and my unconventional conception, we weren't good candidates for the DNA search.

"We'll find her, dear." Tillie's normally smooth forehead, thanks to the best cosmetic surgeon in town, puckered slightly as she frowned. "I just hope it's before my time is up. I so want to get to know my granddaughter."

I felt guilty for having misgivings about finding my sister. This was important to Tillie. I gave her a hug. "I'm sure we will."

"Why, oh why, did my dreadful mother-in-law have to force your mother to do a private adoption with no agencies involved? My investigator hasn't been able to find a trace. Not even a birth certificate. It's like that poor child disappeared into thin air." Tillie's ex-husband's mother had been the force between breaking up my mother and Mr. Skyler and then facilitating the adoption. Her voice hardened. "If that woman were still alive, I'd kill her."

Chapter 9

Tillie had voiced her dislike for her mother-in-law before, but I'd never seen this level of vehemence. "I'll talk to Brian and see if there are other avenues of searches that we can take. Maybe we've overlooked something. We'll find her, I promise."

She dabbed at her eyes with the crumpled napkin I'd given her along with the donut sack earlier. "Enough of that. Tell me everything that happened with the Jorgensens, and let's make a list of suspects."

With another pot of fresh coffee brewed, I recited the sequence of events from the previous two days. Since I'd printed out the guest list I'd found in the pantry, from the photo I'd covertly taken, Tillie studied it while I tried to remember the details of the people sitting closest to the Jorgensens. What I remembered most and made my anger burn anew were the chuckles from the men sitting there as drunken Mr. Jorgensen tried to manhandle me.

"Mr. and Mrs. Jorgensen sat side by side at the head of the table with Mr. Jorgensen to the left of her." I rummaged through Tillie's so-called junk drawer—it was pristinely organized—and pulled out a large scratch pad of paper and a pen.

After sketching a quick rectangle to represent the table, I added the host's and hostess's initials. "Sitting to his left was a platinum-gray-haired woman, perhaps in her late sixties. She was rail-thin and has obviously had augmented surgery for her, um, assets. What struck me most were the huge ruby necklace, ring, and earrings she wore. I've never seen rubies so large, and I'm pretty sure they were real."

Tillie consulted the guest list. "I'm positive that's Ruby Dewitt. Those ostentatious gems are her signature jewels."

"Sitting next to Mrs. Dewitt was a man around her age. He's balding and has a fringe of white hair that makes him look like a friar. He's also quite round."

"That's her husband, Ted." Tillie placed a check mark next to the two names on the list.

"Sitting on Mrs. Jorgensen's right side was a man who looked in his early to mid-fifties, although he's probably had some cosmetic enhancements, which makes it hard to guess his age. His teeth were unusually white and straight, which made me think he'd had orthodontist and veneer work done recently. Plus, he's super-tan with dark-brown hair that curled at the tips a bit."

Tillie went down the list while chewing her bottom lip. "I'm not sure about him. Tell me about his wife. I'm presuming couples sat together?"

"It appeared that way to me. She was in her late fifties and looked older than her husband." I took a moment to close my eyes and tried to visualize the guest. We'd been on the run all through dinner service. I hadn't had a chance to observe many of the guests, and they'd all started blending together. "She had the typical honey-blonde hair, worn in a sleek chin-length bob. Her clothing and jewelry were tasteful. You could tell they were expensive but not extravagant. Slender, of course, and oh, she had violet eyes and wore super-long false eyelashes."

Personally, I thought the lashes looked more like spiders, but it was apparently an accepted fashion style at the moment.

Once again Tillie consulted the list then picked up her phone, opened the browser, and typed in a name. Images popped up, and she enlarged one and handed the phone to me. "Is that the couple? Linda and Martin Irving?"

I agreed it was and added their names to my list. Some of the older men, around Arthur Jorgensen's age, had very young trophy wives—most likely their second or even third. Tillie didn't know their names. Different social circles and all that, I guessed. I was more interested in the two couples who sat right next to the Jorgensens, since they would have had the opportunity to introduce some type of poison into his food. We continued the exercise anyway, until Tillie had identified about half the names. The remaining few guests appeared to be widowed friends of Mrs. Jorgensen or, as in the case of Will Trenton, a relative escorting their elderly family member.

When I mentioned chatting with the attorney, Will Trenton, I remembered I'd shoved his business card into the back pocket of my pants the previous evening. I went to my bedroom and dug the wrinkled and coffee-stained pants out from the hamper. Once I retrieved the card, I showed it to Tillie.

"He said he'd be happy to talk with Sal. I'll call him and let him know about the transfer to the OC jail, and maybe he can find out about bail."

"Tell him I'll pay his retainer." Tillie reached over and scratched Piper's overly furry golden chin, and I realized she was overdue for a day of grooming at the doggie spa.

"That's very kind of you, but I hope he'll make a couple of phone calls without charging a fee. He seemed contrite about sending Sal into the danger zone, so to speak, and wanted to help."

"Let me know, and I'll write the check." Tillie checked her

watch. "I'd better get going. I need to get ready for lunch and a movie date."

"Moving on from Ira already?" I couldn't help but tease my friend.

She snorted. "Frances is more than welcome to Ira. Let's just say this date will have her turning green, and I'll be the one having the last laugh."

With Tillie gone, my pool house seemed quiet. I turned on soft jazz and opened all the French doors that led onto the patio. The cool breezes blowing in from the bay kept the July heat from building. I went to my small kitchen and started on the lemon drop martini cupcakes for my mother. I often used Tillie's large, industrial-sized, and outfitted kitchen for my cupcake catering jobs, but sometimes I liked the coziness of my space and being able to watch Piper cavort outside while I worked.

Since I'd baked several batches of the cupcakes for the Jorgensens' party, I'd prepared extra cupcake and frosting liquid mixture ahead of time to save time for my mother's order. Fresh lemon juice, limoncello, and triple sec provided a tangy bite to the little cakes and buttercream, and the mixture kept well in the refrigerator. It didn't take long to whip the melted butter and sugar together in my stand mixer. By the time the eggs were beaten in, the creamy mixture was ready for alternating the flour and leavening with the limoncello mixture.

Once the cupcakes had sufficiently cooled, I made the buttercream frosting. The flavor of the limoncello comple-mented the combination of creamy butter and confectioners' sugar. As my stand mixture whipped the clouds of sweetness into a fluffy concoction, I had to stop the KitchenAid mixer a couple of times to spoon a dollop out to taste how refreshing it was. I decided I shouldn't have had the apple fritter for break-fast when the sugar rush hit my brain.

While the mixer whipped the buttercream, I scooped a

small portion out of the centers of the cupcakes and filled the holes with lemon curd. I cheated this time and used prepared jarred curd instead of making my own, but I knew the intense flavors of the limoncello and triple sec would cover my short-cut. Once I piped swirls of buttercream, using a large star tip, on top of the cupcakes, I garnished each with a yellow-striped decorative straw. I set a couple cupcakes aside—one for Tillie and one for me—and placed the remaining cupcakes in reusable delivery boxes.

With a shower and clean bike shorts and a T-shirt donned, I shoved my feet into cheap rubber flip-flops. I'd be in and out of my mother's house well before the party started, so I didn't feel the need to look presentable. I called Piper into the house and fed her dinner. The amount of running around the large yard, chasing squirrels and birds, would be sure to cause her to nap the entire time I was gone. Loaded up and ready to leave, I sent my mother a text to let her know I was on my way with the cupcakes. She responded with a thumbs-up, smiley face, cupcake, and heart emoji. I grinned when I received her text.

After my dad abandoned us, I'd been cautious around my mother, Addie Whitendale. She'd been overly strict and prone to criticizing me for not living up to her standards. Reputation was everything, and I often disappointed her. I was never sure why we had a contentious relationship until last fall when she'd finally confided about giving up her firstborn. It was as if her personality had finally been freed from a heavy weight when she stopped hiding her secrets. She'd become carefree, almost playful at times, and I treasured how our relationship had become closer. She still had her moments when she reverted to being prim and proper, but for the most part, that was in the past.

Chapter 10

Post-holiday beach traffic was every bit as snarled as I'd dreaded. The main thoroughfare out of the Balboa Peninsula, where Tillie and I lived, wasn't quite so bad. It was when the road converged onto the Pacific Coast Highway, PCH as locals called it, that cars inched along, bumper to bumper. Throngs of tourists, dressed in colorful beach attire, crowded the sidewalks as they strolled from shops and restaurants and bars. After sitting through a traffic light cycle twice without moving, I sent Randall a text to see if he was available to chat. In mere seconds, my phone rang, and his photo popped up on my screen.

"Hey. How're you holding up?" I longed to brush my fingertips along his strong jawline and breathe in his scent that always seemed to smell of freshly ground nutmeg. It was alluring, especially to a baker like myself.

"I'm fine, except for missing you." His deep voice sent shivers down my spine. "They're releasing Dad tomorrow. Neither of us can wait to get out of this hospital."

"I'm glad he's doing so well. Is your mom coping okay?" After Randall's undercover brother had been killed in a task force operation, his mother hadn't emotionally recovered. She was prone to anxiety attacks and bouts of depression. It was one of many reasons why Randall had quit his vice squad job and left law enforcement all together.

"She's doing better than I expected. I think the new medication she's been taking has helped." The ding of an elevator sounded, and Randall murmured something. "Sorry about that. I was headed to the cafeteria for coffee when you texted."

"I'm so glad it's helping. She sounded super-stressed when she answered your phone a few days ago." A tinny-sounding horn beeped from behind me when the car in front of me moved a bare twelve inches forward and I hadn't raced to catch up. I moved my car to fill in the minuscule space with the hopes of avoiding more honking. The light turned red again.

"Are you on your way somewhere?"

"Yeah. I'm trying to deliver cupcakes to my mother before her party starts." I cranked the air conditioning as cold as it would go when the lowering sun beat in through the window, onto my cheek. My sixteen-year-old Honda didn't respond well to my request, so I returned the dial to barely cool. It didn't take long for perspiration to gather along my hairline. "Traffic is a nightmare. I've moved an entire five feet in five minutes."

"I'm happy to keep you entertained." He chuckled. "While I miss you, I don't miss summer beach traffic. Since you're sitting there with nowhere to go, tell me about the event yesterday. You didn't find any dead bodies this time, did you?"

Randall patiently listened to the events of the previous day, asked probing questions, then predictably told me to let the police handle the investigation if the death was indeed a murder.

"I know you're smart and perfectly capable of taking care of yourself. I just worry about you, Em, and don't want to see you get hurt." Randall was all too aware of the close calls I'd had in the past with deranged murderers after I'd asked a few too many questions. "Let that attorney... what's his name?"

"Will Trenton?"

"Yeah, Will. Let him do what he can for Sal. You really don't need to get involved this time." Randall covered his phone and said something to someone else. "I've got to go. The doctor is here to check on Dad, and I have some questions about his discharge."

We said our goodbyes, and a while later, I pulled up to the gated community in Irvine, where my mother lived with Lars. The guard waved me in when he recognized me, and I wove through the twisty streets carved out of the hillside. I circled the cul-de-sac where my mother lived. Every single space was taken, and her three-car driveway was double-parked too.

I glanced at the clock on the Accord's dashboard and saw I was thirty minutes late. Checking my phone, I was surprised my mother hadn't left me several messages asking where I was. That was a first. The only curbside parking space open, which didn't require me to utilize my nonexistent parallel parking skills, was over a quarter of a mile away. I grabbed a large, sturdy tote bag and filled it with the four boxes of cupcakes.

By the time I reached Mother's house, sweat trickled down my back, and my hair was frizzier than ever. When no one answered the door after I rang the bell several times, I went around to the side of the house and let myself in through the gate. I followed the chatter of voices and the tinkling of music flowing from hidden speakers. Barbecue smoke drifted from the grill that Lars manned, surrounded by several other men, all holding beers. Mother, dressed in white capris and a patriotic-themed T-shirt, and a handful of women dressed similarly, lounged on cushy chairs ringing the firepit. They held glasses of white wine, and two bottles of chardonnay sat on the firepit edge, condensation dripping down the sides.

My mouth fell open, and I snapped it closed when a dragonfly breezed by. Mother didn't do casual get-togethers. She was the queen of formal. The right china with the right crystal and place cards for all attendees. Long tables sat at the other end of her yard, covered in red-checked tablecloths. White-and-red carnation centerpieces accented with American flags graced the tables. I looked behind me then back to Mother, not sure I was really seeing what was right before my eyes.

"Darling! There you are." Mother gracefully walked over to me on wedged espadrilles, another first, and air-kissed my cheek. "I hope traffic wasn't unbearable."

"It was worse than I'd planned for. Sorry I'm late." I shifted the tote bag, worried about what she'd say about my attire. "Where would you like me to set up the cupcakes?"

"Just put your tote in the kitchen then come back out and have a glass of wine."

"Uh, sure. I can put them on a platter for you first."

She waved her hand in a circle. "No need. I'll take care of it later, or we'll help ourselves straight from the box."

Who was this woman, and what had she done with my mother? "Are you feeling okay?"

The tinkling sounds of laughter that fell from my mother's lips almost made tears prick my eyes. Not from sadness but from happiness. I'd never, ever seen her so lighthearted, so carefree. She brushed my cheek with her lips then reached over and wiped the smear of rose-colored lipstick from my face. "I couldn't be better. Grab a glass of wine and give us the scoop on the murder investigation. We have several theories on who killed Arthur."

Now I knew for certain that the woman standing in front of me was a doppelganger. Less than a year ago, she'd been horrified that I'd gotten involved in an investigation after finding the body of my ex-best friend. And almost nine months ago, she'd been aggravated that I'd found the body of a Bavarian barmaid. And now she wanted the scoop?

I found space on the white marble island in her kitchen

and stacked the cupcake boxes. The caterer in me wanted to artfully arrange the cupcakes for the guests, but I did as my mother asked and left them in the boxes. After placing the empty tote by the front door so I wouldn't forget to take it home, I picked up a wineglass and headed to the patio.

An empty chair had been placed next to my mother's lounge chair. I inelegantly plopped down and rested my feet on the edge of the firepit. Too late I noticed my legs needed shaving and my toes were in desperate need of a pedi. I waited for a snide remark from my mother. None came, but I tucked my legs and feet beneath the chair just in case. No need to draw attention to my lack of grooming. The woman sitting on the other side of me passed me a bottle of chardonnay after she'd poured herself a generous portion.

My mother recited the names of the women sitting with us, not that I'd remember. "So darling, fill us in on what happened at the Jorgensens' party?"

For the fourth time that day, I shared the details about the tragic turn of events that had befallen Mr. Jorgensen. I felt like a spotlight was on me as question after question was lobbed my way, and soon most of the men had gathered around to hear my tale. I didn't like being the center of attention in a large group, and I self-consciously tugged the hem of my bike shorts down, trying to cover a little of my chubby legs. When it didn't help, I gulped a mouthful of wine while listening to a few theories being thrown around about who had killed the man. None of them believed that it had been an accidental death.

"Do you remember the scandal involving Arthur Jorgensen and his business partner a couple years ago?" Georgiana—at least that was what I thought her name was—asked the group.

A couple women nodded assent and tsked.

"What scandal was that?" I asked, leaning toward the

stout woman who had dressed in red, white, and blue sports-wear. Even her mani and pedi reflected the patriotic theme.

Georgiana picked up a half-full wine bottle and topped her glass before filling mine. "Well, dear, they owned a small wealth management business, and the business partner"—she snapped her fingers a couple of times—"Pete, I think his name was, embezzled the funds and disappeared."

This opened up a new avenue of suspects. Could one of their clients have killed Mr. Jorgensen for revenge over the stolen money? "What happened? Did they ever find the partner or the missing funds?"

"Nope. Arthur claimed he was a victim just as much as their other clients, and as far as I know, Pete was never heard from again." Georgiana leaned back in her chair and sipped her wine.

"From what I could tell from catering their party, they certainly weren't financially hit by the embezzlement. Wouldn't his company have to make restitution to his clients?"

Georgiana chased a buzzing insect away with a flick of her fingers. "Most of their wealth belongs to Lisette. I'm sure she had the good sense to not invest with her husband, may he rest in peace."

"Did Mr. Jorgensen have a reputation for losing money on investments?" I had to wonder why people would entrust their money to someone whose own wife didn't trust him with her fortune.

"It was rumors only, and I'm sure they surfaced after the embezzlement happened."

"Hey, didn't Pete disappear right around the time the Jorgensen boy was killed in that car accident?" the yoga-pants-wearing woman sitting next to my mother asked. For the life of me, I couldn't remember her name.

Georgiana jumped in. "Yes! It all happened just a day or two of each other. I don't think the investigators ever found a link between the two, though."

"What do you know about their son being killed?" I couldn't believe how much gossip these women had about the Jorgensens. I wished I could've taken some notes on my iPad, but that seemed gauche. This was a party, after all.

Unfortunately, none of them could tell me anything except it had been some kind of car accident.

My mother claimed the bottle of wine being passed around and poured a splash into her goblet. "You have to wonder if it's all connected. The embezzlement, the son's death, and now Arthur's murder."

"It has to have been the wife who killed Arthur," a woman with mousy-brown hair that had frizzed in the heat insisted. "She sat next to him and could have easily poisoned his food or his drink."

"I disagree," an elderly woman with steel-gray helmeted hair interjected. "If you want my opinion, they've already arrested the right man. Arthur rightfully accused him at the party of murdering his son, and if someone like that kills once, they'll kill again."

"Addie, the steaks are ready." Lars rested his hand on my shoulder and gave it a light squeeze. "You'll stay and eat with us, won't you, Emory?"

"Thank you, it smells delicious." It was a good thing Lars interrupted, because I was ready to get into an altercation. Someone who didn't even know Sal or the circumstances had tried and convicted him already. If others felt the same way she did, there was no hope for Sal unless I did something to clear his name.

Chapter 11

Despite Independence Day being over, someone in the neighborhood decided to detonate illegal M80 fireworks for half the night. Piper cried and frantically scratched at her crate walls, so I allowed her on my bed, to snuggle next to me. It took a while of speaking in soothing tones and stroking her ears and back for her to stop shivering. Tillie had said Piper had tolerated the previous evening's fireworks, but then I remembered the photo of Piper sitting on her lap. I should have noticed, since my dog wasn't allowed on any furniture, including my bed… except in the case of an emergency like the Fourth of July. Or whenever anyone decided to create their own holiday and celebrate with M80s, like the Fifth of July.

With Piper distraught, sleep wouldn't come, so I switched the light on, turned on soothing classical music, and grabbed my iPad. Mr. Jorgensen had accused Sal of killing his son, and I wondered if I could find out any information on what had happened. It was slow going, since I didn't know their son's name, plus Mr. and Mrs. Jorgensen had their faces plastered across all the society pages extolling their participation in charity events and galas alike.

Finally, a result popped up, and I clicked through the link to read the brief article. Their thirty-four-year-old son, Nathan, had been involved in a single-car accident. Traveling at a high rate of speed, his Lamborghini had plunged over a beachside cliff early one morning, two years ago after attending a Fourth of July celebration. Large amounts of cocaine and alcohol had been found in his system.

No wonder Mr. Jorgensen had been drinking so heavily. He'd probably been trying to drown his grief. I found it odd, though, that given the anniversary of their son's death, they would choose to host a party. The party seemed to be driven by Mrs. Jorgensen's desire. Was she so heartless that she'd subject her husband to burying his grief by entertaining guests, or was it her way of trying to distract themselves from the tragic accident that had claimed their son?

Morning came too soon, and Piper followed my bedraggled self across the alleyway. She stuck to my side, sniffing the air, hoping I'd drop the frittata filled with vegetables, goat cheese, and more importantly, Italian turkey sausage. My other hand firmly gripped the carafe of freshly brewed coffee. It was going to be my most important accessory of the day after very little sleep.

Once the fireworks had stopped, Piper refused to leave her cuddly spot on my bed. She seemed to move or shake her dog tags the very second I fell asleep, which startled me and started the cycle of trying to drift off to sleep again. It was safe to say I had zero rest over the long night, which had left plenty of time to ponder Mr. Jorgensen's death.

Tillie took one look at me and started another pot of coffee. While we ate our breakfast together, a tradition since I'd moved in, I filled her in on the happenings and gossip I'd gleaned from my mother's party, along with the information I'd found on the internet about Nathan Jorgensen. Tillie seemed inordinately pleased with my mother's high spirits, and I supposed in a way she'd almost been Tillie's daughter-in-law. It was probably why I was so close to Tillie. She was the grandmother I'd never had.

"How was your date yesterday?" I refilled both of our coffee cups. In my defense, Tillie used dainty china teacups for coffee. One slurp emptied the tiny thing, so I was constantly refilling.

Her eyes twinkled. "Better than I'd hoped for. Frances is going to be so jealous when she finds out who I'm dating."

"Yay for you!" Good lord. I dearly loved Tillie, but she sounded like a teenager now, and I was following right along. "So… who's the mystery man?"

She wagged her index finger at me. "Not gonna say until I see how it progresses."

"What! Can't you even give me a hint?" I winked at her. "Is he at least tall, dark, and handsome?"

Tillie waggled her flat palm. "Sorry to say he can't compete in Randall's category. But he does have some redeeming qualities."

"Such as?" I enjoyed Tillie's vivacious banter. It brightened my mood.

Before she could answer, my phone rang. I didn't recognize the number, but I answered anyway, thinking it might be a cupcake catering order. Unfortunately, it was Detective Tran.

"Ms. Martinez, I'd like to drop by and get your statement again. Is now a good time?" The detective wasted no time on greetings or even taking a breath of air.

I looked down at my half-eaten breakfast and the unfinished coffee. "Would a half an hour from now work for you?"

"Not really. I'm sitting outside your gate."

Oh. I tried to hold in the sigh that wanted to escape. "All right. I'm at Tillie's house, but I'll be there in a moment."

The detective disconnected without so much as "I'll see you soon" or "goodbye."

"Detective Tran is waiting outside. I'll come back to wash

the dishes and clean up for you." Typically, Tillie's house-keeper, Dorie, would do the washing up after breakfast, but she was on vacation for the week.

"Nonsense. I am entirely capable of loading a dishwasher and washing dishes." She began stacking our plates. "Refill the carafe from my coffeepot and take it with you. You look like you need the caffeine today."

That was an understatement. Plus I was pretty sure the detective would drink a cup or three of the brew. Unlike Tillie, I served coffee in substantial mugs that held at least fourteen ounces or more.

I called for Piper to follow me, and she gazed disappoint-edly at the remaining frittata sitting on the table. "Don't worry, girl, I'll give you a treat when we get home."

She perked up at the word "treat" and fell into step along-side me after I clipped a spare leash on, which I kept stored in the main house for situations like this. I blew Tillie a kiss then headed to my interrogation.

The detective was dressed in an impeccable white button-down collared shirt that would have looked masculine on me, but she gave it a feminine twist with the way she'd styled the collar and cuffs. Paired with sharply creased black trousers and stylish mule pumps shined to perfection, she exuded professionalism despite the gun holstered around her tiny waist. The closer I got, though, the more evident the dark bags beneath her eyes became.

"I brought us a carafe of coffee. Are you interested?" I held the carafe up while maintaining a firm grasp onto Piper's leash with the other hand.

"That would be heavenly. Thank you." She waited while I unlocked the gate that led to my pool house yard then followed in, close behind me.

I set the carafe on a glass-top bistro table and motioned at the cushioned patio chairs. "Is this okay, or would you prefer to sit inside?"

Detective Tran scanned the perimeter, and I assumed it was to see if there was a risk of a neighbor overhearing our conversation. The large double-sized lot, with its generously proportioned pool, was ensconced with privacy walls. To add another layer of privacy, large, leafy trees had been planted just inside the perimeter of the lot on all three sides. Unless someone sat in a tree close to where we spoke, I doubted they'd be able to hear anything but murmurs.

"This is lovely." She gracefully lowered herself into a chair. "It has a peaceful feeling, which isn't something I get to experience much these days."

I unclipped Piper's leash, and she bounded off to romp in the grass without giving the detective a sniff. It was unusual, but perhaps my dog had picked up on the way I held myself aloof from the woman. "I'll bring out the coffee mugs. You like cream with your coffee, right?"

She nodded absently, her eyes dreamily gazing at the shimmering pool.

I walked into my house, and Piper skittered close behind me, making a beeline for the kitchen. She hadn't forgotten about the promised treat. Once she'd snarfed down the liver treat, she bounded back to cavort in the yard, on the hunt for any squirrels or birds who might dare invade her kingdom.

I warmed two leftover blueberry muffins from the previous day in the microwave and poured cream into a pitcher. Placing everything needed on a large tray, I returned to the patio. It appeared Detective Tran was napping. I set the tray down as quietly as I possibly could, but in the process, I stubbed my toe on the chair, which caused the chair to scrape across the patio concrete. She startled, and her hand immediately flew to her gun.

"I'm so sorry. I didn't mean to startle you." Backing away, I held my palms up in front of my body.

The detective raised her hands to her face and rubbed. Her deep breaths and exhalations sounded noisy in the quiet yard. She lowered her hands to her lap. "I apologize. It was completely unprofessional, and if you feel you must file a complaint against me, I understand."

"No! I'd never do that. It's obvious you're running on fumes and coffee." I plopped down on the cushioned chair across the table from the detective and rubbed my now-throbbing toe. "Just how much sleep did you get last night?"

"It doesn't matter. I have a job to do and prove myself worthy of the position." She again sighed deeply. "Women have to work so much harder and longer than our male counterparts to prove we can do the same job."

"That's kind of hard to accomplish when you're sleep-deprived. Can you go home and take a nap at least?"

"That doesn't work. My daughter is ambitious about claiming my time whenever I'm home." She sighed. "Maybe I'll check into a motel for a few hours this afternoon. I've tried that before, but it's usually too noisy for me to sleep. Why do people feel the need to slam their doors no matter what time of day or night it is?"

"You could nap here, er, if you don't feel too uncomfortable." What was I thinking? I didn't need to get friendly with the investigating detective. She would probably do the bare minimum of looking for any other evidence that would clear Sal's name.

"Thanks, but that would be unprofessional and a potential conflict of interest." She picked up the carafe of coffee. "For now, I'll stick to more coffee and one of these muffins."

We ate and sipped in silence for a few minutes. Piper, weary from squirrel hunting, plopped down next to my feet, her pink tongue lolling from her mouth as she panted. I absentmindedly stroked her golden fur.

Detective Tran daintily wiped her mouth with the turquoise floral-print napkin I'd placed next to her. "That hit the spot, but it's time to get to work. I need to go over the sequence of events again."

Unfortunately, I knew the drill all too well, so I started from the beginning and retold the story for the umpteenth time. Detective Tran periodically glanced at notes on the iPad Mini she'd pulled from the small black leather-stitched satchel she'd brought with her. She also stopped me several times to clarify who had been where and at what times.

"Do you mind if I have a look around your property and inside your house?"

"I don't have anything to hide, so help yourself." I took a sip of the now-cold coffee sitting in my mug while she returned the iPad to her satchel. "Can you tell me what you're looking for?"

"Do you or Mrs. Skyler have any oleander bushes on the property?"

"Oleander?" Why was she asking about a shrub? Then a childhood memory came flooding back. Oleanders were highly poisonous. I swallowed hard. "Mr. Jorgensen was poisoned by oleander?"

"How do you know that?" Detective Tran slammed her flat-palmed hand onto the tabletop.

Holding up my hands, palms facing out toward her, I spluttered, "I didn't poison him!"

Chapter 12

I watched the retreating back of the petite detective as she strode to my tiny kitchen to search the contents. With the numerous French doors that led from my pool house to the patio, I could easily see what she was doing. Piper lifted doleful eyes up at me, huffed, and fell back asleep as soon as I bent down to scratch behind her ears.

The door that led from my house to the garage slammed shut, and I presumed the detective was now searching the nearly empty space. After an unfortunate death had occurred over Halloween, the garage had been thoroughly torn apart and searched. Tillie had taken the opportunity to discard most of the contents, and I was certain the detective wouldn't find a thing except the odd dust bunny.

She reemerged and motioned for me to stand up. "Come walk around the property with me and tell me what you know about oleander."

Piper sprang to her feet and then dipped into a down-ward-facing-dog pose. It made me want to join her. Instead, I fell into step beside the detective as we walked along the boundaries of Tillie's property. The copious flowers, shrubs, and trees were well trimmed and thrived, thanks to her team of gardeners. If left to my ministrations, they'd all be dead sticks poking up from either parched dirt or mudholes from chronic underwatering and then overwatering thanks to my neglect. A green thumb wasn't my forte.

"If you grew up in Southern California, you knew oleanders were poisonous." I shuddered at my close call as a very young girl. "They're not as prevalent now, but it used to be oleanders flourished in many yards because they made good privacy shields thanks to their rapid growth and the fact that they were drought-resistant and hardy. And of course, everyone liked the pretty flowers. They also used to be planted as freeway dividers. There were miles upon miles of oleanders. It was pretty when they were all in bloom."

She opened the gate to the alley and motioned for me to follow her.

"Hang on, let me get a leash for Piper." If we were going on a neighborhood stroll, I might as well let Piper enjoy an outing. In less than a minute, Piper and I were back.

"But they're poisonous. Why would people want a plant like that around kids and pets?" She led us down the alleyway and peered over fences as we passed each house.

"I guess most people just assumed kids wouldn't be stupid enough to ingest a yard plant." I gulped and wiped the prickle of perspiration away from my forehead. "Although when I was five, I wanted to have a surprise tea party for my mother and sister. I crumpled oleander leaves for the tea then floated their pink flowers in the liquid. I already had the teacup at my lips to taste the tea when my mom noticed and slapped the cup away, just in the nick of time. You can bet that those shrubs in the yard were pulled out the very next day, and I never forgot that lesson."

Detective Tran swiveled on her heels and placed her hands on her narrow hips. "Are you telling me you have personal knowledge that oleanders are poisonous?"

"Are you telling me Mr. Jorgensen was poisoned with

oleander?" Uh-oh. Had I just incriminated myself? I gulped again. "I didn't do it, and neither did Sal."

"I should be reading you your rights and hauling you in right now." Detective Tran rubbed her forehead with her fingertips. "But I can't think straight, and there's no evidence of oleanders on the Skyler property or in your neighborhood. My gut feeling is telling me it wasn't you."

"Thank you, thank you." Tears pricked my eyes. I'd been arrested enough to last a lifetime.

"That doesn't mean your employee is in the clear. Just the opposite." She was back in investigative mode. "I counted ten mature oleander bushes in his neighborhood, and there were traces found in your sister's catering van. We're going on the assumption that oleander was added to the victim's meal somehow. There are several eyewitnesses who say that Mr. Cruz had plenty of opportunities to do so. Combined with the erythromycin antibiotic the victim was taking for bronchitis, the results were deadly."

The unwelcomed news made me reel back, and I stumbled. Detective Tran reached out to steady me, and Piper took the opportunity to stand on her hind legs and lick her hand. A smile broke out on her face as she released my arm and bent over to scratch behind Piper's ears once she'd plopped back down to all four legs.

"You don't think my sister had anything to do with it, do you?" The oleander in the catering van wasn't what I wanted to hear. I didn't think the detective would be willing to part with any additional information, but I had to try. With an infant and two young daughters to care for, my sister didn't need the added stress of being a suspect. It was bad enough having her sole employee arrested.

"No, I don't consider her a valid suspect." She twisted her shell-pink lips in a wry smile. "I'd appreciate it, though, if you kept this conversation to yourself. I shouldn't have been so forthcoming, but I blame it on sheer exhaustion."

"Um, yeah, sure." There was no way I'd be able to keep this from Tillie. She'd pry it out of me in a heartbeat. And I'd have to discuss the implications of the oleander found in Carrie's catering van with my sister. Who put it there? Were they trying to frame one of us?

"Never mind. I see you'll have an impossible task of keeping a secret from your posse." The detective shook her head, and the sunlight accentuated the dark-blue highlights in her black hair. "Just try to limit how many people you share the information with, and see to it that they don't spread it around as gossip."

"That I can promise." I returned her smile. It worried me a bit that I felt comfortable with Detective Tran and even liked her. Did she use her friendly persona to get information out of unsuspecting witnesses instead of using an interrogation method? I'd have to watch what I said during our easy conversations.

"Thanks for the coffee and the muffin. It made me feel almost human." She shifted the satchel slung over her shoulder. "I'm sure I'll be in touch soon with more questions."

Once she had strode down the alleyway and turned the corner, Piper and I went back to Tillie's. It wouldn't have surprised me if the octogenarian was on the other side of her security gate, trying to eavesdrop on the detective. But she wasn't. Instead, Piper pulled me through the house and onto the patio that fronted the bay. Piper loved to chase the seagulls that tried to land on the glass half wall that kept brisk breezes from disturbing the patio occupants. I enjoyed watching the colorful sailboats and electric Duffy boats motoring by, as the occupants took in all the sights that Newport Bay had to offer.

Tillie sat in a cushioned chair and held a brightly colored mystery book in her hands. Reading glasses were perched on the end of her nose. She placed the book onto the glass tabletop just as Piper bounded up to her, and she bent over to give my pup some love.

"How did it go with the detective? Are you a suspect?"

"Surprisingly, no, and neither is Carrie, despite oleander being found in her catering van." I wasn't even going to pretend I couldn't wait to share this news with someone.

"So that was how the old goat died? Oleander?" Tillie tsked and shook her head.

"Apparently he was also on some kind of antibiotic that, when combined with oleander, produced a deadly effect." I wondered again if the copious amounts of alcohol the man had consumed had contributed to his death.

"Your pool house area had a slew of them planted alongside the wall adjacent to the main thoroughfare when I bought this place. I had them yanked out first thing, even though they provided a nice sound barrier and the flowers were pretty. I couldn't risk that rascal grandson of mine getting it into his head to put it into his pretend food and actually eat some when he was a young lad."

"Brian liked to cook even when he was a small boy?"

"Oh, yes. I don't know what his father was thinking trying to keep Brian from his passion." Tillie paused and dabbed at her eye. "I couldn't be prouder of him and his restaurant."

I had to agree. His Laguna Beach restaurant, Oceana, not only served award-winning food, it had amazing ocean views and the ambiance was divine. Once word had gotten out about the new eatery, there was now a month-long, or more, waiting list for reservations. Tillie had also made it very clear that she wished I could return Brian's romantic interest in me, which was another reason I rarely visited his restaurant. I couldn't tell her that while I was attracted to her grandson, he was too much of a player and had left a string of broken hearts up and down the Newport coast. I couldn't get involved with another man like that. My ex had been a player, and I'd never subject myself to someone like that again.

"What else did the detective have to say?" Tillie's voice cut into my thoughts.

"Not too much. She thinks Sal added oleander to the food he served to Mr. Jorgensen. She said plenty of the guests indicated Sal had ample opportunities to do so."

Tillie snorted. "Of course, they pointed the finger at Sal, and the chief finger pointer was certainly the killer."

I shivered and not because of the pleasant breeze blowing in from the bay. "It's hard to imagine I actually interacted with and served a killer. They all seemed so rich and la-di-da without a worry in the world, and now they couldn't care less that an innocent young man is taking the blame."

Chapter 13

I hung out with Tillie for a while longer. She tried to get me out of my funk by dropping hints about her new beau, but even that didn't improve my sour mood. I decided a brisk walk, or even a jog, might be the best solution, and Piper would never disagree with that choice.

Once I'd changed clothes and applied a liberal amount of sunscreen—as a redhead, I easily burned within minutes of sun exposure—Piper practically pulled my arm off as we headed out. Summer on the Balboa Peninsula is always crowded, particularly around the Balboa Fun Zone with its carnival rides, fair-type food, and entertainment. With the Fourth of July holiday occurring right before the weekend, many tourists had extended their stay, making the area unbearably packed.

Instead of heading to the downtown area, I led Piper toward the end of the peninsula, where most tourists didn't venture unless the waves were huge and the surfers swarmed. There, a long rocky jetty jutted out into the water where the Pacific Ocean convened with the Balboa Bay. There were several fishermen casting lines as they perched on the large rocks that formed the jetty.

It would be difficult for Piper to navigate the large rocks and chunks of concrete that made up the jetty, so I decided to stay on the sand, close to the lapping waves. Piper strained against her leash, wanting to frolic in the water, roll in the sand, and chase seagulls. I kept a tight hold of her and chided myself for not bringing treats to work on training her. I'd started doggie training but hadn't followed through, and at moments like this, I regretted it. So intent on keeping Piper away from a pile of pungent kelp-fly-and-beach-hopper-ridden seaweed, I didn't notice the tall man approaching until he stopped right in front of me.

"Emory?"

My head snapped up, and then I pulled Piper away from the odiferous mound before she had a chance to bury her snout into it.

"Will! What are you doing here?" I wanted to smack myself. It was obvious he was out for a walk.

"I decided I needed a break from visiting with my aunties." He half grimaced and half smiled. "For the past two hours, I've been trying to make my three eighty-something-year-old aunts understand why I'm over forty and not married. I was either going to bang my head on the table until I was unconscious or leave the house before I strangled them. Since it's a nice afternoon, I chose to leave and take Missy for a walk."

It was then I noticed a curly-furred small red dog sitting patiently by Will's feet.

"What a cute dog!" I knelt and offered the back of my hand to the dog. "What kind is she?"

"Missy's a mini goldendoodle." Will scratched his arm. "I have terrible allergies and my doctor thought I would do well with her breed."

"Oh! Piper's mom was part goldendoodle and terrier, but her father was quite a mixture of other things." I'd finally had a doggie DNA test done to see if there were any future medical issues I should be aware of due to her heritage.

Piper and Missy took the opportunity to sniff each other and become acquainted. It didn't take long for them to romp together as well as their attached leashes allowed.

"Do your aunts live nearby?" I tried to get Piper to sit after the two leashes tangled, but she wasn't having any of that, especially when a kid whizzed a Frisbee next to us, narrowly missing Will's head. Piper's paws scrambled in the soft sand, trying to chase the flying object, and it took all my strength to rein her in. "Yikes! Maybe we should move."

"Probably a good idea as long as it doesn't take us anywhere near my aunt's house at least for another hour." Will's shoulders drooped. "I guess after that I'll have to suck it up and collect my other two aunts and drive them back to Dana Point. I doubt they grasp the concept of Uber to get themselves home."

"You're a good man, Will Trenton." I gave him a sidelong glance. His skin didn't seem quite so sallow as the night of the party, and again I wondered if he was ill or was recovering from an illness. It wasn't my place to pry, so I didn't say anything.

"I've been worried about your employee. Sal, is his name?"

"Yes. It's Salvador Cruz. I'd planned on calling you tomorrow, once the holiday weekend was over." I thought carefully about what to say, not wanting him to think I was trying to get free legal advice. "He's been moved to the Orange County jail in Santa Ana, but he doesn't have an attorney, nor has he made a call to anyone to ask for help. I know you live in San Diego, but could you recommend someone up here to represent him? My friend, Tillie, said she's willing to pay his bail and legal fees."

"I can do better than that. I'm happy to be his attorney if he's willing to let me." Will urged Missy to follow when she got distracted by a potato chip bag discarded in the sand.

"Won't that be difficult living in San Diego while he's up here?" I picked up the pace, hoping to tire Piper out as we trudged through the sand, then slowed when I noticed Will's labored breathing.

"Can we find a quiet spot to sit for a moment?" Will pointed at a spot about twenty yards away from the water. "I don't have the energy I used to have after going through chemo."

"I'm so sorry. I didn't realize."

He waved away my concern. "It happened several months ago, and my cancer is in remission. But it's taking a while for my energy to return. It's one of the reasons I'm up here staying with a friend, with time on my hands. I didn't feel like I could go back to work, and he, ah, needed some assistance I could provide."

He flopped down onto a patch of sand that seemed far enough away from potential eavesdroppers, and Missy climbed into his lap. Piper flopped down, too, then rolled over on her back and squiggled. Belatedly, I realized I'd be spending most of the evening bathing and brushing her in order to get rid of the sand sure to be trapped in her thick fur. Perhaps we should have gone the route of the Balboa Fun Zone after all.

"What can you tell me about Sal's arrest and the ongoing investigation? I meant to follow up, but my aunts had their own agenda for me over the last two days." He groaned and drew Missy up to his chest. "They've had an endless stream of divorcées parading through for brunch, afternoon tea, and cocktails. I welcome the thought of immersing myself in defending your innocent young man from murder charges."

I double-checked to make sure there were no other beach-goers within listening distance then filled Will in on what I'd learned. By the time I finished talking, I wished I'd thought to bring a bottle of water. "I think there are plenty of other unknown suspects, thanks to the embezzling by Mr. Jorgensen's partner, to cast reasonable doubt on Sal's arrest."

"Let me make some calls first thing tomorrow morning, and I'll schedule a meeting with Sal, I hope by mid-morning. Will you be available to go with me?"

"Will they let me in as a visitor? I thought there were scheduled visiting hours that had to be adhered to."

"It won't be a problem. We'll just tell them you're my assistant." He glanced at me. "You don't happen to have any paralegal training, do you?"

"Nope. It's fine just as long as it doesn't create any issues for Sal."

Will stood, gently placed Missy down, and brushed off the sand clinging to his pants. He held his hand out to me, and when I grasped it, he pulled me to my feet. Piper scrambled to stand up and shook herself, which sent sand flying everywhere.

"I'll call you just as soon as I have a meeting scheduled. I hope it'll be around ten, so we'll need to be there around nine thirty." He pulled his cell phone from his pocket and opened the contacts app. "What's your cell number? I'll text you with the time and the address where we can meet in Santa Ana."

I recited my number then made sure I had his cell phone keyed into my own contacts list.

"Would you like to come back with me and meet my aunts?" He ran a bony hand through his thin hair. "I know it's a huge favor to ask, but it might get them off my back if they saw me with a woman."

"Really? They're that relentless?" Piper nudged my hand. "I'd need to drop Piper off at home first. She's too sandy to go anywhere."

"It's not a problem. I'll have to stay out on the patio anyway until I can clean Missy." He glanced at his watch. "They're probably having their tea and scones right about now, and honestly, I could use a wing-woman."

"If you're sure Piper won't be a problem, then I'm game." I was a bit hungry anyway, and maybe the aunts would share their scones.

"Thanks. You have no idea how much this means to me." He flashed a sheepish smile. "And you don't have to worry about me getting the wrong ideas about there being an 'us,' no matter how my aunts misinterpret your visit."

"No problem. I can't wait to meet your meddlesome aunties." I gave him a reassuring pat on his arm then turned to follow him toward the line of houses that lined the beach. Will and Missy trudged ahead of us, leading the way. His steps were plodding, and his shoulders bent forward. His dog stayed close beside him. I hoped getting involved in Sal's case wouldn't be too taxing on the man. He may claim his health had improved, but from my observation, he still looked quite ill.

About fifteen minutes later, Will led us onto a patio that faced the ocean. The unobstructed views were breathtaking. A round stone firepit was central to the patio, and three elderly women sat beside it, their pedicured toes resting on the ledge that ringed the pit. Small flames flickered across the crystal pieces that formed the base of the firepit. It was quite cozy.

Three sets of amber-colored eyes examined me the second I followed Will and Missy in.

"I ran into friends on the beach. This is Emory and Piper." Will had straightened up, and his voice sounded energetic. Did his aunts not know how ill he'd been or still was? "Emory, these are my great-aunts, Pansy, Petunia, and Poppy."

The women each gave a little finger wave as Will called out their name.

"Welcome, dear. Have a seat and help yourself to a scone and tea." The three women gazed at their nephew then back to me. Smiles broke out across their wrinkled faces.

"It's so nice to meet you." My dog gazed at the small cart that held a heaping plate of scones and a fat teapot that emitted steam from the spout. I pulled her leash tighter. I gestured around the patio. "You have a lovely home, and your view is spectacular. I imagine you see the most amazing sunsets."

"Yes, that is true, dear," Pansy said. "I've lived here for close to forty years and wouldn't dream of moving anywhere else, even though the crowds and traffic can be unbearable at times."

The three women all began talking at once, fussing over tourists and how crowded the freeways were. I looked around for Will, uncertain where to sit or what I should do. Missy had made herself comfortable on a large padded cushion lying on the floor in the corner. Piper tugged on the leash, wanting to join her new friend. I walked Piper over and got her settled, and the two dogs curled together.

Will was in the process of pulling a chair over to the firepit. He winked at me and patted the cushion for me to sit. "I'll get you a scone and some tea. Do you prefer milk or lemon in your tea?"

"Plain is fine, but I can get my own cup."

"Now, dear, let him wait on you. He's such a darling that way. Knows how to treat a lady. You can't do any better than being with someone like our Will." I half expected Pansy to ask us what date our wedding was scheduled for already. No wonder Will wanted a wing-woman.

"Now Aunt Pansy, Emory and I are only friends. We just met at the Jorgensens' party on Friday."

"Oh! Did you attend with your grandparents or an aunt? Do I know your people?" Pansy leaned toward me as if to examine my face for recognition. She wrinkled her nose a bit when she took in my frizzy red hair. The humidity from the beach wasn't kind to my hair.

"My sister and I were the caterers." I took a nibble of the scone then placed the concrete block back on the dainty china plate. The pastry was so hard I could've chipped a tooth.

"Ohhhhh…" Pansy let the drawn-out word linger in the air. She squinted her eyes at Will, drew her mouth downward, and gave an imperceptible shake of her head. Apparently, she didn't want her grandnephew fraternizing with the help.

"It really was an amazing dinner, and Emory's cupcakes were"—he hesitated for a moment—"er, out of this world."

I realized he'd just about said "to die for" before he remembered someone had died, maybe even from my cupcakes.

"But didn't the caterer intentionally poison Arthur Jorgensen?" As one, Pansy, Petunia, and Poppy scooted their chairs away from me.

Chapter 14

I'd beaten a hasty retreat with Will apologizing profusely for his aunts' behavior. I didn't blame him in the least and in fact felt quite sorry for leaving him to face his aunts on his own. By the time I'd pulled Piper home—she didn't want to leave her new friend or the excitement of the beach—and spent time grooming her to get the sand out of her fur, it was almost dinnertime. Tillie had sent me a text letting me know she had plans with her "new" friend and not to worry.

I opened the fridge and stared at the container filled with buttercream and the few remaining eggs left over from baking. The two limoncello cupcakes I'd saved from my mother's order sat encased in tightly sealed plasticware. There wasn't much else to eat. I dreaded a run to the grocery store but knew it was a must so I'd have something healthful to feed Tillie for breakfast.

After feeding Piper and grabbing a few stale crackers to snack on, I headed out. Traffic wasn't nearly as thick as it had been the day before. Ideally, that meant most holiday tourists had made the journey home and I wouldn't have to fight crowds of sunburned parents and cranky, hungry kids while standing in line to purchase groceries.

Claiming a lone shopping basket stuck in an outer corner of the small parking lot, I pushed it, wobbly wheel and all, to the brightly lit market. The smells of freshly baked bread mingled with brewed coffee, and my stomach rumbled. It wasn't nearly as busy as I'd feared, and I quickly gathered fresh fruits and vegetables and a few dairy products and then headed to the deli to find something quick for my own dinner.

"Hey, you." Someone jostled my arm, and I yanked on the cart to keep it from crashing into a display of packaged cookies and cupcakes. I whipped my head around and stared into the dark-green eyes of Brian Skyler, Tillie's grandson.

"Brian! I didn't expect to see you grocery shopping." I tried to casually smooth back my frizzy hair. While I'd shampooed and brushed Piper out after our trip to the beach, I hadn't done a thing about my appearance. I probably looked frightful.

"A guy can't eat out every meal." He shrugged. "Actually, I'm craving some Chunky Monkey ice cream, so here I am. After cooking brunch for over two hundred at Oceana today, I definitely deserve a reward. Care to join me?"

"Wow, you had some turnover today. Is two hundred a record?" I purposely ignored his invitation.

"It is. We had three seatings, thanks to the holiday weekend." Brian used his palm to rub the back of his neck. It was hard to tear my eyes away from his well-defined biceps and the T-shirt that hugged his six-pack abs. Despite being a busy chef, Brian spent a lot of time working out and surfing. "What's Tillie up to?"

"She went out to dinner with some friends. Andrew drove her, so she's well taken care of." I wasn't entirely sure that was the case, but Brian had a protective streak when it came to his grandmother.

She called it overprotective almost to the point of being

intrusive, so I tried to mediate and keep him from inhibiting her zest for life. He certainly wouldn't approve of her dating, and I did everything I could to protect her secrets. Her other grandson, Theodore, whom she called Teddy to his great annoyance, wanted to contain his grandmother with the intent of gaining control over her fortune. At least Brian had altruistic intentions. He really did love his grandmother and didn't want to see any harm come from her unconventional—according to their social standing in the community—lifestyle.

He grunted. "Well, my offer stands to share my container of ice cream. You can tell me about the latest murder you've found yourself wrapped up in, and I'll share the gossip I heard today about the victim."

I knew it was a bad idea, but my interest piqued with his offer to share gossip about the Jorgensens. Brian's Laguna Beach restaurant wasn't that far from where the Jorgensens resided. Perhaps he had something new that would shed light on exonerating Sal.

"Well…" I twisted my mouth in a wry grin. "I haven't eaten dinner yet, and I can't leave Piper alone for too long."

"Tell you what, buy your groceries, and I'll meet you at your place with dinner and ice cream." He smirked. "I knew my offer of gossip was too good for you to pass up."

I lightly punched his shoulder, which was rock-hard. "Fine. But I want Super Fudge Chunk ice cream."

Brian bumped my shoulder back. "You got it. See you in about thirty minutes."

I hurriedly finished my shopping, and as soon as I'd popped the groceries into the trunk of my car, I sent Tillie a text letting her know Brian was coming over. I knew he'd repeatedly monitor his grandmother and make a big deal when she returned home. Then, if past experience was any indication, he'd question her about who she'd spent time with and where she'd been. It was all thanks to Tillie's former daughter-in-law, a trophy wife with bad intentions, who convinced the family that Tillie had dementia and could no longer care for herself. There was zero truth in those accusations.

Tillie responded with a palm-over-face emoji and said she'd be home soon. I hated that she had to cut her date short, but there wasn't any way I would invite myself to Brian's house. That seemed dangerous in the emotional boundaries sense to me, and I had to remind myself, again, that Randall and I were dating, no matter how much Brian's appeal might be growing on me. I sent Tillie a text back and told her to come to my place when she got back, and she could have dinner with us. Tillie didn't answer, and I knew it was because she wanted to play matchmaker.

Once I returned home, I let Piper out and put the perishables into the refrigerator. Before unpacking the remaining groceries, I brushed my hair and put on a subtle shade of lipstick after washing my face. I wished I'd taken a shower after bathing Piper earlier, but it was too late for that.

By the time Brian arrived, carrying takeout sacks from the best Italian restaurant in the county, iconic Antonio's, I'd managed to clean the kitchen and put away the stacks of clean laundry I'd allowed to build up. Piper pranced around Brian's feet as she sniffed the mouthwatering aromas emanating from the bags. I had to admit I was about doing the same as Piper, since my stomach growled loudly enough for Brian to hear.

"Why don't you plate up the food, and I'll open the wine." Brian rummaged in my freezer, trying to find space for the two pints of ice cream.

I bumped him out of the way and found a miniscule crevasse and wedged them in. It didn't much matter if the lids were a bit misshaped from the shove it took to fit them in. "Whad'ya bring from Antonio's? I would've been content with deli fried chicken and potato salad."

Brian whirled around to look at me and placed his hand

over his heart. "You wound me after all the effort I went into picking up dinner. Besides, deli fried chicken isn't real food."

I felt my face flame hot. "No, that's not what I meant. Of course I'm beyond grateful you brought this feast. I just feel bad you went to all the effort and expense. Let me know how much I owe you for my share."

"It's no trouble." He waved away my offer. "My treat, although if it's fried chicken you want, I'll bring that next time. Except it'll be my own home-cooked chicken and not from some nasty deli."

There really shouldn't have been a next time, although home-cooked fried chicken certainly sounded tempting as did the way those dark-green eyes gazed at me. I shook myself and pulled two plates from the cupboard then opened the takeout sacks and pulled out containers of eggplant parmigiana, garlic bread, and Caesar salad. My mouth watered.

Brian busied himself by pouring two goblets of ruby-red wine, and I caught a glimpse of the winery label. He'd brought a top-notch bottle. Letting him come here was a very bad idea, but I hoped any information he could provide about the murder would offset the downside.

Once we'd settled at the kitchen table with plates piled high with the food and Piper curled beneath our feet, hopeful that a morsel might fall her way, I brought up the murder. "Okay, spill your gossip. I've been on pins and needles wondering what you know about them."

Brian picked up his wine goblet and swirled the red liquid, then took a sip of the wine. "We'll get to that, Emory, but for now, enjoy the food and the wine. They're meant to be experienced together and savored."

He had a point, and I did love food. I couldn't stop myself from comparing his view with Randall's outlook on food, which was that it was mere sustenance for him. He generally shoveled it in so fast, he almost couldn't taste it. I gave myself a mental slap. I couldn't compare the two men. Randall's fast-paced, high-profile security company kept him on the go with extensive travel. As he'd told me before, he often didn't know when he'd get to eat next, so when a meal came, he ate it quickly, since regular interruptions came. When we did see each other, it wasn't leisurely with time to linger over a bottle of wine and a good meal. Instead, it was snatches of time squeezed in between catering jobs, especially after Carrie's baby arrival and his flights in and out.

The sound of Brian clinking his wineglass to mine tugged me from my musings. "Tell me what cupcake flavors you've been working on. Perhaps we can feature some at the restaurant."

"Uh, I don't know about that. Oceana is so"—I struggled to find the right word, thrown off-balance by his offer to feature my cupcakes—"elegant. Or perhaps 'sophisticated' is a better word. My cupcakes wouldn't really fit in."

Brian threw his head back and laughed. "Everyone, no matter how sophisticated they may pretend to be, loves cupcakes. What did you serve at the Jorgensens' party?"

"Limoncello cupcakes were the biggest hit, but I also served lower-calorie champagne cupcakes."

"Do you have any cupcakes already made I could sample?"

"Actually, I just happen to have two limoncellos leftover from my mom's party yesterday. I'll set them out so they come to room temperature while we eat." I went to the fridge and placed the cupcakes on the counter. "I don't think the ice cream flavors will go very well with the limoncello, and I'm pretty sure I don't have any vanilla ice cream, although I can check with Tillie."

Surprisingly, Brian waved away my offer to check with his grandmother. It made me think they were both in cahoots in coordinating this dinner. After all, Tillie knew Randall was still in Florida and wouldn't be home for another week.

"We'll eat the cupcake first, and then we can eat the ice

cream if we're still hungry." He looked down at the plate of eggplant parmigiana and shook his head. "Maybe I shouldn't have gotten a double order. These are huge portions."

"I'll box it up, and it'll reheat just fine for your lunch or dinner tomorrow."

"You keep the leftovers for you and Tillie." He took another large bite and swallowed. "I've got a double shift at the restaurant tomorrow, and I'll eat there. We're finally training a new assistant executive chef, so I hope I'll start seeing some consistent days off."

Chapter 15

We spent another hour chatting about the restaurant, and we brainstormed seasonal flavors of cupcakes that I could create that would complement tasting menus he had planned for the holiday season. I jotted notes and couldn't wait to start experimenting. By the time Brian tasted the limoncello cupcake, he'd already decided to pair it with limoncello sorbet and add lemon piccata scallops to the menu. I could barely contain my grin when he placed an order for five dozen cupcakes to start out and wanted them delivered on Thursday.

Brian quickly did the dishes while I took Piper outside. He joined us and handed the half glass of wine I'd left inside to me then motioned at the patio chairs. "Shall we sit out here and I'll tell you everything I've heard about the Jorgensens? Or would you rather talk while we take Piper for a walk?"

Considering how tight my waistband felt, a walk wasn't a bad idea. Piper, hearing the word "walk," ran up to us and danced on her hind legs.

"I don't think my dog is going to give us a choice. Let me grab her leash and put on better shoes." I still wore the dollar-store rubber flip-flops I'd put on to bathe Piper.

It didn't take long until we were walking on the now quiet, dark streets. Brian headed toward the end of the peninsula.

"Do you mind if we stick to sidewalks instead of the beach? Piper already had a long romp in the sand today, and it took me over an hour to get the sand out of her fur."

"Whatever you want. Just lead the way." He swept his hand in front of us.

Despite having had a long walk already, Piper was eager to move. We picked up our pace to match hers. I checked our surroundings to make sure no one was within earshot and found the streets empty. "No more procrastinating. Tell me what you've heard about the murder."

Brian chuckled. "Obviously, the caterers are the killers."

"Argh. It's going to be the final nail in finishing off my sister's company." Business had been bad since the Halloween party, but this would make it doubly worse.

"Don't worry. I set those people straight." He brushed my bare arm with his fingertips. "Perhaps I can work something out with your sister and send some business her way if she wouldn't mind using my recipes. Maybe create a catering extension of Oceana until I can get my own staff hired and trained?"

"You'd do that for us?" Brian was proving to be full of surprises tonight.

"It's actually a great solution for both of us. I've had several customers want to hire us to cater, and I simply can't take it on right now. Your sister has the experience and the cooking expertise to pull it off. Have her give me a call tomorrow. You have my cell number, right?"

I nodded, relieved that there might be hope for Carrie's business. "Thanks. I'll send her a text tonight with your information."

"I also heard that Arthur Jorgensen had dementia and was a handful to keep out of trouble."

"He definitely was a handful at the party. Do you think that was why Tiny was always around?"

"Tiny? Who's that?" He placed his hand beneath my elbow and pulled me to the side of the sidewalk as a man, pushing a doublewide jogging stroller containing two small wiry-haired dogs, ran past us.

"He's huge, think NFL huge, bald, carries a gun. He's maybe in his early forties. I think he's their bodyguard."

"Ah, you must mean Carlton, although I don't know his last name. He's Lisette's nephew, but they treat him like an employee instead of a family member."

"You've met him before?" I let Piper reel out the retractable leash as she rushed to sniff a lone tree planted in a bitty patch of dirt that was surrounded on all sides by concrete.

"Lisette and Arthur have dined at Oceana a few times, and Carlton has been there, standing at attention, so to speak."

"But why would they need a bodyguard, especially one so visible as Tiny, er, Carlton?"

"They claimed—now, mind you, this is all hearsay—that their son was murdered and the business partner who absconded with their investors' money had put a hit out on them too."

"That's awful! Did the police find any evidence that their son was murdered?" We'd caught up to Piper, and I gave her leash a gentle tug to pull her away from the tree's scents that intrigued her.

"Unless someone forced him to booze and coke it up at the party, there wasn't any evidence of foul play. But honestly, it wasn't much of a surprise he died that way."

"Did you know their son, Nathan?"

"I'd met him a few times years ago, but I didn't really know him. He was a couple years ahead of Theodore in school, and they were on the tennis team together. I think they continued to play tennis together off and on even after college." He huffed out a breath of air. "I suppose I could ask my brother what he knew about Nathan, if you think it'll help."

There wasn't any brotherly affection between the half brothers Brian and Theodore, for which I placed the blame entirely on Theodore. He was pretentious and greedy. I'd had my own run-ins with him, and none had been pleasant. "Don't bother. He won't give you any information without demanding something in return. Besides, Nathan doesn't sound like someone your brother would have anything to do with."

"True. Nathan was a trust fund baby, and nothing was ever expected from him. It's probably why he was such a huge partier." Brian pursed his lips. "Although it seems to me Arthur finally made his son start coming to the office several days a week in the months leading up to Nathan's death."

"Perhaps there is a connection between the partner absconding with the funds and Nathan's death after all."

He shrugged. "Hard to say, but as far as I know, the investigators never linked them together."

"Do you know the partner's name?" I hadn't thought about researching that angle until now and wanted as much information as possible to pass on to Will.

"I don't remember. But I think their company was called Seacliff Investments."

Hmmm, that company name meant nothing to me. "Any other tidbits of gossip you've overheard?"

"Actually, there is, and I think you might be able to clarify it for me." He leaned in toward me until his lips were close to my ear. "I hear my grandmother is dating some mega-wealthy British baron."

I stumbled and would have fallen if Brian hadn't grabbed my arm to steady me. Piper paused mid-step and looked back. My mind raced to recall what Tillie had said. I knew for certain she hadn't mentioned a word about nobility, only that her nemesis, Frances Allain, would be green with envy. "What!? I haven't heard a peep. Where did you hear that from?"

His chuckles filled my ears. "Oh, I have my sources."

No matter how much I cajoled, Brian wouldn't tell me anything further about Tillie's new beau, although by the same token, I wouldn't confirm that she even dated. In fact, I stated the opposite. She only had friends.

"Speaking of dating, is my dad seeing anyone that you know of?" Brian kept his gaze facing forward. His father, David Skyler, had made a couple monumental mistakes with matrimonial choices, and it had almost torn the family apart.

"The only time I hear from him is when he sends me a text with instructions on where to FedEx a packet of mail. The last I heard from him was well over a week ago when he was in Paris." I paused, wondering how much my boss wanted his sons to know where he was. He'd traveled to Europe numerous times for extended periods ever since his last trophy wife met with a tragic ending. I thought his travel started out because he wanted to escape the press coverage surrounding the death, and then he found he enjoyed it. Theodore had proven himself capable of taking over the family business, which made it feasible. "I think his plan later this week is to head to Lake Geneva in Switzerland and stay for a month."

Brian snorted. "He must be getting another face lift. At least that means he doesn't have a new girlfriend yet, but I'll bet there'll be one hanging around just as soon as he recovers. It's his MO."

I shrugged. It wasn't any of my business, and I'd always suspected Mr. Skyler had already indulged in cosmetic surgery long before I'd started working for him. I didn't care about a new girlfriend, either, as long as she didn't try to turn the family against one another.

Chapter 16

B y the time Brian left, I was too exhausted to do an online search on Seacliff Investments. Instead, I sent my sister a quick text with Brian's catering job offer along with his cell number. She responded with three red heart emojis, which made me smile. Next, I chopped up fresh fruit for breakfast and prepared the coffee machine to automatically begin to brew at six.

My conversation about Brian's father reminded me it had been almost a week since I'd attended to my part-time accounting job for Mr. Skyler. I knew mounds of mail and bills awaited me at his home, and it was time to get them taken care of. He'd made it clear from the first day he hired me, at my mother's behest, that I could set my own hours and days. My first and foremost responsibility was to cook for his mother, Tillie, and keep her out of trouble. Getting her to avoid trouble was easier said than done.

I sent a quick text to Hannah Olsson, Mr. Skyler's live-in housekeeper, letting her know I'd be there early. Since I had my own entrance and alarm code for the house, I shouldn't be a bother to her, but I still didn't want to startle her should she hear me come in.

Between all the walking, fresh air, good food, and wine I'd had, I slept soundly until my alarm shrilled. I wanted to bury my head beneath the pillows and go back to sleep, but instead I pulled myself out of bed and headed to the shower. Fueled by coffee and a microwave-defrosted muffin I'd dug up from the depths of my freezer—don't think I wasn't tempted by the ice cream Brian had left behind—I headed to Mr. Skyler's home. As the crow flies, he wasn't that far away from my home, but since he lived on the opposite side of the bay, I either had a twenty-minute drive—assuming there wasn't traffic—or a ten-minute bike ride plus a ten-minute ferry ride to get to his house. Since tourists were still snug in their beds, I drove and happily found curbside parking around the corner and half a block down from his residence. Sometimes I ended up parking a half mile away when summer crowds swarmed the area.

The huge, stuccoed edifice, painted a light cinnamon color, took up half the block. After punching in the security gate code, I pulled the house key from my purse and climbed the outside spiral wrought-iron staircase to the small second-floor balcony. The views of the bay from the little balcony couldn't be beat, and I often liked to sit and watch the boats float by while I ate lunch or sipped coffee. I kept my gaze from looking down toward the crystalline blue pool. It held too many horrific memories.

After letting myself into the office and punching in the alarm code to disarm the security system, I rifled through the neat piles of mail Hannah had set on my desk. She'd separated them into stacks of catalogs and advertisements, bills, invitations, and miscellaneous. It wasn't the housekeeper's job to do that for me, but I suppose being by herself with little to do except some dusting and general cleaning had to be pretty boring. When Mr. Skyler was in residence, she'd prepare meals and run errands for him, but for now, his visits home were few and far in between.

I paid the bills from the generous checking account Mr. Skyler had set up for me to use. Next, I declined all the invitations he'd received for a variety of galas and charitable events. If the events and donation requests were on his list of approved charities, I wrote out checks for their fundraising efforts. Mr. Skyler, and his family, had proven to be quite philanthropic, and I was impressed by the breadth of needs that they contributed to.

Hannah interrupted me just as I began weeding through the stack of catalogs and advertisements. I'd learned the hard way about tossing the pile before making sure an important document hadn't accidentally gotten stuck in between a page.

"Excuse me, Miss Emory, can I make you a latte or a chai?" Hannah stood in the doorway, dressed in a simple floral-print dress and her gray hair neatly braided. She was on the stocky side and looked to be about fifty. Soft-spoken, Hannah brought a calming influence to the household that was much needed after the events that occurred around Halloween last year.

"Thanks, a latte would be wonderful. Is everything going okay around here?"

"Yes, Miss Emory." She seemed to hesitate but didn't say anything.

I raised my eyebrows, hoping it would prompt her to speak up.

"Well…" Again, she paused. "I don't know if I should say anything, but maybe you'll know if it's okay… Mr. Theodore… he's been coming around and removing items."

"Items? Like what?" Neither Mr. Skyler or Tillie had mentioned to me that Theodore would or should have access to the house.

"First it was an old book from the library that he said he needed to do some research on and then a silver tea set that he said Mr. Skyler wanted professionally polished." She looked down at the floor and wouldn't meet my gaze. "I keep the silver polished, and there wasn't anything wrong with the tea set. I don't want to get in the middle of a family squabble, but I don't want to be blamed for things missing either."

"I can make sure that doesn't happen." I had the access codes to all the security cameras that surrounded the Skyler compound. I'd definitely be making a backup copy of the video feed showing Theodore's forays into his father's house, even though the ongoing video would be on file for at least a month. "Did he take anything else?"

"Yes." Hannah smashed her lips together until they almost turned white. "Yesterday."

"Hannah, trust me, you won't get in trouble with Mr. Skyler." I stood and reached out to give her arm a gentle squeeze. "If Theodore has permission to take those items, Mr. Skyler will be grateful that you're keeping a close watch on his property in his absence. If he doesn't have permission, then it's our duty to protect Mr. Skyler's assets."

The housekeeper still remained silent, and a tear trickled down her cheek.

"Did Theodore threaten you somehow?" I couldn't see him threatening violence, but I could certainly see him bullying this soft-spoken woman by telling her she'd be fired if she said a peep. "Did he tell you you'd lose your job?"

She gave a tiny nod. "And said I'd go to jail for anything that's missing from the house."

"That's not going to happen. And, if for some bizarre reason you lose your job, I promise you that Tillie will see to it that you're well compensated and will find an even better position for you. Okay?"

She nodded again. "Maybe I should show you the blank wall, and you can say you noticed the painting missing and that you checked the security video and saw him take it. I don't think Mr. Theodore knows about the video recordings."

I had a very bad feeling about the blank wall Hannah wanted to show me, but I agreed. If my premonition was correct, Mr. Skyler would need to catch the very first flight available and come straight home.

I followed Hannah out into the hallway and down the wide curved staircase that led to the ground floor. A long gallery-type hallway ran from the massive front door to the great room that looked out onto the patio and pool deck. Paintings by both notable and obscure artists alike hung on the walls lining the hallway. But the most cherished painting, given a prominent placement, was missing. Worth several million, the Jackson Pollock had vanished. I felt my knees wobble, and I abruptly sat and leaned against the wall.

I waved my hand at the empty spot. "Did Theodore say why he took this painting?"

"He said it belonged to his mother and that Mr. Skyler agreed it should go back to her."

I knew for a fact that Theodore was straight-out lying. He'd just committed a felony, because no way did Mr. Skyler give that painting to his son or his ex-wife. The Pollock was his pride and joy after purchasing it only two years ago. It wasn't that long ago that I'd scanned the purchase authentication along with an updated appraisal for the insurance policy. How was I going to break the news to Mr. Skyler?

I climbed to my feet, my knees still wobbly. "I'll make a backup copy of the security video showing Theodore leaving with the painting, and then I'll call Tillie for advice."

Hannah stood there wringing her hands. "I'll get the latte for you."

I shook my head. "No. I don't think I could drink it right now. Maybe later would be better."

She nodded then fled to the sanctuary of her kitchen. I trudged up the stairs and made my way to the A/V room. After keying in the passcode, I scanned the recorded video feed from the day before. Sure enough, around ten yesterday morning, Theodore, dressed in a suit, let himself into the house. He clearly had used a key, and not once did I see

Hannah at the doorway. Ten minutes later he left the house, this time carrying the almost two-foot-by-three-foot painting. I cringed when he almost knocked a corner of the painting on the security gate as he exited to the street.

Why hadn't he wrapped it in protective covering before he left? The video provided clear evidence that it was indeed the Jackson Pollock painting and Theodore was in sole possession of it. I made three copies of the incriminating video. I'd scan the previous days and make copies of the other items he'd pilfered, but right now, the theft of the painting needed to addressed before it disappeared into a private collection.

Chapter 17

I pulled my cell out and called Tillie. Before she even had a chance to say hello, I started jabbering.

"Whoa, Em. Slow down." Tillie chortled. "Did someone have a bit too much coffee this morning?"

"Sorry." I sucked in a lungful of air. "The Jackson Pollock is missing. It's been stolen by Theodore."

Nothing but silence filled my ear for what seemed like minutes. Finally, a squeaky voice came through. "Could you repeat that, Em? I thought I heard you say the Pollock has been stolen."

I closed my eyes. "I'm so sorry. But yes, Theodore waltzed in here yesterday and took it. I found it on the security video."

Tillie never swore, but today words came from her mouth that I wouldn't have thought she even knew. "That stupid, stupid boy. Have you gotten ahold of David yet or called the police?"

"No! I haven't done either. That's why I called you as soon as I saw the video. I have no idea what to do."

"Okay, this is what we're going to do. Put me on a three-way call with David. It's what time in Paris right now, or wherever he is?"

"I think it's either four or five in the afternoon." I opened the world clock app on my phone and checked while I walked back to my office. "It's definitely five. Once I connect the three of us, do you want me to break the news to him?"

"I'll do it, but when he picks up, let him know all three of us are on the call, and then I'll take over. I want you to stay on so you can facilitate any instructions he might have." Tillie muttered something, and I thought I heard her say "stupid boy" again. "Let me know when you have David connected to our call."

With shaking fingers, I called David's cell phone and prayed he answered. It rang five times, and just when I thought it would switch to voice mail, he answered.

"*Bonjour*, Emory!" He sounded quite jovial. Perhaps he'd been sipping wine in a Paris bistro, although I didn't hear any background noise.

"Hi, Mr. Skyler. I have Matilda on the line with us. She'd like to chat with you for a moment." Tillie's son detested his mother's chosen nickname and insisted on calling her the more formal Matilda. Not once had I ever heard him call her Mom or even Mother.

"Matilda, what can I do for you?" His tone had turned formal and stiff.

"David, I hate to be the bearer of bad news, but your son seems to have borrowed your Jackson Pollock painting."

His roar filled my ear, and I pulled my phone away from my head. I put it back just in time for him to blame Brian for the theft.

"No, Mr. Skyler! It was Theodore!" I couldn't hold my tongue while Tillie collected her thoughts to redirect Mr. Skyler away from blaming Brian, who had never been the favored son. "This morning I saw the empty space where the painting should have been, so I scanned the security feed. It's all there showing Theodore came yesterday at ten and walked off with it."

"It can't be," he sputtered. "Please tell me this is a sick prank."

"Son, I'm afraid it's true." Tillie cleared her throat. "What do you want us to do? Call the police?"

"Absolutely not. This stays in the family." He was back to roaring, and I hoped he wasn't in a public place. "Do I make myself clear?"

"Yes, sir." I wasn't going to be the one to get on this man's bad side.

"Emory, get me on the first direct flight from Paris to LAX. Coordinate with Janelle on having my driver meet me curbside. I won't check luggage." He whispered something to a person in the background, and a female voice answered. Perhaps there was a new woman in the picture. "Matilda, hire that private investigator we used last year and have him track Theodore. He's not to confront my son unless Theodore tries to hand the painting over to a collector. As long as it remains in his possession, I'd like to leave well enough alone until I'm back to straighten out this mess."

While he'd been talking, I'd pulled up a website for flights and had just about finished booking his business class seat on Air France. "Mr. Skyler, the first flight out is tomorrow morning, ten fifteen, from Charles De Gaulle landing at LAX at two fifteen in the afternoon. They only offer business class."

"Fine. Let Janelle know."

"Is there anything else you need for us to do before you arrive?" My finger hit the purchase button, and once the confirmation of the flight popped up, I printed out a copy.

"Just keep this quiet. Don't breathe a word of it even to Brian." He cleared his throat. "I'm sorry I jumped to the conclusion that he was the cad who took advantage of me. I know you're close to that boy, Matilda."

Tillie didn't respond, just harrumphed a couple times. For a family who had so much, they certainly were dysfunctional, and for certain it bothered Tillie.

The call disconnected without Mr. Skyler saying another word. I scanned the flight confirmation and sent it attached to a text to Mr. Skyler and to his company assistant, Janelle, with a message for her to coordinate his driver. She responded immediately with a "got it" and a smiley face. I thought I should forewarn Brian that his father was coming back but decided it could wait. I had other more important issues to attend to.

My call to Tillie went directly to voice mail, and I assumed she had called the private investigator the second Mr. Skyler disconnected the call. I returned to the A/V room and continued scanning the recorded feed going backward, looking for proof of other items Theodore pilfered. All the while, my mind tried to puzzle out his motivation. He was paid handsomely by his father's company, and while he might not have ownership, he knew it eventually would be passed down to himself and his brother. Had he gotten into financial trouble somehow? Had he invested with an unscrupulous company, similar to what happened with Seacliff Investments? Or did he have a gambling problem? I shook my head to clear my thoughts and refocused on the video feed whizzing by.

I found him again, on the afternoon of July fourth, entering the house and then removing a large cardboard box that contained the Tiffany silver tea service that had been passed down from Mr. Skyler's paternal grandmother. While worth only several thousand dollars, nothing in the vicinity of the Pollock painting, had it been a trial run for the larger theft? Or had it proven effortless and paved the way for the greater temptation?

Using the intercom, I called down to Hannah and asked her to bring me a glass of ice water. I could have gotten it myself, but I wanted her to confirm that Theodore had only entered the house three times that she knew of. I plugged the flash stick containing the theft of the Pollock painting into the laptop that stayed in the A/V room and brought up the video to make sure it worked properly.

Once Hannah set the crystal tumbler down beside me, I motioned for her to take a seat. I started the video and pointed at Theodore exiting the house, painting in hand. "Here's the evidence that Theodore was the thief. You're nowhere in sight, which exonerates you. I found where he took the Tiffany tea set, and I'll continue looking for the book he stole. Do you know the title or the exact date he took it?"

"I don't know which book he took. I looked in the library after he left, but there are so many books on the shelves, I just couldn't tell." She appeared to be counting as she moved her lips silently. "Maybe he took the book on the first, or maybe it was the second? The days kind of run together."

"That's all right. Are you sure those three days are the only time he came and removed items from the house?"

"Yes, although I suppose he could have let himself in when I ran errands or on my day off when I went to visit my mom in San Diego."

"What day was that?"

Hannah twisted her hands together. "It was Sunday, June twenty-ninth. Sundays are usually my day off, but I had a migraine, so I stayed home yesterday."

"Perhaps Theodore didn't expect you to be here yesterday, and you surprised him."

"I guess that's possible. He was definitely angry when I questioned him about taking the painting, even though I tried to be polite about it."

It would explain why he made up the lie about the painting belonging to his mother and trying to intimidate Hannah. "All right, I'll keep scrolling back for at least another couple of weeks. If you notice anything else missing in the house, no matter how inconsequential, let me know."

"Thank you for believing me, Miss Emory."

"Oh, before I forget, Mr. Skyler is flying home tomorrow.

He lands in LAX at two fifteen, so I suppose you'll need to have food prepared for him." I glanced back down at the video playing in a loop on the laptop. "He also doesn't want a word of the theft to leak to anyone. No police, no outsiders."

She nodded. "I won't say anything to anyone. It's for the best."

Once Hannah headed back to her domain, I continued my scrolling. The monotony of the video running backward almost made me miss Theodore's visit on July second. I slowed the playback down and tried to focus on the book he carried in his hand as he departed the house. It was thick, maybe four inches, and the cover appeared to be tooled leather. But no matter how I squinted at the frame I'd frozen in place, I couldn't make out the title. I snapped a photo with my cell phone and tried zooming in that way but to no avail.

After saving the footage to the flash stick, I continued the monotonous scrolling again. When I came to the twenty-ninth, Hannah's day off, I slowed the video back down. Sure enough, at noon sharp, Theodore let himself into the house. Fifteen minutes, later he exited, carrying a small framed paint-ing. I stopped the video and used my cell phone to take a picture and zoom in.

I stood up abruptly, and my chair fell over backward and clattered on the hardwood floor. Rushing to the master suite, I bypassed the bedroom and hurried to Mr. Skyler's private study. There, on the wall behind his desk, an empty space stood with a hook still sticking out from the wall. Once again, my knees felt like they would give way. Theodore had taken another valuable painting from his father—this time it was a Picasso.

Chapter 18

Hannah must've heard the crash of my chair, because a minute later, she rushed into the room, breathless. "What's wrong?"

And then she noticed the empty wall and crossed herself. "Oh my God! Not the Picasso, too."

"I found the video. He took it last Sunday while you were out." I glanced over at the ashen woman. "Do you need to sit down?"

She shook her head. "I can't believe this is happening. Why did he do this to his father?"

"You haven't been in this room since last Sunday?" I was certain that if she had, Hannah would have immediately noticed the missing painting.

"No. With Mr. Skyler traveling so much, I take two weeks to rotate through the house, deep cleaning as I go." She pulled her phone from a pocket in her dress, opened the calendar app, and scrolled through several days. "I cleaned this room on Saturday, June twenty-eighth. The day before he took it."

"All right, let's close the door, and I'll copy the video footage to the flash stick then call Tillie. It's probably best to wait until Mr. Skyler returns home to let him know, since I'm assuming he'll want to handle this the same way as the Pollock."

She looked at me with fear-filled eyes. "I think I should quit and disappear for a while. I can't be implicated in these thefts."

"Please don't do that. There's enough evidence to exonerate you while convicting Theodore of the crimes. I promise, you have nothing to fear."

She gave me a wary gaze then turned her back and plodded downstairs and back to the kitchen. I hoped my promise held true, but I honestly couldn't see Mr. Skyler throwing this kind woman to the wolves in order to protect his son. Tillie would stand by Hannah as well.

Returning to the tedious chore of copying the video footage to the flash stick, I continued to view additional days to determine if Theodore had taken other items. I put off calling Tillie with the unsettling news of the missing Picasso for now. I might as well have the full picture before I added to her burdens.

I found only one more instance of Theodore entering the house on Hannah's day off, Sunday, June twenty-second. He left twenty minutes after entering but held nothing in his hand. Instead, his left hand was jammed into his suit jacket pocket, and he kept it there as he locked the front door and exited the security gate. He must've swiped some small knick-knack or an inconsequential piece of jewelry his father had lying around. Whatever it was, I'd never be able to tell, and I doubted Mr. Skyler would notice something that small missing.

Once I was certain there weren't any other intrusions, I copied the video files to three separate flash sticks—thanks to having a multiple pack I'd picked up from Costco—and hid two of them. One I placed at the bottom of a file cabinet in my office, another I put into a ziplock bag and buried in a sack of flour after Hannah left for the grocery store, and the last I tucked into my purse and would hide at home. I also copied the files to the cloud and emailed myself. Honestly, I couldn't believe Theodore was so stupid to overlook the security cameras. He was a sharp guy. Did he want to be caught, or was he so arrogant that he thought he was above suspicion? No matter what, if it dawned on him that he should destroy the footage stored at his father's house, I had insurance that the footage would remain intact.

Once the task of protecting the video was complete, I fixed myself a cup of chamomile tea. I was wired enough without adding extra caffeine to my system in the form of a latte. I settled back into my office and called Tillie. She wasn't quite so chipper as she'd been earlier.

"I'm sorry I didn't make it back in time to fix your breakfast. Did you eat?"

"Phew, I'm perfectly capable of scrambling some eggs for myself and peeling a banana. Don't you worry about me." She snapped her fingers, and the sound of Piper's nails skittering over her kitchen floor came over the phone. "I knew you'd be busy the rest of the morning, so Piper and I are hanging out. She likes scrambled eggs too."

"Thanks. I worried about her, but it's been too crazy here."

"Why? David said not to do anything until he returns." Piper's grunt filled the phone, and I assumed Tillie had lifted my dog into her lap. Piper was spoiled by Tillie, but it made me smile. "I hired the PI, and he's on the case effective immediately. My God! What was my grandson thinking? I can't wrap my head around it."

"Look, I'm going to wrap things up here and come straight over. We need to talk."

"You're scaring me, Em. What else happened?"

"We'll talk when I get there in about thirty minutes. Hannah's grocery shopping for Mr. Skyler's return, so I want to make sure the house is locked up tight."

"Uh-huh. Kinda like locking the barn after the horse escapes."

"Yeah, something like that." Boy, Tillie had no idea. "Anyway, I'll be there soon. Do you have plans for lunch? Brian left eggplant parmigiana, and I can heat it up when you get hungry."

"That'll work. I wish we could tell Brian what happened. He might be a big help in making sense why his brother would do something like this."

"Maybe. Or it might drive a wedge further in between them." I waited until Piper's jangling dog tags quieted after she shook her fur. "Let me wrap things up here, and I'll be there soon."

Disconnecting the call, I looked at my watch. It was only ten. It felt like this day had been a lifetime already. A nap and a carafe of coffee sounded perfect right now. But then the pile of catalogs I'd planned on combing through before Hannah dropped the bombshell caught my attention. I really didn't want to go through them, and I almost dropped the whole lot into the recycle bin. Except a yellow piece of paper peeked out from the edges of a sporting goods catalog. It looked out of place from the rest of the pile. I tugged on it then dropped it as if a snake had struck.

In super-bold magazine cutout letters, someone had written:

Stop being a nosy parker or you'll be next

Hannah wasn't a nosy parker, and I doubted Theodore would have left this for either of us, since he couldn't have known he'd been caught. It could only mean that someone associated with Mr. Jorgensen's death knew where I worked and wanted to scare me off from clearing Sal's name.

Chapter 19

I ran downstairs and plucked a large ziplock bag from the organized paper goods' drawer then ran back upstairs and, using a tissue, shoved the offending note into the bag. After sealing it shut, I put it into my purse. After quickly rifling through the remaining catalogs to make sure there were no other surprises—there weren't—I placed the ads into the recycling bin. I couldn't get out of the huge, empty house fast enough, and I speed walked while checking every door and window to make sure it was locked up tight. After locking the front door behind me, I sent Hannah a text to let her know I had left.

I paused a moment, thinking about who could have left the note for me. Surely it wasn't Hannah. Anyone could have accessed the across-the-alley garage, where the mail drop fed the daily mail into a box sitting on the pristine floor. Had I jumped to conclusions that Hannah wasn't involved with Theodore and the thefts? Theodore knew all about my proclivity for investigating. Had he coerced Hannah into leaving the note for me just in case I decided to implicate him in the thefts?

No doubt about it. I was seeing monsters where they didn't

exist. I ran to my car and stopped short. Another message, in the form of spray paint, covered my car.

Nosy Parker, Killer, and Snitch were spray-painted in blood red over the hood and windows of my car. I collapsed onto the curb and tried to control my shaking limbs. It took several minutes until I felt calm enough to look around for security cameras. I'd parked around the corner and halfway down the block from the Skyler compound, and all other residences in the area had their cameras facing inward, toward their own property. Public roads, in the low crime area, didn't have any coverage. I pulled my cell phone out and called Detective Tran. When she didn't answer, I left a detailed message, walked two blocks away, and tapped my Uber app for a ride. I'd deal with my vandalized Honda later.

Reaching Tillie's home, I let myself in and had just locked the front door behind me when Piper skittered around the corner and launched herself at me. Laughter then a sob bubbled from my lips as I hugged my furry beast.

"She acts like she hasn't seen you in weeks." Tillie appeared around the corner, her eyes fixed on my face. "Come to the kitchen, and I'll fix us a cup of tea with a splash of brandy."

Swiping the tears from my cheeks with the palms of my hands, I followed the stately woman. "Sorry about this. It's been a heck of a morning."

Her long sigh was barely louder than a whisper, but it held so much meaning. I squeezed her shoulder and directed her to sit down. "I'll fix the tea. We probably need something to eat if you want brandy too."

With the teakettle heating, I rummaged in the freezer and found individually wrapped brownies I'd stored in there the previous month. Chocolate was just what we both needed. I popped a couple into the microwave and started the defrost cycle.

Sipping the brisk Irish breakfast tea with its bracing

splash of brandy and nibbling on the warm brownies, I broke the news to Tillie about the Picasso being stolen. Her hands began shaking, and her lips quivered. Taking the teacup from her hands, I returned it to the saucer, and in that moment, I saw Tillie's true age instead of the force of nature she showed to the world. She was frail and frightened, and I'd never forgive Theodore for doing that to his grandmother.

"We'll get through this, Tillie. I'm sure Theodore has a logical explanation for his behavior." I wanted to gag while trying to defend him, but right now Tillie needed to be soothed. "Mr. Skyler will be here tomorrow, and things will be put to rights and go back to the way they were before this incident."

Tillie rolled her eyes at me. "You can stop trying to make me believe those lies, Em, just to make me feel better. You know good and well it'll never be the same between my son and Theodore."

"Maybe, maybe not. It will all depend on the reason why Theodore felt he had to steal from his father. What if his life depended on it?"

She snorted. "Like he got involved with the mob and they forced him to steal the paintings?"

"Something like that. Theodore's a private person, and it's impossible to know just what he's gotten mixed up in."

"All right, you've made me less angry, and now I'm frightened for that boy." Tillie dabbed at her eyes with the napkin I'd placed beside her teacup. "It seems like just yesterday he was scraping his knees while learning to ride a bike out in front of my house. Where did the time go?"

I reached over and gave her a gentle hug. Her shoulders felt bony beneath my arms. When had Tillie become so frail? After releasing my grip, I stood and refilled our teacups. Despite having inhaled the brownie, I was still hungry. "I'll bring the eggplant parmigiana over and reheat it for lunch. I think there's some garlic bread, and I have fresh fruit salad. Is there anything else you'd like?"

"That sounds more than enough, dear. I'm not terribly hungry."

I noticed she'd barely touched the brownie. "Drink some more tea, and I'll be right back. We both need to keep up our strength."

Piper followed on my heels, but I sent her back to Tillie. My dog knew how to provide comfort, and if anyone needed comfort right now, it was my friend. It took mere minutes to collect the leftovers and the fruit salad I'd made the night before and return to the main house. Tillie still sat where I'd left her, her tea and brownie untouched. Piper's head rested in her lap, and she absentmindedly stroked the dog's head.

After plating the microwave-warmed eggplant on the table along with the toasted garlic bread, I took a bite. The eggplant dish was every bit as rich and delicious as the night before. I might have moaned a little.

It elicited a chuckle from Tillie. "I see Brian knows the way to your heart."

Heat flooded my cheeks. "No, nothing like that. But he certainly knows about great food."

"Uh-huh. Sure." Tillie toyed with the eggplant but didn't take a bite.

"Try it. Brian picked out the best thing on Antonio's menu." I nudged her hand. "Just one bite?"

She did as I asked and managed a few more bites with my cajoling. "Speaking of Brian, he told me your mystery man is a baron! Is that true?"

Tillie's eyes twinkled, and a smile almost appeared. "How did that whippersnapper figure it out? We've been so cautious."

My eyes widened. "So, it's true?"

"It's true he's a baron, but there's nothing serious going on between us. Although I certainly wouldn't mind if Frances

Allain thought otherwise, so feel free to spread the gossip." A real smile finally broke free, and her face lit up. She took a larger bite of eggplant.

"How did you meet a baron? And why is he even in Southern California in the first place? Does he live in a castle?" I was most curious about the castle.

"You've watched too much *Downton Abbey*. He's just a normal man, my age." She dabbed the corner of her lips with the linen napkin.

"Yeah, normal except for being a baron." I sipped the now tepid tea. "How did you meet?"

"I've known John since college days. He attended Yale and was roommates with a young man I dated for a while. That was back before I met David's father." She shrugged. "We've kept in touch over the years. It's no big deal."

"No big deal that you know a baron? But seriously, does he live in a castle?"

"No. He has a beautiful home in London."

"How long is he staying here, and are you going to see him again?"

"You're certainly being inquisitive. Perhaps if you tell me about your date with Brian last night, I'll share some details about John."

I choked on the sip of tea I'd just taken and bent over at the waist as I tried to get my coughing under control. "Ugh, sorry. Tea. Wrong pipe. Not dating."

Tillie had her arms crossed in front of her chest by the time I'd straightened back up.

"What?" I asked and pointed at her crossed arms. "I didn't mean to choke."

"You know that's not the problem." She pointed her index finger in my face. "It's time you admitted to yourself that your relationship with Randall isn't going anywhere. He knows it, but you're the one avoiding the truth."

I tried to interrupt, but Tillie would have none of it.

"Hear me out. You met each other when you both needed the emotional support after the death of that dreadful floozy your ex was involved with. It was good for both of you to lean on each other. At. That. Time." She relaxed her arms to rest her hands in her lap.

I, on the other hand, crossed my arms in front of my chest and tapped my toe impatiently. Tillie had been trying to push Brian and me together for months.

"You've grown and matured, Emory, and while you enjoy Randall's company when he's around, you're not in love with him. Heck, you haven't even fallen a tiny bit in love with him." She raised her eyebrows at me as if daring me to argue. When I didn't say anything, she continued.

"Then there's Randall. Granted, he was smitten with you starting out, but in context, you were the one who brought closure to his brother's murder and gave comfort as he grieved. It provided a strong emotional base for your early relationship. Now that he's dealt with his loss, he's emotionally moved on. I'm sure he'd never admit it, even to himself, but you might be a painful reminder of that dark period in his life."

I slowly nodded. "I can see how that might be."

"It's obvious that Randall is keeping himself inordinately busy without carving out any time to spend with you. I don't want to see you get hurt or caught unaware, which is why I'm bringing it up."

"You might be right, although Randall does have valid excuses for never being around." My cheeks flushed warm. "But I can't deny that there are sparks between us when we do get together."

"Anyone with a beating heart would feel sparks when Randall turns those gorgeous eyes their way. But that doesn't mean it's a good basis for a long-term relationship." She circled her hand in the air. "You and Brian have a lot in common, and I think you have what it takes to make a great couple. But truly, that's not my motivation for saying anything, and I promise not to play matchmaker between you two."

"All right. I'll consider it." I huffed out a sigh. "He's in Florida with his family for another week anyway."

Tillie raised her eyebrows and started to say something. When I narrowed my eyes at her, she mimicked zipping her lips closed. Her antics made me laugh, and I knew no matter what happened with Randall, Tillie would always have my back.

Chapter 20

My cell phone rang, and I checked the display. It was the attorney, and just in the nick of time. I was emotionally exhausted talking about what amounted to my failed relationship with Randall. I didn't want to admit it, but Tillie was right. "Hi, Will. Did you get an appointment to see Sal?"

"It's set for two this afternoon. Can you meet me there at one thirty?"

I glanced at the clock. It was just before noon. "It shouldn't be a problem, but I'm going to have to Uber it. I'm having, ah, car trouble."

"I'll swing by and pick you up in about forty-five minutes. We can head over to the jail together."

"I don't want to inconvenience you." I needed to schedule a tow truck to pick up my car just as soon as Detective Tran saw my tagged vehicle. But there wasn't anything I could do about it right now.

"It's no trouble, and it'll give us some time to talk about the case before we see Sal."

"All right. I'm texting my address to you right now." I'd

put the call on speaker and worked on sending him the information.

As soon as I ended the call, Tillie asked the obvious question. "What happened to your car?"

"Taggers spray-painted it while I was at Mr. Skyler's this morning."

"And what aren't you telling me?" Tillie was sharp, no doubt about it.

"I found a warning note stuck into the mail when I worked this morning, and then when I left to come home, taggers had basically left the same warning all over my car." I tugged on the plastic-encased note and showed it to her.

Tillie sucked in her breath. "Why haven't you given this to Detective Tran yet?"

"I called and left a message, but she hasn't returned my call." I put the note back in my purse. "I'll show Will the note."

"Did you park your car in the garage? I can let the detective in when she comes by." I was happy to see color returning to Tillie's cheeks, and her eyes looked brighter. She loved being in the middle of investigations.

"I left it parked around the block from Mr. Skyler's. I couldn't drive it, and I wasn't in the right state of mind to deal with it, so I Ubered home." I cleared the empty plates from the table and began to wash the dishes. "As soon as I hear from the detective, I'll call a towing company and have it taken to a repair garage to clean up the graffiti."

"Feel free to use Andrew as much as you need." Tillie's long-term chauffer was magazine-model gorgeous and just as kind to me as he was to Tillie.

"Thanks, but my bicycle should get me around town, and if I need to go farther, Uber works just as well." I didn't feel comfortable taking advantage of Tillie's generous offer. Somehow it felt like I'd lose my hard-won independence if I relied upon someone else to drive me around. Uber didn't count.

"Suit yourself, but if you change your mind, you have Andrew's number."

I kissed Tillie's cheek. "Thanks. I'd better take Piper for a power walk and change clothes before Will comes to pick me up."

"Bring Piper back here before you leave. She can hang out with me on the patio." A wistful look passed over her face. "I think I'll try to lose myself in a good book instead of dwelling on what I have no control over."

"Sounds like a plan I need to implement too."

After a power walk around the block, I left Piper in my yard to frolic in the sun while I changed clothes. Will had indicated he'd planned on passing me off as his assistant, so I pulled out black wool slacks and a crisply starched button-down pale-pink shirt—clothes left over from my long-ago accounting firm days. Tugging the slacks up, I realized, with growing horror, that they barely fit halfway up my thighs. There was no way I'd be able to get them over my hips in an attempt to button them. All the cupcake and frosting sampling I'd done since starting my cupcake catering company probably wasn't a good thing for my waistline, but this was the first solid proof I'd had. I took the offending slacks off and tossed them onto the bed for recycling. The label caught my eye just as the pants flew from my hand.

I picked them up and found they were Dolce & Gabbana —an expensive designer brand I'd never buy in a million years —and the slacks were size thirty-two. I had no idea what that meant, so I held the pants up. I could clearly see that the length was a good eight inches too long for my short legs and the waist was teeny-tiny. There was only one person these slacks could have belonged to, and she'd put them in my old closet, probably over a year ago, for me to find later. I hadn't noticed them when I'd moved to Tillie's pool house and unpacked. Tori—my ex-best friend. I shivered. Her taunts were still finding a way to reach me from her grave.

By the time Will showed up, I was a shaky mess. At least my dress slacks actually fit, more or less, and I'd managed to brush off most of Piper's fur after taking her back to Tillie's. I tried to calm myself as I slid into the buttery leather seat in his cherry-red Mercedes sedan. It was an older model, but it appeared to be in pristine condition.

I handed him the retainer check Tillie had written for Will to represent Sal. "You can send her an invoice if that's not sufficient."

He glanced at the check, and his eyes widened. "That's more than enough, unless we end up in a long court battle."

"With any luck, it won't come to that." I shut the door and clicked the seat belt on.

"You look professional." Will swept his gaze over me. "I guess we should have discussed wardrobes."

As he tucked the folded check into his pocket, I took notice of his faded blue jeans and Hawaiian-print shirt. He wore flip-flops on his feet, and it looked like grains of sand still clung to the shoes. "Maybe I'm your public image while you're the behind-the-scenes guy."

"Works for me." He flashed a grin, but to me, it looked like it took some effort.

In between pausing for the navigation system to call out directions, I brought him up to speed on what I'd learned about the Jorgensens from Brian, along with the threatening note I'd received and my car getting tagged.

"As soon as we're done with our interview at the jail, you need to be calling the detective every thirty minutes until she answers." Will put his blinker on and merged onto the freeway that would take us to Santa Ana. So far, there wasn't a lot of traffic going in our direction, but the cars were backed up for at least two miles on the opposite side of the freeway. Their occupants were heading into Newport Beach for an afternoon in the sun.

I waited to speak until Will chose a lane and sped up to keep pace with the flow of traffic. "I realize she's busy, and I didn't want to be a pest."

"Trust me, it's the squeaky wheel that gets the grease. Receiving warnings like you did means the killer thinks you know more than you do. It could become dangerous, and I'd never forgive myself if something happened to you."

"It wouldn't be your fault. I'm the one who dragged you into representing Sal." I looked out the window and watched the scenery fly by.

"But I encouraged you to ask questions."

I didn't recall it happening that way, but I wouldn't argue. Instead, I changed the subject. "I hope your aunts didn't harass you too much yesterday afternoon. They probably had a lot to say about you inviting a killer back to tea with the family."

Will smiled. "It was perfect. Not once did they bring up finding a suitable wife for me. Instead, they theorized why you killed Mr. Jorgensen and how you've gotten away with murder."

Burying my face in my palm, I groaned. "That's not good. They're going to gossip to all their friends, and then it'll be all over Newport Beach before cocktail hour tonight. Did they forbid you to ever talk to me again?"

"More or less." He swerved to miss hitting a car that had crossed over multiple lanes in front of us in order to take an exit. "But I don't think you have to worry about my aunts being the source of gossip."

I pried my white-knuckled hand from the door rest after the near miss. How had Will remained so calm? He acted like we hadn't been inches away from a horrific accident. I gulped in air, unaware I'd been holding my breath. I attempted to refocus on our conversation. "Err, why is that?"

"The three of them are reclusive and only socialize with

each other." He checked over his shoulder before switching lanes. "That is unless they're trying to set me up with someone, then they put aside their reluctance. I think something happened in their late fifties that caused it. It was right around the time Pansy's husband passed away, from a heart attack. Petunia and Poppy moved in with her for several years then bought their own place down in Dana Point. Neither of them have married nor had children, and as the years passed, they stopped socializing with anyone except a few select family members. Lucky me."

"I thought your aunt was supposed to attend the Jorgensens' party, which was why you attended." It didn't seem like the Jorgensens' soiree was an event a recluse would even be invited to in the first place. "I'm glad you were there. I don't know what we'd have done without you stepping in to help Sal."

"Ah, yes. The party." He paused a moment while he checked the navigation map. "My Aunt Pansy is godmother to Lisette, which was why she received an invitation. Lisette knows my aunt doesn't attend large gatherings, but she tried to guilt-trip her into coming, since it was the anniversary of their son's death. Lisette thinks she's entitled to whatever she wants, so my aunt said yes and sent me instead."

"What about your parents or grandparents? Do they visit your aunts?"

"My parents don't. They retired to Florida several years ago, but even before they moved, my mom had no patience for the meddling biddies, as she called them. My grandmother, their sister, had a falling out with them before I was even born. But she's long gone, too, so basically my only relatives here in California are those three aunts." He shrugged. "They're an acquired taste, and they're usually not quite so meddlesome as they were yesterday."

As the navigation system directed us to exit the freeway, I remained silent so that Will could follow the prompts and execute the necessary turns. When he pulled into the large government multi-building complex to make his way to the parking structure, the imposing concrete edifice that comprised the jail gave me the shivers. Poor Sal. Stuck in there all alone.

Once Will found a parking slot, he pulled a briefcase from the back seat along with a printed-out map showing the various government buildings. He traced the walking route from the parking structure to the men's jail with his index finger then put the map into his briefcase.

"You ready to do this?"

I nodded, although my heart was in my throat. It was distressing that Sal languished here. I had to figure out a way to prove his innocence.

Chapter 21

After going through the rigamarole of producing our IDs, going through a metal detector, and having our personal belongings searched, we were finally taken to an interview room. I jumped when the heavy-duty door clanged behind the guard when he left to retrieve Sal. Taking deep breaths in, I tried to calm myself. Will, on the other hand, looked like he could take a nap, and his skin had turned ashen. I hoped this outing wouldn't be too much for him.

I jumped again when the door banged open and the guard brought Sal in. The orange jumpsuit looked baggy on his slight frame, and the sight of handcuffs encircling his wrists just about made me cry. Sal sat down in the plastic molded seat, which was the color of oatmeal and dingy. Will indicated that the guard should remove the handcuffs, which he did. Once we were alone with Sal, the young man straightened his spine and looked less shrunken into himself. Perhaps that was his coping mechanism, making himself seem as small and unassuming as possible in this place.

"Sal, I'm so sorry you're in this mess." I placed my hand over my heart and willed the water in my eyes not to overflow onto my cheeks. "This is attorney Will Trenton, and he's agreed to represent you. We're doing all we can to get you out of this place."

"I didn't do it, Emory. Please believe me." Sal's soulful brown eyes shimmered, and a bruise discolored his left cheek. Had he been beaten?

"We believe you, Sal, which is why we're here." I pointed at my left cheek. "Did the officers do that to you?"

"When the *jefe* shoved the cupcakes at me, the corner of the serving tray caught my cheek. It's nothing." He touched the bruise and looked at Will. "But I can't afford an attorney. You should just leave."

"Your legal fees have been paid by a concerned citizen, Sal." Will pulled a sheaf of papers from his briefcase and handed a page to the young man, along with a pen. "Can you sign this contract allowing me to represent you? You'll see it clearly states that you aren't liable for any costs associated with the representation."

"Why would someone help me?" Sal pulled his gaze from the paper and looked at me. "I know Carrie is hurting for money, and if she's risking her home or something, I won't accept."

Tillie hadn't said she wanted to remain anonymous, and I worried that if Sal thought my sister was financially jeopardizing her family, he wouldn't sign the contract. "It's Tillie Skyler. My friend and employer."

Sal's eyes widened. "Why would she do this for someone she's never met?"

"Because Carrie and I both know you're innocent, and that's the kind of person Tillie is."

He shook his head but took up the pen and signed his name after carefully reading the agreement. "It's loco, but tell her *gracias*. I'll never be able to repay her, although I'll do everything I can for the rest of my life to do so."

Will took the signed contract. "She doesn't expect repayment, so rest easy at least on that point."

"How long am I going to have to stay in this place?" Sal waved his hand around the room forlornly. "Don't they have to take me before a judge to keep me here?"

"They'll arraign you forty-eight to seventy-two hours after your arrest, but unfortunately holidays and weekends don't count. Since the Fourth of July holiday was on a Friday, the arraignment countdown started today."

Sal hung his head, looking even more dejected. "I don't have money for bail, but I keep thinking if I get in front of a judge, they'll finally realize they've arrested the wrong guy. This has been a huge mistake."

I wanted to reach over and hug Sal to provide some comfort. Instead, I kept my hands firmly in my lap. I wasn't sure what was permitted in a place like this in case we were being monitored. "Tillie has offered to post bail when it's set. We don't want to see you stuck in here either."

Sal shook his head. "I can't accept it. It's one thing to pay Mr. Trenton attorney fees, but fronting bail money is too much."

"But she wants to do this for you." It broke my heart to see him unwilling to accept help.

Sal looked around the room as if checking to see if someone were listening in then lowered his voice to a whisper. "I know myself. If I get out of here on bail, knowing I'm going to face life in prison if I'm convicted, I'll disappear over the border. It's best I stay put and not betray your boss."

"Oh, Sal. I'm so sorry this happened to you." I pulled a tissue from my purse in case my eyes released the tears that threatened to spill. Being less than one hundred miles from the border with Mexico, Sal's chances of disappearing were very high. "We're doing everything we can to find out who killed Mr. Jorgensen."

Will cleared his throat and handed me a legal pad and pen. He didn't give me instructions on what to do, but I supposed he wanted me to take notes of anything important.

"I agree with Emory. We're going to do everything possible to prove your innocence. We don't have a lot of time, but I'd like to not only find out what your perspective is on what happened Friday night but also get to know a little bit about you." Will checked his watch then settled into his chair as he gazed into Sal's face and started asking questions.

I listened and jotted down most of the information Sal provided, even though a lot of it seemed inconsequential as it pertained to the murder. Will dug into Sal's background, who his friends were, and if any of his extended family members knew the Jorgensens. I'd known Sal had had a rough life, but his story was eye-opening and heartbreaking. After Carrie hired this unassuming, talented young man, he'd thought he'd finally gotten a break in life. Instead, he'd been handed a nightmare. I vowed, again, to do everything I could to get him out of here.

Sal said he'd never met the man until the day of the party, and he'd never heard of Nathan Jorgensen. Sal didn't think he had any enemies and hadn't gotten involved in any of the gangs, even in high school. While he'd been bumped around between his extended family from the age of eight, after witnessing his mother's death at the hands of a drive-by shooter, he felt like the majority of the families who had sheltered him had been decent, despite not providing a permanent home for him. Most had tried to do the right thing for him by instilling the belief that education was the key to making a life for himself. Unless Sal was lying, he'd been a good kid and had worked hard to get through school and the culinary program.

When Will and I left the complex an hour later, we still didn't have any ideas about who'd killed Mr. Jorgensen. Driving back toward Newport Beach, using surface streets to navigate around a five-car pile-up on the freeway, Will reminded me to call Detective Tran. I called and was immediately dumped into her voice-mail system. I left a short message asking her to call me.

"You should have left a detailed message," Will chided.

"I did that earlier today."

"Well, it doesn't hurt to keep leaving those details every time you call." Will inched the car forward a foot. Even the surface streets were jammed, and it looked like it would take a very long time to get back home.

"I hope you didn't have another appointment anytime soon today." I pointed at the triple line of cars stacked up in front of us while we waited at yet another red light.

"No. This was it for the day."

"Your aunts didn't rope you into another afternoon tea?" I hoped my tone came across as teasing and not as a jab.

He barked out a humorless chuckle. "I may have led them to believe I'm back working full-time. At least it keeps them from bothering me during the week. Weekends are a completely different matter. According to them, San Diego is practically down the street, and it's my familial duty to make the drive up to chauffer them around and let them meddle in my life."

"Like I said before, you're a good man, Will Trenton." My phone chimed with a text, and I glanced down at the screen. It was from my sister, who was wondering how our visit with Sal went. Traffic had picked up speed, now that we were around the stalled-out vehicle that had caused the backup, and Will's gaze fixated on the road. "Do you mind if I give Carrie a quick call? She's been stressed out about Sal, and I want to put her mind at ease."

"Be my guest. Had the jail not had a limit on the number of visitors, she could have gone with us." He tapped a button on the navigation screen, and the view changed to show greater detail. "If she wants to visit Sal, let me know, and I'll schedule a time to go with her."

"Thanks. I'll make the offer, but I'm afraid she'll have

trouble finding someone to watch her kids." In reality, our mother could watch them, but Carrie didn't want to impose too often and instead saved it for when she desperately needed the assistance when a catering event and her husband's job conflicted. After the financial difficulties they'd endured, their normal babysitter wasn't an option.

Chapter 22

Carrie answered on the first ring with a brisk hello as Tommy wailed in the background. While I loved my nephew, I missed the days of long chats over coffee and cookies, or working together as we prepped for a catering job.

"It doesn't sound like now is a good time to fill you in on our visit to Sal."

Exasperation filled Carrie's voice. "He's teething, and nothing seems to be soothing him. Mother recommended rubbing whiskey on his gums, as if I'd even consider such a thing. Doesn't she Google before offering her advice?"

Carrie criticizing our mother meant things really were dire in her household. My twin was the favored child, and she'd always been close to our mother. "I'm on my way home and wanted to give you a quick update on Sal. He's doing as well as can be expected, but nothing new has popped up to exonerate him."

"Maybe you should visit Lisette. Take Tillie and make a condolence call and see if you can find anything out."

I pulled the phone away from my ear, checking the display, to make sure it really was my sister on the call. Aside from trying to prove her husband's innocence last fall, Carrie thought I should leave investigating to the professionals. I put the phone back to my ear. "That's not a bad idea. Tillie can probably get us in to see the other couples sitting close to the Jorgensens as well."

Tommy's wails increased in volume. "I gotta go. Maybe a drive will calm him down."

"Do you want me to come pick the girls up? I can do an auntie sleepover with them."

"Thanks, but they're already at mother's house. She took them this morning after Kaylee and Sophie swiped my phone and called her begging for help." Carrie giggled. "I might just accidently leave my cell in the TV room all the time so those imps can call Grammie for rescue."

"She can't tell your daughters no, that's for sure." I smiled, thinking how having grandchildren had changed my mother for the better. "I'll plan on having a sleepover with them next weekend."

Will had jumped back onto the freeway, which was now flowing at high speed, just as I ended the call. "I couldn't help but overhear your conversation about visiting Lisette and some of the other guests."

Somehow, I assumed Will would be against the idea, but he surprised me when I confirmed what Carrie had suggested.

"That's a good idea, especially if you can get Tillie to pave the way for you. While she runs in different social circles than Lisette, she's well-known and admired in the community." He tore his gaze from the road and gave me a quick glance. "Seeing how I was at the party and Lisette is my aunt's goddaughter, perhaps I should tag along with you. I wouldn't feel comfortable going on my own. Besides, three pairs of eyes are better than one."

"That's a great idea! Tillie will love the chance to feel like she's helping the investigation along. I'll send her a text and see if she can set something up." Plus, it would provide a much-needed distraction from Theodore. My fingers flew over the screen, and within a minute of my text being sent, she responded with YES, sent in all caps, along with a thumbs-up emoji. She'd probably have an appointment scheduled for us before I even reached home this afternoon.

Will dropped me off at home with the promise he'd let me know when Sal's arraignment had been scheduled, and I promised to let him know what time we planned on visiting Mrs. Jorgensen. My stomach rumbled, and I was in desperate need of bathroom facilities, so I popped into my house to freshen up and change out of my overly tight slacks into stretchy yoga pants and a loose T-shirt. Perhaps I ought to lay off sampling the cupcakes and buttercream. My stomach rumbled again, so I grabbed an apple, congratulated myself on making a healthier eating choice, and walked to Tillie's house.

Once again Piper greeted me with love, and I followed her out onto the patio. Tillie had a plate of assorted cheese and crackers sitting on the table and a bottle of crisp sauvignon blanc chilled on ice. Two unused wineglasses sat beside the ice bucket.

"I'm sorry, I should have called instead of barging in." My face heated as I pointed at the wine. Had I interrupted a romantic interlude? "Are you expecting someone?"

"This is for our investigation strategy meeting." Tillie said, guffawing. "If I'd had a romantic tryst going on, I would have sent you a text and told you to stay away."

I looked down at the apple then at the cheese and cracker plate. The siren song of my favorite appetizer with a scrumptious glass of wine was too much temptation. I set the apple on the table and poured us each a glass of wine then clinked my glass to hers.

While we sipped and ate, I filled Tillie in on the visit with Sal. She looked just as heartsick as I felt, as I told her about

Sal seeing his mother murdered right in front of him and then being shuffled around from family to family after that.

"Andrew will be here at nine thirty tomorrow morning to drive us for a visit with Lisette. She's expecting us at ten." Tillie piled cheese onto a cracker and took a nibble. Despite her indulgences, she never gained an ounce.

"Do you mind if Will meets us there? He would like to give his condolences to Mrs. Jorgensen but didn't want to go on his own." I sent the attorney a quick text after Tillie gave her assent. He immediately responded with a "see you there."

"It'll be good to have another set of eyes casing the joint." Tillie tried to inflect her words with an exaggerated 1920s gangster affectation. "Maybe we'll find evidence to spring Sal out of the pokey."

"Isn't Mrs. Jorgensen going to throw a fit when she realizes I'm one of the caterers who hired the person who supposedly killed her husband?" It reminded me of a time, not so long ago, when I'd been banished to wait in the car while Tillie "interrogated" a society maven.

"If you dress professionally, flat-iron your hair, and wear copious amounts of makeup, I doubt she'll even recognize you." She studied my features. "Women like her rarely give 'the help' more than a passing glance."

"So basically, I need to be up by five to change my appearance." I knew Tillie was right, though. Even if all I did was dress in professional attire, Mrs. Jorgensen wouldn't recognize me.

She patted my hand. "Beauty always comes with a price."

My phone rang. It was Detective Tran, so I immediately connected.

"I'm in front of your house. Are you home or not?" She sounded put out and a touch snarky.

"Come over to Tillie's gate, and I'll let you in." As soon as nothing but dead air filled my ear, I turned toward Tillie.

"That was Detective Tran. Can you brew a K-cup of coffee for her?"

"Or you can offer her a glass of wine. She sounds like she needs it."

"She's on duty and has a toddler at home. Coffee is a safer bet." I ran through the house and out the front door and opened the security gate.

Detective Tran stood there, scrolling through messages on her phone and tapping her toe impatiently. "I'd just about given up on you."

"Sorry. Come on in. We have coffee brewing."

A brief smile passed over her lips before she reverted to looking grim. "I don't have time for a social call. Tell me about the threatening note and your car being vandalized."

"I have the note in my purse. Come on in and I'll get it for you." I pointed toward Tillie's house. Just then Piper bounded out, probably because Tillie had put the cheese out of reach of her snout, sniffed the detective, and wagged her tail.

She absentmindedly reached down and scratched behind Piper's ears. "Fine, but let me check out your car first."

"Um, it's still parked on the street close to Mr. Skyler's residence. I didn't know whether I should have it towed or wait until you could take a look at it."

Her sigh hung heavily in the air. "Text me the location, and I'll take a look at it once I'm done here."

I led her to the patio and introduced Detective Tran to Tillie, who'd placed a cup of coffee on the table with a small jug of cream.

Tillie motioned at the coffee. "Have a seat, young lady. You look like you've had a long day."

"You have no idea." Detective Tran sat, and Tillie took the chair next to her.

"Have you made any progress in finding out who killed that awful Mr. Jorgensen?" Tillie leaned forward and edged the plate of cheese and crackers toward the detective.

Detective Tran shot me a panicked glance. Tillie could be a bit much if you didn't know her. "Uh, Mrs. Skyler, I really can't discuss the case with you."

"Fiddlesticks. We're concerned citizens who don't want to see the wrong man convicted of a crime he didn't commit."

"I realize that, but I really can't talk about an ongoing case." The detective busied herself by pouring cream into the steaming mug. "I'm here to take possession of the threatening note Ms. Martinez received."

Taking the hint, I retrieved my purse from beneath the chair I'd been sitting in and handed the plastic-encased note to her. "I found it stuffed in between some ads and catalogs at Mr. Skyler's residence. There's no telling how long ago it was delivered because it'd been almost a week in between my visit to his house."

She held it up and examined each cutout letter before snapping several photos with her phone. "I'll have it checked for fingerprints, but chances are there won't be any. Where is the mail deposited at Mr. Skyler's residence, and who has access to it?"

"There's a mail slot in his detached garage that sits across the alleyway from his house. Hannah—that's his live-in house-keeper—has a remote control to open the garage door as well as keys to open the side door. I have keys as well."

"How secure do you think the side door is?" She took a sip of the creamy brew.

"It's pretty flimsy, but there is a security camera on each side of the garage." I twisted my mouth as I thought. "It would be pretty easy for someone to break in without us noticing for quite some time."

"I was afraid you were going to say that." She gulped the remaining coffee in the mug. "Perhaps it would be better for you to meet me at the Skyler residence. We can take a look at your car and examine the garage door lock."

"That'll work, except I don't have a car, and neither does

Tillie." While Andrew was convenient, he wasn't available at a moment's notice. "I'll have to call for an Uber."

After opening the app, I showed the detective the screen. "There's a twenty-five-minute wait for a car."

She huffed. "Fine, you can ride over with me and then take an Uber back home. It's been a long enough day already."

I looked at Tillie and nodded my head toward Piper. "Do you want me to put her into my house?"

"She's fine. Come back here when you're done with Detective Tran." Tillie winked at me. "We still have a lot to talk about."

Chapter 23

I had just closed the security gate and stepped toward Detective Tran's unmarked Honda Pilot when the figure of a muscular man rounded the corner, walking in our direction. His stride was purposeful, and my heart leapt into my throat while butterflies danced in my stomach. It was Randall!

I broke into a trot to greet him with a hug. "What are you doing here? I thought you were staying in Florida for another week?"

He held me at arm's length and gazed at me with his piercing sapphire-blue eyes. "I knew you'd put yourself into the middle of this murder investigation, so I came home to keep you out of trouble."

My ego was a bit deflated. I'd rather have been told he missed me, but maybe that was his way of doing it. I held out my arms and twisted them back and forth. "I'm fine. See? No one's attacked me, and I don't have any bumps or scrapes."

I looked back up, expecting to see him watching my antics. Instead, his eyes were riveted on something over my shoulder, and his mouth hung open. His Adam's apple bobbed when he swallowed. I turned to see what had caught his attention, and there stood Detective Tran. Her gaze was transfixed on Randall, and a pink flush had appeared on her neck and cheeks.

"Nattie?" Randall's gulp sounded loud.

"RB? What are you doing here?" Detective Tran looked from Randall then to me and then back to him.

Nattie? RB? They had nicknames for each other? What was going on? I stepped to Randall's side and faced the detective while I waited to see what my boyfriend had to say.

He ran long fingers through his chestnut-colored hair that curled just over the tops of his ears. The strange thought that he usually didn't let it get that long flitted through my brain. "I. Uh, I heard Emory had gotten herself mixed up in another murder and thought I could help. What are you doing here?"

"I'm investigating the murder." Her gaze never left Randall's face. It was as if I didn't exist and as if we weren't on our way to take a look at my tagged car and find out who might be threatening me.

"You look good. How've you been?" Randall's gaze was still locked onto the detective's face.

"Fine. And you? Did you leave Florida for good, or are you just visiting?" For the briefest of moments her gaze flitted to me then fixated back onto Randall.

"I'm living out here after starting up a security firm." He shifted his feet. "How about you? How long ago did you move here?"

"A bit before your brother's, ah, accident." She scuffed her high-heeled foot on the asphalt. "I'm really sorry you lost him."

Randall's undercover brother had died during a vice squad raid in Florida. Randall had quit the force to spend the next two years hunting for his brother's killer when our paths crossed. I wondered if Detective Tran and Randall had worked together but then concluded it didn't matter. No matter how they'd known each other, it was clear they'd meant more to each other than simply coworkers or friends, and it was apparent their attraction was still in place.

"Thanks." His voice sounded stressed. "Were you on your way somewhere?"

She glanced at me. "I'm taking Ms. Martinez to examine her car and Mr. Skyler's garage."

He finally tore his gaze away from the detective and looked at me. A frown deepened the line between his eyebrows. "What happened to your car?"

"A tagger got to it. Plus, it appears someone broke into Mr. Skyler's garage and left a, um, anonymous note for me."

Detective Tran snorted. "You mean a threat, don't you?"

"I don't understand why you put yourself in danger, Emory." Randall's frown became a scowl. "Nattie is more than capable of solving the murder. You need to step back and let her do her job without interfering."

"First off, I didn't go interfering. People talk to me, and I'm not about to step back, as you say, and let an innocent kid be convicted of a crime he didn't commit. Those people at the party were horrible, and just because of Sal's heritage, they think it's okay to let him take the blame." My temper rose, and I fisted my hands on my hips. "You don't get to swoop in here and tell me what I can and can't do without having any context of what's going on."

"She sure told you off, RB." Detective Tran's face held a smile. "And she actually has a point. Where have you been for the last four days, and how do you know what's going on?"

I mouthed the words "thank you" to the detective. She didn't have to stick up for me, but then again, she probably got mansplained to, even more than I got.

"Well, I, uh, well, uh…" Randall ran fingers through his hair again. He looked pointedly at Detective Tran. "Perhaps you can fill me in on the investigation so we can keep Emory from harm."

"You should probably stop digging yourself into a hole,

Randall." I brushed past him and walked toward Detective Tran. "We've got places to go and people to see. You didn't need to fly back to keep me safe. Detective Tran's here to do that."

She shrugged at Randall then turned and followed me to her SUV. Using her remote, she unlocked the vehicle and pointed at the front passenger seat. "You can sit up here."

Relief flooded me. I was afraid I'd have to ride in the caged back seat. It would've been beyond humiliating with Randall looking on. Once I slid into the leather seat and shut the door, I chanced a peek back at him. He still stood in the middle of the alleyway with his mouth hanging halfway open. I giggled, and Detective Tran joined me.

Once she'd pulled on the main thoroughfare, Detective Tran asked, "How long have you been dating Randall?"

"It's that obvious?" I didn't think there'd been any affection between us aside from my initial hug. "We met last summer when I'd been accused of killing my ex's girlfriend."

"Ah yes. I do remember a bit about that case, but I wasn't aware that Randall was involved."

"He was more on the periphery." I cleared my throat to give myself time to figure out how to word my question.

"I know you want to ask how we know each other." The detective put her blinker on and merged to take the road to the other side of the bay. "We worked together in Tampa and dated for a couple of years. I didn't like how undercover had changed him. It wasn't good, for either of us, but he wouldn't see it or admit there was a problem. Long story short, I moved here, back home with my parents. We had mutual need of each other at that point, so the timing was good to be with family."

I wondered if impending single motherhood had caused her to return home. It wasn't any of my business, so I squelched the desire to ask about her child, and she didn't offer any further explanations. Asking about her previous relationship with Randall seemed reasonable, though. "It seems like there's some unfinished business between you two?"

The detective grunted but didn't answer. Instead, she asked, "How serious are you and Randall?"

"Not very. He travels all the time." I picked at the cuticle on my thumb, all too aware Tillie and I just had a discussion about this very same thing. It was time to face facts. "Truth be told, periphery is probably the best word to describe it, and I've been okay with that."

"Just so you know, I'm not going to come between you two, no matter what Randall meant to me all those years ago." She heaved out a long breath of air. "God knows I don't need any more complications in my life, so just forget about this unexpected reunion."

"Yeah, that's not going to happen. And if you know Randall, he's not going to let it drop either." I fingered my cell phone. "I should probably text him an apology for huffing off like that. After losing his brother, he goes into protective mode without realizing he's smothering. But I know he means well and has the best intentions."

"You're probably right on both accounts."

Chapter 24

Randall didn't reply to my short apology text. We rode in silence until I gave her directions on where I'd left my car. Bloodred paint still covered the windows and sides of the vehicle, and now, all four tires were missing, the hood of the car gaped open, and the bumper was gone. I groaned. "I should have had it towed this morning. What was I thinking?"

"It looks like it might be time for a new car." Detective Tran retrieved a Maglite and switched it on as twilight descended. She circled my vehicle. "It's been pretty well stripped."

Groaning again, since I could ill afford to purchase anything right now, I peeked into the car as the detective continued to shine the light around the interior. The seats were gone, as was the stereo system. As we circled to the front of the car, it was obvious that parts, names unknown to me, had been removed from the engine compartment.

"I think it's safe to say that the taggers and the parts theft were committed by two separate parties." She turned to me. "I'll have it towed for inspection, but I'd suggest you contact your insurance company right away and place a claim. Your car is totaled."

Nodding, I swiped at my eyes as the detective went back to her SUV and made the call. When she returned, she scanned the area as if to look for security cameras. Unless they were well hidden, I was certain there weren't any.

"Show me the garage."

"It's around the corner on the next block. Do you want to walk or drive?" With parking spaces at a premium, I always walked.

She looked pointedly at my car. "We'll drive."

"It's probably a good choice." I gave her instructions on where to park next to the garage then called Hannah. I didn't want her to be startled, thinking someone was breaking into the garage. Besides, the detective would probably want to talk to the housekeeper anyway if we found signs of a break-in.

Hannah immediately answered and said she'd meet us at the garage.

Once parked, Detective Tran hopped out of the vehicle and headed down the side of the garage where I'd indicated the door stood. I took the opportunity to send Hannah a quick text reminding her to not say anything about the stolen artworks. That would be entirely up to Mr. Skyler to report the theft or deal with his son on his own terms.

I walked down the narrow sidewalk, relieved to see the security lights had automatically clicked on when the detective had passed by. The bright lights illuminated the space, although Detective Tran still used her flashlight as she examined the locked door and took a few photos with her cell phone.

She pointed at the security camera strategically placed on the corner of the building and aimed toward the walkway and entrance. "How many cameras are on the garage, and do they record?"

"There are four, one covering each side." I exhaled my breath in a long stream, exhausted just thinking about spending another several hours searching through security footage. I couldn't risk Detective Tran going through the records and seeing Theodore leaving with the paintings. "And the video recordings are held for thirty days. I'll review the footage and see if I spot anything, and if so, I'll copy it onto a flash stick for you."

"Guess that'll have to do. We don't have the manpower to examine the video, unless you come up with something concrete." She swung the Maglite along the edges of the door. "Do you have a key to open the lock?"

I dug through the crossbody purse slung across my chest and pulled out a key ring. The multi-colored pom-pom and yarn-tasseled ring holding the keys made me smile. My twin nieces had found the craft project on Pinterest and insisted I immediately take them to the craft store to buy the supplies. My reward for indulging their creativity was a lifetime supply of key ring decorations. I located the correct key, inserted it into the lock, twisted, and pushed the door open. I stepped through the doorway with the detective right on my heels.

I found the light switch and turned it on. Bright overhead lights illuminated the pristine oversized four-car garage. The floor was shiny, as if it had recently been waxed. Built-in cabinets surrounded two walls, and I knew the tools and objects they held were clean and organized. Mr. Skyler's black Maserati held center stage, and strategically placed spotlights made me feel like I'd stepped foot onto a showroom floor. I startled when the left-side garage door began opening, then realized, when Hannah's sneaker-encased feet and jean-clad legs began appearing, that she'd used the remote to join us.

I introduced the two women. Hannah barely made eye contact with the detective, and I worried that it might be perceived that she was trying to hide something. The last thing we needed was for word to get out that Theodore was a multi-million-dollar art thief.

"Ms. Olsson, would you mind showing me where you collect the mail from and tell me how often you pick it up?"

"I check every afternoon, around three." Hannah's voice could barely be heard in the cavernous space, and there was a faint quiver at the end of her sentence. She walked to the side of the open garage door and pointed at the built-in slot situated halfway up the wall. Below the slot, sitting on the floor, was a box to collect incoming mail. It was empty.

"Have you noticed anything different over the last week or so with any of the incoming mail?"

"No, ma'am." Hannah shook her head but wouldn't meet the detective's gaze. "I take it to Emory's office and divide it into piles. Can you tell me what this is about?"

"Someone put a threatening note in one of the catalogs on my desk." I jumped in, not giving the detective any time to intimidate Hannah further. "We're trying to find out how the note got there."

"I never saw anything that didn't belong." Hannah's eyes grew wide, and her face paled. "But I don't look closely at the mail, either, so it might have been hiding."

"Thanks, Ms. Olsson. I have one more question for you, and then you're free to go." Detective Tran scanned the walls of the garage. "Is there a security alarm on the garage? I'm not seeing a panel."

"No, ma'am. Just the security cameras."

She nodded. "Okay. I think that's all I need from you. We'll close the garage door and lock up when we're done here."

Hannah didn't wait another second and instead scurried across the alleyway and back to the house. Detective Tran never took her gaze from the woman's fleeing form until she was hidden by the security gate that she closed behind her.

She turned to me. "She's hiding something. Do you know what it is?"

"Who, me?" My voice squeaked. I cleared my throat.

"Uh, no. It could be that she's nervous about Mr. Skyler returning tomorrow and him finding police activity at his house. She might be worried he'll blame her."

"Is she to blame?"

"Definitely not. She couldn't possibly have anything to do with Mr. Jorgensen's murder." I was pretty sure I'd told the truth. Or at least I hoped it had been the truth.

"The side door doesn't appear to be broken into, which means someone with access to the house left you the note or someone put it into a catalog and dropped it through the mail slot." She turned to face me. "Did you take a look at the catalog that held the note? Did it have the Skyler address on it?"

I wrinkled my brow as I tried to remember. "I didn't pay any attention other than it was a sporting goods catalog that held the note. I put it, along with the other ads and whatnot, into the recycling bin."

"Would the catalogs still be in the recycler? I'd like to take a look."

"Let me call Hannah. She usually cleans my office the second I leave."

Hannah answered on the first ring and confirmed what I'd suspected. She'd already emptied my recycle bin into the curb-side can, and the trash company collected it a few hours later. I told Detective Tran as much.

"Are we about done here? I need to call an Uber." I tapped open the app and felt like whining. There was a thirty-minute wait for a ride. It'd take me less time to walk home via the ferry, but I didn't feel safe doing so in the dark without Piper.

Again, Detective Tran audibly exhaled as she slowly blew her breath out. "I'll give you a ride back. I can't have it on my conscience if something were to happen to you on your way home. But do yourself a favor and call your insurance company first thing tomorrow. Your policy probably covers a rental car until they settle your claim."

"Thanks for the advice. I hadn't thought of that." It would be a godsend if it worked out that way. Uber could be convenient when cars were available, but the costs also added up. Who knew how long it would take for me to purchase another reliable but cheap car to replace my trusty Honda?

We rode most of the way in silence, aside from the detective's loud yawns that filled the cabin of her vehicle. When she pulled up in front of my gate, I hopped out then stuck my head back into the vehicle. "Do you want a cup of coffee for the road?"

"No, thanks. I'm heading straight home." She swiveled in her seat to face me. "I meant what I said about Randall. I have no desire to come between you, so do what you must to make your relationship work."

I shook my head. "It was already ending, but neither of us wanted to admit it. Unless you strongly object, I'm going to text him your phone number. You have some unfinished business with him, and until it's resolved, neither of you are going to be able to move forward."

She turned back in her seat to gaze out the front windshield. The silence lay heavily in the air between us for what seemed an hour. "You could be right. Send me his number as well. I should probably get it over with."

"Good luck, and I truly mean it." I liked Detective Tran and wouldn't begrudge her if things worked out between her and Randall. My mother had warned me that he'd been a rebound guy for me, after my marriage disintegrated, and it wouldn't last. I hated that she was right, although I'd never admit it to her.

Once the detective had turned the corner, I sent Randall a text and sent his phone number to "Nattie," then made my way to Tillie's. Over a bottle of wine, I told her about the whole sordid mess that had become my life.

Chapter 25

T he alarm clock went off at what seemed like o'dark thirty. Grit filled my eyes, or perhaps it had it been from the tears that fell as I told Tillie about my breakup with Randall. I checked my phone, for the millionth time, and still hadn't heard back from him in response to the text I'd sent. Honestly, I didn't break up with him via text. I wasn't that emotionally broken. Instead, I'd sent him "Nattie's" phone number and suggested he work out his unfinished business with her. I also apologized, again, for my reaction to his need to protect me. It wasn't hard to fathom that after losing his brother in such a violent manner, he'd never want to experience the loss of someone he cared about again.

I mixed up a batch of blueberry muffins and popped them into the oven then clipped the leash onto Piper's collar. She practically pulled my arm off as I took her for a quick walk around the block. I hadn't spent nearly enough time playing with her to burn up her excess energy. By the time we returned home fifteen minutes later, my heart rate was up—in a good way—and I felt less stressed. Brad stood by my gate, holding up two cups of coffee and a pastry bag.

"You're out and about extra early." I unclipped Piper's leash then opened the security gate. She bounded in and rolled around in the grass.

"I have to pick Gabe up from the airport, so thought I'd stop by."

"Uh-uh. You and I both know you're here for some gossip, since I'm not anywhere close, or conveniently on the way, to the airport." I checked the muffins for doneness then removed them from the oven and put them onto a cooling rack. Piper came running into the kitchen as I filled her food bowl and freshened her water.

"I brought you an apple fritter. Trade you for a hot muffin?" Brad's gray eyes almost looked black in the early-morning light.

"Sure. Help yourself." I picked up the to-go coffee cup, sat next to him at the table, and took a sip. "Thanks for the coffee."

"So..." He nudged my elbow. "How's the investigation going?"

Groaning, I cradled my face in the palms of my hands. "It's not. I feel so bad that Sal's still in jail and I have barely figured out any suspects. Tillie, Will, and I are visiting the grieving widow this morning."

"Will? Who's he?"

"He's an attorney who attended the Jorgensens' party." I stared at my best friend and realized it'd been days since we'd talked. "I'm such a bad friend. How've you been without Gabe around to keep you out of trouble?"

"I'm fine, though a little exhausted. The company had a deadline for software delivery yesterday, and Sunday morning my analyst found a bug in the code." He rubbed a hand over his smooth jawline. "We worked on it twenty-four hours straight, but at least I delivered the product on time."

Brad owned a successful gaming software company that

had expanded over the years. He'd done remarkedly well for himself, and despite his wealth, he still lived a low-key, down-to-earth lifestyle. In fact, if they didn't know better, most people pegged him for a surfer dude who'd rather hit the waves than hold a job.

I bumped my coffee cup to his. "Cheers and congrats! I'm surprised you're up and around this early after that."

"I had to check in on my bestie." He gave me a half grin. "And I really am picking Gabe up at the airport in ninety minutes, so spill the beans."

"Fine, but I need to get Tillie's breakfast to her, and I'm supposed to go incognito to our visit with Mrs. Jorgensen. It's going to take some time to get myself ready."

He lifted one sandy-blond eyebrow. "Incognito?"

"Yeah, you know, full-on make-up, straightened hair, jewelry, and nice clothes." I rolled my eyes. "Kind of an anti-slob look."

Brad's chuckle was low. "Show me what to take over to Tillie's for breakfast, and then you can talk to me while you get dolled up."

I pulled two yogurt and granola fruit parfaits from the refrigerator that I'd assembled the night before and set them in a sturdy tote bag. Several still-warm muffins went into a small bread basket, and I covered them with a linen napkin. I handed the tote to Brad along with a sealed carafe of coffee and pushed him toward the door. "I'll let her know you're on the way and will be joining her for breakfast while I take a quick shower. After that, we can have a chat while I get ready."

Tillie adored Brad, and I knew she wouldn't mind his company. Piper followed on Brad's heels. When I called her back, she turned and gazed at me with mournful, sad-dog eyes. I relented.

"Do you mind taking Piper with you? She's used to hanging out with Tillie most mornings."

"Not a problem. Can you open the gate for me, though?" He tilted his head toward the closed security gate. "I don't want to drop anything."

I led the way through my gate, across the alleyway, opened Tillie's security gate, then unlocked Tillie's front door. Before I could call out, Piper made our presence known as she sang out her singsong-y whine and scampered to find her favorite friend. We made our way to the kitchen, where we found Tillie sipping a cup of coffee while solving a crossword puzzle, in ink.

"Brad!" Tillie rose and held out her arms. "Come give me a hug and kiss. We've missed seeing you around lately."

Brad did as she requested once he'd placed the tote and carafe on the granite island countertop. "I'm having breakfast with you this morning, if that's okay. I heard our Em has to get dolled up, and she thinks it's going to take all morning."

"You know it's more than okay." Tillie eyed me up and down, taking in my ratty T-shirt and tattered pajama bottoms. I'd twisted my frizzy hair into a messy bun after dragging myself from bed this morning, all without benefit of a mirror or brush. I knew I looked a hot mess. "Perhaps she does need some extra time, but no matter, at least you're here to keep me company."

"Fine, but no gossiping about me behind my back while I get ready."

Brad placed his index finger at the side of his cheek and twisted while posing with duck lips. "Don't be a spoilsport. We have so much to dish about you."

"Whatever." I waved away his playful attitude. "Tillie, you might as well tell him about the latest soap opera going on with me, especially since Brad's met Detective Tran a few times."

I left the pair of them giggling to get ready for the foray into Mrs. Jorgensen's home, knowing I wouldn't see Brad the rest of the morning. It didn't bother me, since I needed to focus on the questions I wanted to ask Mrs. Jorgensen. Brad, on the other hand, would have wanted to dissect my ending relationship with Randall, whether I was ready to do so or not.

AS SUSPECTED, Brad was long gone by the time I stepped into the town car where Tillie waited for me in the back seat. She'd dressed in a stylish knit three-quarter-sleeves black suit, from the St. John collection if I had to guess. A strand of pearls adorned her neck, and several dainty gold bracelets encircled her left wrist. As usual, her makeup appeared flawless and complemented the fine job her plastic surgeon had performed on her now unlined face. Very few women who resided along the Newport Coast ever looked their actual age, and most, in the social set, had their cosmetic surgeon on speed dial.

Tillie's pale-blue eyes swept over my appearance, and she nodded her approval. "Much better, my dear. Perhaps I should take you shopping and schedule a makeover for you now that you're back on the market."

"Tillie!" My skin flushed hot. Without a doubt, the heavy amount of foundation I'd troweled on to cover the generous number of freckles sprinkling my face wouldn't hide the red that I knew colored my cheeks. Tillie had always seemed accepting of my lack of adherence to her social circle's norms. I was happier without wearing makeup, and I'd learned to love my wild red hair instead of spending copious amounts of time and money in an attempt to tame it.

"I'm teasing you." She patted my hand. "You look lovely, my dear, with or without makeup on. Besides, now that Randall is moving on, perhaps you should give my grandson a chance."

I wanted to scream *no, no, no,* but I held it in when Tillie's hopeful face beamed at me. "Brian's nice, but I've decided I don't want to date right now. It's time to focus on me. Look what happened when I went from my ex straight into dating Randall. I don't want to go through that again."

"We'll see." She patted my hand again while Andrew skillfully drove down the Pacific Coast Highway.

Chapter 26

Exiting the car in front of the colossal three-story Spanish-style house, I noticed Tillie had an ornately carved cane in her hand.

"What happened? Did you hurt yourself?" My heart plummeted. Mr. Skyler would blame me if his mother injured herself. I was supposed to be keeping an eye on her.

She beckoned me closer. "It's a prop. While you and Will distract Lisette, I'll do some snooping. She'll never think to have her bodyguard follow a frail old woman like me to the powder room."

With that, she leaned heavily on the cane and slowly limped up the steps, not giving me even a second to argue with her. Will made his way from his car and stood beside me as Tillie rang the bell. As happened on my first visit, Tiny opened the opulent door and greeted us, with a gun. At least this time it was holstered instead of pointing directly at me.

"I'm Mrs. Matilda Skyler." Tillie drew into herself until she seemed much smaller than her five-four height. Perhaps she used the cane to promote the reduction in her stature and give credence to her frailty. "We have an appointment with Lisette."

Despite the dark-blue stiletto heels I'd crammed my feet into, I still felt short and dowdy beside elegant Tillie. The navy-blue sheath dress with cap sleeves I wore felt overly tight around my waist, and even though I'd ironed it before putting it on, wrinkles had appeared around the hip area where it had pulled tight while seated for the drive. I tugged the hem down, hoping to smooth the wrinkles out. At least my hair had remained straight and silky, thanks to the flat iron my sister had gifted me last Christmas. I guiltily thought how today had been the first time to use it, and I reminded myself to thank her.

Tillie lightly touched my arm as if to scold me for fidgeting. I stilled my hands.

"Follow me." Tiny waited to see that we were behind him then led the way into the house. He slowed his walk to allow for Tillie's tottering, as she used the cane to aid her balance.

Being the last one to enter, Will closed the front door and followed behind me. I glanced around to see if he needed assistance. While standing on the front steps waiting for Tiny to answer the door, I'd observed that Will looked even paler than the day before, and his hand had a slight tremor when he'd reached out to shake Tillie's hand after I'd introduced them. He also seemed to struggle with catching his breath. I desperately wanted to ask what was wrong but knew it would most likely be an unwelcome intrusion into his personal life.

Once again, I walked down the corridor lined with objets d'art and fresh floral arrangements, different from what had previously been displayed on my last visit. Tiny led us into the great room where Mrs. Jorgensen waited for us, perched on one of the plump white sofas. A silver coffee service sat on the low marble table in front of her. As on my previous visits, I couldn't pull my gaze away from the blue expanse of the Pacific Ocean that shimmered in the sunlight. The doors that led onto the patio were closed, and I longed to feel the cool ocean breeze instead of the stifling heat emanating from the fire that burned in the stacked stone fireplace.

Using her cane, Tillie hobbled over to the sofa where the widow sat. She stretched out her hands and took Lisette's right hand and held it. "Thank you for agreeing to see us. May I offer our sincere condolences on your tragic loss, my dear."

"Thank you, Mrs. Skyler. It has truly been a trial." Lisette pulled her hand away and used an embroidered handkerchief to dab at her eyes. She then gazed over Tillie's shoulder toward us and raised her eyebrows. "Please, won't you have a seat?"

Tillie slowly lowered herself onto the sofa where Lisette sat. "I think you know Will Trenton? He's your godmother's nephew."

Will strode over and shook her hand before taking a seat on the sofa opposite from where Lisette sat. "My aunt Pansy sends her sympathy. She's still under the weather and asked that I visit you to offer our support in any way you need."

"Oh, dear Pansy. I was so sorry she missed our soiree." She dabbed at her eyes again. "I hope her ailment isn't too serious?"

"Nothing that a little bit of time and rest won't cure." Will rubbed his hands along the top of his slacks. "I'll let her know you asked about her."

"And this is my assistant, Ms. Gosser." Tillie had decided I should be introduced as her assistant, using my maiden name. Neither of us wanted my married name to bring any association to the murder investigation I'd been involved in when my marriage disintegrated, in case Lisette had followed the progress in the news.

I nodded and carefully took a seat beside Will.

"May I offer you a cup of coffee, Mrs. Skyler and Mr. Trenton?" Lisette reached over to lift the brightly polished silver coffeepot, pointedly ignoring me.

"Yes, please, but Ms. Gosser can serve us if you'd like." Tillie nodded at me.

"You're too kind to offer her services." Lisette withdrew her hand. "Thank you. It's been a struggle after my husband's death and the way my household staff have abandoned me."

I wanted to roll my eyes, but Tillie had been right. As soon as Mrs. Jorgensen associated me with the hired help, she'd not given me another glance. I stood and as carefully as I could poured coffee into three white bone china cups rimmed with silver and perched on matching saucers. I'd practiced lowering my voice on the ride here, so I'd sound different than the catering woman I'd been for the party. "Would you like cream and sugar, Mrs. Jorgensen?"

"Black is fine."

I handed her the cup. My mother had drilled into me that guests were to be served first, no matter the circumstances, but Mrs. Jorgensen's lack of decorum didn't surprise me. She was a self-absorbed woman.

"Mr. Trenton? How would you like your coffee?"

"Please, serve Mrs. Skyler first, then I'll take mine with a bit of cream." Will looked like he'd bitten his lip to keep from laughing at our ridiculous tableau.

I stifled a giggle before adding cream and two lumps of sugar to Tillie's cup. She took it from me but wouldn't meet my gaze. She probably knew I wouldn't be able to contain the laughter that wanted to bubble up. I splashed some cream into Will's coffee and handed it to him, avoiding his amber-eyed gaze. Without pouring a cup for myself, I sat back down. Will used his chin to point at the silver coffee service and raised his eyebrows, but I returned his gesture with a brief shake of my head. Mrs. Jorgensen would be sure to find it unseemly if the help partook of refreshments. I most likely pushed the envelope by sitting with them, and I expected at any moment to be told to wait in the kitchen.

Tillie and Mrs. Jorgensen chitchatted about the weather

and mutual friends while Will chimed in with anecdotes. His charming manner contributed to a relaxed conversation between the trio. Will would be able to keep Mrs. Jorgensen entertained just as we'd planned. I, of course, kept silent, as did Tiny, who lurked in the far corner, closest to the corridor that led to the front door.

Fifteen minutes into the visit, Tillie placed her hand onto Mrs. Jorgensen's arm. "Please forgive an old woman, but would you be so kind to point me in the direction of your powder room?"

"Tiny can show you the way." Mrs. Jorgensen waved the large man over.

"Ms. Gosser can aid me. Please, just point the way." Tillie stood, using her cane for balance, then hobbled toward me. "I hate to bother this young man."

I stood and placed my hand beneath Tillie's elbow as if providing support. She took a few more shuffling steps.

"Nonsense. It's easier if he shows you." Mrs. Jorgensen finished her coffee then looked pointedly at her empty cup. I ignored her unsubtle hint that she wanted a refill. Will, on the other hand, leapt up and offered to pour for her, then sat beside her.

Tiny swept his arm in front of him and pointed the way toward the area that I knew held the kitchen and a bathroom the staff used. I'd hoped there would have been a guest powder room closer to the front entrance and the stairs that led to the upper floors. Tillie and I had decided that would be the best place to do some quick snooping. But it wasn't meant to be. Tiny walked slowly so Tillie could easily follow with me holding on to her.

Once Tillie was inside the bathroom and the lock clicked, I headed back toward the way we'd come.

"Shouldn't you wait for her?" Tiny looked from the locked door then to me.

"She'll be at least ten and more likely fifteen minutes in

there." I lowered my voice to almost a whisper. "She's been having tummy issues lately, and she'd prefer some privacy."

The pallor of his face turned a bit yellow. He glanced at the door again then decided Tillie couldn't get into any trouble. I appeared to be the greater risk as he walked closely behind me.

I intentionally raised my voice as we walked through the kitchen, so Tillie would know the coast was clear for her to come out. "Do you mind if I go out onto the patio and take a look at the view?"

Chapter 27

I opened one of the French doors, out of sight from the bathroom, and stepped out into the sunlight without giving him a chance to reply. Once Tiny followed me, I shut the door behind us and walked the distance to where the railing overlooked the cliff drop-off. Too late I realized I stood right where Mr. Jorgensen had collapsed and died. I swallowed down my panic and looked out to sea. Boats, some with sails billowing in the wind, a few speed boats churning up wake, and mega cargo ships chugging in the far distance, dotted the water.

"This view is spectacular." I tried to keep my voice low as I reminded myself that Tiny had met me twice before. But so far, he hadn't indicated any recognition, and I hoped my luck held while Tillie snooped around. "How long have you worked for the Jorgensens?"

"A long time." Mr. Chatty he was not.

"So, are you her bodyguard?"

"You could say something like that."

"Do you get bored standing around all day?" I tried to channel a bored personal assistant, a bit on the airhead side. "My days are impossibly boring. She doesn't want me to be on my cell phone checking Instagram even when there's nothing going on. If I didn't have so many credit card bills, I'd quit in a heartbeat."

Tiny didn't answer except for a grunt, like he'd tuned me out. I decided to press for some information like we were just two bored employees passing time and gossip.

"Mrs. S—don't tell her I call her that—said that Mr. Jorgensen was murdered. Is that true? Were you here when it happened?"

"That's what the cops say. He died right where you're standing." A smile finally flitted across the big man's lips when I screeched and jumped back.

"Oh my gawd! Are you kidding me? Is his ghost still here?" I clutched my hand to my chest.

He shrugged.

"How did it happen?" I glanced around furtively then lowered my voice to a whisper. "Do you think the wife did it?"

Tiny's eyes turned sharp and dark as his gaze focused on my face. He grabbed my arm. "Why would you say something like that? Who's spreading those rumors?"

"Chill, dude. It's always the spouse who does it in all the movies." I held my hand up, palm facing him, and he released my arm. "OMG, I didn't even know anything about this until Mrs. S told me why we were making this condolence visit on the drive here. No one's said anything about who did it. I'm just shooting my mouth off until it's time to get out of here."

I breathed a little easier when his shoulders relaxed and he took a step back. "Don't get so wound up. I'm not spreading rumors."

"Here's a fact you can spread if you feel you've got to keep shooting your mouth off. The caterer poisoned Mr. Jorgensen." He crossed his arms in front of his chest and glared at me.

"Really? Did they arrest him, or was it a her?" I gazed out at sea to calm my nerves.

"Yeah, he was arrested right after it happened. I hope he gets the death penalty."

The venom in Tiny's voice stunned me, and I was greatly relieved that California had a moratorium on sending convicted criminals to their death. I swallowed hard to settle the quiver that threatened to overtake my lips. "That's awful he'd do something so horrific like murder. Do you know why he killed your boss?"

"Who knows why psychos like that punk kill? Maybe it was a gang hit or something," Tiny muttered, furrows appearing in his brows as he frowned.

"OMG! A gang hit?" This man was stretching what little acting ability I had. I wondered how much longer I could hold on, waiting for Tillie to send me an all-clear text. Was he making this stuff up to try to impress me, or was he trying to cover something up? "I guess you're lucky only your boss was poisoned. Do you think the gang was trying to kill a bunch of people?"

He shrugged. "With psychos like that, who knows?"

"But no one else got sick, did they? Ya know, how scary to think a murderer served you food at a party!" I gasped and widened my eyes, hoping the brown contacts I'd worn didn't slide around and show my natural green eyes. "Did you eat any of the killer's food?"

Tiny glared at me like I'd finally worn down his patience. "If I ate the poisoned food, do you think I'd still be standing here listening to you yak?"

I tilted my head back and forth and batted my eyelashes. "I don't know. You're a big guy, so maybe it didn't affect you the same way."

He turned away from me, and I thought I heard him mutter something akin to "unbelievable bimbo" beneath his breath. I wanted to laugh out loud, but I had to find a way to keep him engaged and away from finding Tillie where she wasn't supposed to be.

"Maybe your boss was on some kind of medication that interacted, and the caterer was only hoping to make a bunch of people sick." I drew my brows together and pursed my lips. "Did you say anyone else got sick?"

"No. No one else got sick." He scowled at me. "Can you just drop it and go check on your boss? Hasn't she been left alone too long?"

I looked at my watch. I'd stretched our conversation out to ten minutes. We'd hoped Tillie could have at least fifteen. "She usually sends me a text when she's, ah, um, emptied out."

Again, Tiny's face appeared a little green. "Just stop. I don't need the details."

"Okay, so back to the murder mystery."

"You can just stop with that too." He huffed out a breath of air. "Why don't you admire the view or meditate or do something quiet?"

"If you don't want to chat, feel free to return to your boss." I felt certain this was an idle suggestion. He'd been given orders to keep his eyes on me. What were they afraid I'd do? Steal one of their valuable objects? Or were they hiding something?

He closed his eyes and shook his head.

I was frantically searching for another topic to annoy Tiny with when, thank God, my phone chimed with a text. I pulled my cell from the itsy-bitsy over-the-shoulder evening bag I carried. It was Tillie sending a thumbs-up emoji.

"It was great getting to know you, Tiny, but I need to go assist Mrs. S." I headed to the door. Before I could swing it open, a meaty hand held it shut, and his hot breath on my cheek made my skin itch.

"You are not free to wander around without an escort, Ms. Gosser. Do I make myself clear?" Before I could collect my thoughts for a smart comeback, he twisted the handle and pushed the door open.

I entered and made my way back through the kitchen to the bathroom. Tillie stood, leaning against her cane, outside the bathroom with its door shut tight.

"Mrs. Skyler, are you all right?" I offered her my elbow.

"Right as rain, now." She turned to Tiny. "Young man, you might want to tell the housekeeper to restock the Febreze in this bathroom. I might've used it all up."

I stifled a giggle when he took a big step backward. Tillie shuffled forward, using her cane and grasping onto my arm as we made our way back to the great room. When we entered, a wave of relief passed over Will's face before he stood to allow Tillie to reclaim her seat.

"Ah, Lisette, my apologies for the delay. I've been having some gastrointestinal issues—old age and all that—and I've just about given up my outings." She smoothed down the hem of her jacket. "Now tell me, dear. Have you planned the funeral yet? I'd like to attend if I can and of course either make a donation to your favorite charity or provide a lovely bouquet of flowers for the service."

"That's very kind of you. I'm still waiting on that horrid detective to give me information on when my husband's body will be released." Out came the embroidered handkerchief to dab her dry eyes. "I can't plan anything until then."

"Of course, dear. You'll keep me apprised, won't you?"

"Naturally." Mrs. Jorgensen stood, which appeared to be our cue to leave.

Tillie struggled to her feet and I rushed to help her, while Will moved to stand on Tillie's opposite side for support. Her feebleness almost had me fooled. I had no idea she was such an accomplished actress.

"I'll be sure to bring Aunt Pansy to the service. She's simply bereft over your loss." Will reached over and briefly clasped the widow's hand.

We shuffled down the long corridor with Tillie between us. Tiny kept his eyes glued on our group the entire way while

Mrs. Jorgensen disappeared the moment we left the great room. When the massive entry door clanged shut behind us, we moved to the town car where Andrew stood holding the back door open.

Once Tillie eased into the seat, she motioned for Will to lean toward her. "I'm sure we're being watched, so we need to reconvene elsewhere to talk about this visit. Follow us."

She motioned for him to straighten up, and then she reached out her hand and shook his. "Thank you, Mr. Trenton. It's been a pleasure meeting you today, although I'm sorry it's been under such tragic circumstances."

"Perhaps we'll encounter each other at the funeral, and you can meet my aunt Pansy." He released Tillie's hand and nodded at me, still standing next to Andrew. "Ladies, it's been a pleasure. Have a lovely afternoon."

I gave a quick wave then made my way to the opposite side of the car and slid onto the seat. I longed to lay my head back onto the headrest, but I still had to play the part of professional assistant until we were away from the cameras and prying eyes. Instead, I sat rigid and kept my eyes straight in front of me. Tillie remained uncharacteristically quiet until we were well out of sight of the house.

Chapter 28

"Andrew, please take us to Oceana. We'll have an early lunch there, and you're more than welcome to join us."

"Thank you, Mrs. Skyler, but I'm happy to wait in the car for your return."

"Oceana's not open for lunch." I had to remind myself that Tillie wasn't the feeble elderly woman she'd portrayed. Of course, she knew the restaurant was closed. "Never mind. Brian would never turn his grandmother and friends away in need of a private place to reconvene and enjoy sustenance."

Tillie was already thumbing away on her cell, sending a text to her grandson with directions to prepare a meal for us. I turned in my seat to make sure Will hadn't gotten lost. He was there, two car lengths behind. I waved then turned back around as we made our way to downtown Laguna Beach and to the best restaurant in the state.

Andrew parked the car alongside the curb that fronted Oceana. The restaurant was a stone-and-glass building that featured a unique mixture of contemporary and traditional architecture. The name was etched, in a swooping font, on a rubbed bronze metal sign that contrasted against the patina-hued copper-clad domed roof. It was elegant yet inviting, and the view of the ocean with Catalina Island in the distance must have upped Brian's rent to the stratosphere.

Brian greeted his grandmother with a kiss on the cheek and introduced himself to Will. He glanced from me to Will, and I wondered if he was trying to determine if we were on a date. No doubt Tillie had already told Brian about my impending breakup with Randall, who still hadn't answered my text. I found it a bit worrisome.

Brian locked the mahogany-stained door as soon as we entered the restaurant. Tillie made a beeline for the ladies' room while Brian led us to a table topped with a crisp white linen tablecloth and hydrangea-blue linen napkins. It was set with four place settings. A carafe of chilled water waited for us, and perfectly formed purple irises sprouted from a crystal bud vase. To the side of the table, a stand held a silver bucket with a bottle of sauvignon blanc sitting on ice. The vintage was from a charming winery in Temecula, a short distance east of us, that Brian had contracted with to provide the house wine. Our table had a perfect view of the ocean.

I was on pins and needles, dying to hear what Tillie had found in her snooping, but she wouldn't say a peep to me in the car. She'd told me she'd share her findings after we met up with Will. Once Tillie rejoined us, we sat down, including Brian, and a server brought out crisp green salads topped with grilled baby artichokes, goat cheese, and sun-dried tomatoes. The lemony vinaigrette was light and refreshing, and the wine paired beautifully.

"What did you find out, Tillie?" I tried to keep the impatience out of my voice. "Do you know how hard it was to keep Tiny occupied and unsuspecting?"

Brian lifted his eyebrows and gazed at me over the bridge of his nose. "*Tiny?* And just what did you have to do to keep this Tiny occupied?"

I quickly explained who Tiny was and what our mission

had been that morning. Brian started asking another question, but I waved him off. "We need to hear what Tillie found out, or I'm going to burst. Please tell me it was something more than just a stash of toilet paper or empty vodka bottles piling up."

"You hit the nail on the head on both the century-worth stash of TP and the empty vodka and whiskey bottles. Are you sure you didn't breeze through the garage when I wasn't looking?" Tillie blotted her lips with the linen napkin and took a sip of wine. "Of course, it could have been empties from the party, but you'd think the bartender they hired would recycle all that."

Some catering companies were full-service, which included the food and the alcohol. My sister didn't have a liquor license, so her customers had to provide bartending services on their own. We had, on occasion, provided adult libations, but it was for friends only, and my sister never charged for it and told them to consider it a gift. She was generally tipped extravagantly on those occasions.

"Nope, I didn't get a chance to do anything. Tiny had me in his sight at all times. In fact, he threatened me after I tried to leave him behind when I went to assist you after your bathroom break. It was bizarre." I picked at my salad. It was delicious, but I worried our subterfuge had been in vain. "Is that all you found?"

Tillie took another sip of wine, drawing out the suspense. "As you're aware, the only place I could snoop at without being seen by Tiny or Lisette was the garage. I found it highly intriguing that Theodore's Jaguar is parked in the Jorgensens' garage, right alongside a white Mercedes sedan that's registered to Lisette."

"Are you sure it's Theodore's car?" Brian looked concerned. "You must be mistaken."

"I recognized the license plate number." She opened her phone, clicked on the photo app, and handed it to Brian.

"See? It's his. I dug through the glovebox and console until I found the registration. It's his all right. Swipe to the next photo, and you'll see for yourself."

"I don't understand." Brian handed the phone back to his grandmother. "Do you think he sold his car to them?"

"Perhaps, although if that were the case, why didn't Lisette say something about it? There aren't any other Skylers in the area, so you'd think she'd have realized I was related to Theodore."

Brian and I exchanged a worried look. Theodore had been friends with Nathan Jorgensen in high school and beyond. It didn't look good now that there had been another death in the Jorgensen family and Theodore's vehicle was at the scene.

"Have you talked to your brother recently?" Tillie's voice interrupted my thoughts.

"You know I haven't. How about you?" Brian signaled the server to clear our plates and bring the next course.

"It's been a while," Tillie admitted and bent her head over the phone. "I'll send him a text to check up on him."

I hastily finished the last few bites of the perfectly grilled artichokes then passed the plate to the server. The lettuce wasn't something I'd regret skipping, although Brian's garden had grown most of the baby organic leaves, which made his salads better than most. Within moments, small bowls of steaming soup were placed in front of us. The aroma of lemon wafted up, and the plump bits of orzo floated in the delicate broth alongside carrots and fresh dill. I carefully tasted a spoonful, checking the temperature with the tip of my tongue. It was flavorful, and the warming comfort of the soup relaxed me. I sank deeper into the cushy chair and finished the bowl before everyone else.

"Did you find anything else?" I shook my head. "Not that finding Theodore's car isn't huge!"

Seated directly across from Tillie, I could tell by the way

she tightened her lips together and narrowed her eyes that she had found something else but didn't want to talk about it. Something was definitely bothering her.

"What else did you find?" I couldn't help myself. I had to know, so I prodded her again.

Her pale-blue eyes shot daggers at me, and then she gazed first at Will and landed on Brian. After making sure none of the servers were in our vicinity, she lowered her voice to barely above a whisper. "The paintings."

Chapter 29

I gasped loud enough to make everyone turn my way, but before I could pry information from Tillie, the soup bowls were whisked away by attentive servers. Plates, holding petite filets of pan-seared fish, were immediately placed in front of each of us, so I held my tongue. Simply prepared and garnished with a sprinkle of fresh dill and a wedge of lemon, the flavor of the sea shined, and the succulent fish melted in my mouth. Crisp-tender asparagus accented the plate, and like everything else, it had been cooked to perfection. Brian poured more chilled sauvignon blanc into our glasses, although Will had barely touched his wine.

"We're serving California yellowtail, freshly caught this morning." Brian flaked his fish with his fork. "I prefer it simply cooked and garnished, but we do offer it blackened if you'd prefer to try it that way."

After we'd taken a bite, we all agreed this was the perfect preparation. Brian beamed at our compliments as we dug in, and he waved the servers back to the kitchen.

"Now, Gram, what's this about finding paintings?" Brian

placed a morsel of fish into his mouth, and from the look on his face, he was pleased with the flavor.

"This goes no further than the four of us at this table. Your father wants to keep this private and doesn't even want you to know, my dear. I happened to disagree. This is a family matter, and I don't want you to be blindsided. However, if David decides to confide in you, I hope you'll do an admirable job of pretending shock and dismay." Tillie sighed and pushed her plate away. "Since I've already hired Will in the capacity of attorney, I trust client confidentiality will prevail regarding this conversation."

Will nodded his agreement but didn't say anything.

Brian sat back and folded his arms in front of his chest. "Does this have something to do with you finding Theodore's car?"

"Over the last two weeks"—Tillie looked at me to confirm the timing, and I nodded—"your brother managed to walk out of your father's house with both the Pollock and the Picasso paintings."

"What!" Brian stood abruptly, and his chair tipped precariously and almost fell over. I shot my hand out to settle it.

Two servers rushed from the kitchen, a look of terror on their faces. Brian turned toward them with a reassuring smile. "There's no problem, guys. Sorry. I just got carried away over my grandmother's news. Give us some privacy, and I'll let you know when we're ready for the next course."

Once his employees returned to the kitchen, Brian sat back down. "Can you please start at the beginning? No. Wait. Are you really saying David's two paintings are now sitting at the Jorgensens' house?"

"That's exactly what I'm saying. The two paintings are in the trunk of Theodore's car, which is parked in the Jorgensens' garage." Tillie took several swallows of wine then dabbed at her lips with the cloth napkin. "Emory will catch you and Will up to speed on how this came about."

So, I did. Will sat silent and toyed with the food on his plate. Brian glowered and shoveled in his food as I relayed the facts, while Tillie sipped her wine.

By the time I'd finished detailing Theodore's thefts and how he'd been caught on the security video, Brian had pushed his plate away and leaned his face into the palms of his hands. He straightened and gazed at his grandmother. "And you walked away and left the art at the Jorgensens' house? What if they move the car or get rid of the pieces before David can retrieve it?"

"Really, Brian, give me a little credit." She patted his cheek and smiled to soften her chiding. "I texted the private investigator as soon as I saw the art and had him stop watching Theodore and instead begin surveilling the Jorgensen residence. If they move the car or the art, he'll be able to track it."

"But if they move the art without the car, like say put it into the Mercedes and drive off, how will he know?" I could see so many ways this could turn out bad.

"I believe our private investigator has many talents, including accessing secure areas without detection and fixing tracking devices to a multitude of objects." Her pale-blue eyes sparkled. "I might have unlocked the side door to the garage to facilitate his entrance too. Unless they move the car or pieces within the short time it took for me to text and for the investigator to get a person into place until he could arrive, I think we're covered."

"That could be a large enough window of time for them to move the paintings." With several millions of dollars' worth of art on the line, I broke out in a sweat thinking about what could have happened to Tillie had Tiny found her snooping. No wonder Mrs. Jorgensen had him keeping guests from wandering around on their own.

"He thought it might take about ten to fifteen minutes for one of his associates to arrive to monitor the house, and he

167

thought he'd arrive about fifteen minutes later." A grin broke out over Tillie's face. "I dawdled quite a long time, and I'm pretty certain I saw the associate already parked down the street when we left. We did good, Em."

"Which brings us back to Theodore. The investigator has been monitoring his movements since yesterday?" Brian's face had turned pale.

"Yes, so we know he's around." Tillie checked her watch. "Thanks to my desire to not get caught snooping, I told the PI I'd touch base with him this afternoon and get the details on what my grandson has been up to. I'd like to have something to report to David before he arrives home."

"It's going to be tricky getting the paintings back without the police, don't you think?" I asked.

Tillie shrugged. "It'll be up to David on how to proceed. Perhaps he'll simply have someone steal them back."

Somehow that didn't seem like a good option either. There were too many things that could go very, very wrong. But I kept my opinions to myself.

Chapter 30

Tillie's discovery left our group silent. I mulled over how it would be possible to retrieve the paintings without causing a major scandal or someone getting seriously injured. Tiny's free use of his firearm came to mind.

Brian stood. "I'll have them clear our plates and bring out dessert."

It wasn't long before plates of strawberry shortcake with fresh whipped cream sat in front of us and a carafe of coffee was placed in the center of the table. Silence returned as we forked up the succulent red berries and flaky pastry. When I couldn't eat another bite, I leaned back in my chair and observed the group. Will had barely touched his dessert, and Tillie had poured herself another glass of wine, not that I could blame her. Brian kept glancing at his phone. I wondered whether he was expecting a message or if he was concerned about the time and needed to get back to work to prep for dinner service.

"Will, did Lisette say anything of interest while Tillie and I were out of the room?" I'd felt guilty leaving Will to keep Mrs. Jorgensen entertained, but he'd been the logical and only choice.

"You wouldn't believe the number of medications Arthur was on." Will leaned in toward the center of the table and lowered his voice. "I'm certain he would have died sooner than later from the interaction of those drugs, especially with the amount of alcohol he drank."

"Did she tell you specifically what medications he was on?" Despite our server being nowhere in sight, I followed Will's lead and kept my voice quiet.

"He was on digoxin for his heart, plus lisinopril for high blood pressure." Will took a sip of water. "I think he was on acid reflux meds too."

"The detective let it slip that he was on some sort of antibiotic as well. I think it started with an er-something and ended with 'sin.' Oleander, which he somehow ingested, apparently enhances the toxicity levels. It was what killed him." I opened the search app on my cell and typed in antibiotics starting with "er." I had to scroll down the page for a while, but Wikipedia gave me the answer. "Here it is. Erythromycin, and it can cause heart issues. Don't you think his doctor would track which medications he took and how they interacted with each other, especially if he already had heart problems?"

Brian, Tillie, and Will opened their cell phones and started tapping away. Will was the first to share his find. "It looks like the antibiotic should never be combined with digoxin. Even without the oleander, considering how much alcohol he drank, the combinations would have been lethal."

"Why would his doctor combine the two medications?" It seemed to me a wrongful death suit could be filed by Mrs. Jorgensen.

Brian held up his cell phone. "If he was on high blood pressure meds plus a proton inhibitor med for his acid reflux, they could have interacted with the digoxin as well with lethal results."

I gazed at each of my friends. "Even without the oleander,

someone must've been trying to kill him before we showed up for the party. Or else Mr. Jorgensen had a death wish after losing his son."

Tillie rested her hand on Will's arm. "I think Emory and I will pay visits to the two couples who sat next to Arthur and Lisette. Can you go with us after lunch?"

"What are you hoping to accomplish?" Brian leaned back in his chair and crossed his arms. "It seems like you should let the detective know what you've found out this morning and let her take it from there."

"Emory will relay the information to her, but most people aren't exactly forthcoming when questioned by the police." Tillie crossed her arms, mimicking Brian. "On the other hand, most will gossip with a doddering old lady like myself."

Brian snorted and shook his head. "As if you'll ever be a doddering old lady."

An overly full stomach and the two glasses of wine I'd indulged in made my eyelids droop as Will chatted with Tillie about humorous happenings he'd witnessed at the courthouse. He really was a good conversationalist when he tried.

Brian filled one of the coffee cups with dark brew, added a splash of cream, then pushed it my way. "If you're going to keep up with my grandmother this afternoon, you'd better drink this."

I flashed him a lazy smile, picked the cup up, and took a sip. I tried to avoid looking at the reddish-gold stubble that made his jawline appear more masculine. "Umm. You've got a new blend? I like the cocoa undertones."

"Yeah. It's from a local family-owned roaster up in Costa Mesa." He took a sip of black coffee. "I'm partial to their Sumatra beans, but the Brazilian single-sourced beans are good too. I also like that they purchase the coffee from family-owned fair-trade organic farms from around the world."

From the very first conception of Oceana, Brian had been committed to purchasing local, organic ingredients and supporting small family-owned businesses for the restaurant. The freshness of the produce was evident in each mouth-watering dish served. Living right on the coast also had the added benefit of serving same-day catch from the sea. It wasn't any wonder that his restaurant received accolades and every table was booked.

"Next time you order some, send a pound or so our way." I took another sip and concentrated on the undertone flavors. It was similar to tasting wine. "I think Tillie will enjoy it, since it's less acidic."

Brian waved the server over and mumbled some instructions in the young man's ear then turned back toward me. "He's going to vacuum-seal a pound for you and Tillie to share."

"Thanks, but we could have waited."

He waved away my suggestion. "It's the least I can do after all my grandmother has done for me, or for what you've done for my family. Let me know when you need replenishing."

"Thanks. I will."

When the restaurant had gone through a rough patch starting out, Tillie had loaned Brian quite a bit of money to keep Oceana afloat. I wasn't certain Brian was aware I knew the amount of the extensive loan, but in truth, a pound of coffee here and there was a pittance token of thanks for the help Tillie had offered. It wasn't any wonder that Brian pulled out all the stops to provide a fabulous lunch at the drop of a hat anytime his grandmother had a whim to stop by. I was happy to see that Brian appreciated the gift he'd been given to stay in business and had continually done everything he could to express his gratitude. His brother, Theodore, on the other hand—well, he was sour lemons, to say the least. I couldn't help but wonder if Tillie had received a text back from him yet.

Tillie practically sprang from her seat, back to her

sprightly self after playing the tottering elderly grandmother. "Time to move on and question our next witnesses."

We all stood, and Brian rounded the table and kissed his grandmother on her cheek. "Don't get into trouble. Okay?"

"My middle name is trouble, and don't you forget it." Tillie cupped Brian's cheek in the palm of her hand. "Young man, you forgot to shave this morning. How do you expect to find a girlfriend if you're going around looking sloppy like that?"

Brian blushed and shrugged his shoulders. "It's the fashion. Besides, I had to hit the docks at five this morning. If I hadn't, you wouldn't be eating the freshest yellowtail in Orange County."

"If sloppy hygiene is what it takes to get a seafood meal this good, then I'll forgive you." Tillie could barely keep a straight face, which meant she'd imbibed a lot more wine than usual and was in a teasing mood. I, for one, was happy to see that she had a small reprieve from Theodore's betrayal.

Worried about what might come out of her mouth next if she'd happened to notice me talking quietly with Brian during lunch—who was I kidding, of course she noticed—I hurried to usher our group out of the restaurant. "Will, you're coming with us, right?"

After Will acknowledged he would, I turned to our host as the server thrust a brown paper bag in my hands. I peeked inside and found the coffee beans. "Thank you for such a lovely lunch, Brian. As usual, it was spectacular, and I can't wait to relax over a pot of coffee with Tillie tomorrow morning."

"Ha, good luck with that." Brian smiled then jerked his head toward his grandmother. "But in all seriousness, please keep her safe and let me know if she hears back from my brother. I have a hinky feeling about his car and the paintings being at the Jorgensens'."

I nodded then tugged on Tillie's elbow. "Do you have the addresses we need to stop by for our investigation?"

I knew my question would divert Tillie's attention from playing matchmaker, at least for a while.

Tillie sent Will a text with the Irvings' address, in case he lost sight of the town car, while Andrew drove us to our destination. Since Tillie hadn't given her driver an address, I questioned if she'd planned our visits with Mrs. Jorgensen's guests in advance.

"Of course I did. We didn't need any surprises like a door slammed in our face or no one home to question." She checked her reflection in a handheld mirror she'd pulled from her purse, touched up her lipstick, and patted her carefully coiffed platinum-blonde hair into place. She handed the mirror to me. "You could probably do with a little lipstick, dear."

I did as she suggested then handed the mirror back. "Have you heard back from Theodore?"

"No, but that's not terribly unusual." She gazed wistfully out the window. "Sometimes it's a day or even two before he responds to me, especially if I don't give him specifics in my text."

And this was one time when specifics would have Theodore catching the next flight out and disappearing to a country with no extradition laws. We'd just have to be patient.

Once we'd made it through a security-manned guard gate, Andrew parked the car in front of an imposing mini-mansion, modeled after an Italian villa. Will parked right behind us. Tillie must've noticed my puzzled expression because she nodded. "You've been in this neighborhood before. Vivienne Gainer lives right around the corner."

Oh, goodie. We were in that kind of neighborhood. Tillie and I had visited Mrs. Gainer last fall, when we were hunting for answers on the death of a Bavarian barmaid. She wasn't a nice person and had kicked me out of her house. Luckily, she was happy to chat with Tillie, someone she deemed her social equal. I wondered if I'd get the same treatment from the Irvings.

Strolling along the herringbone-patterned brick walkway, the three of us made our way to the huge door made of intricately carved wood with inlaid glass panels. Tillie pushed the doorbell button, and chimes could be heard ringing in the house.

A young towheaded boy, perhaps six or seven years old, answered the door. Long, dark lashes framed his violet eyes. At the party, I'd thought that Mrs. Irving had been wearing violet contacts, but this child proved he'd inherited the color from the woman I presumed to be his grandmother.

"Hello." Tillie offered her hand to the child to shake. "We're here to see Linda Irving. Is she home?"

The boy solemnly shook Tillie's hand then turned on his heels and ran down the wide hallway, yelling, "Gram! Gram! Some old people are here to see you."

I suppressed a giggle while Tillie harumphed next to me. Will remained silent, but then again, he'd seemed subdued by the time lunch had ended. I wondered if he felt all right.

Chapter 31

Linda Irving came down the hallway, carrying a toddler with curly golden-blonde hair and violet eyes, on her narrow hips. I did a double take. She'd looked older than her husband at the party, but now, dressed in black yoga pants and a flattering periwinkle knit T-shirt with bare feet and devoid of makeup, she seemed much younger.

"Come on in." She put the little girl down and came to greet us, her hand outstretched. Except she got no more than one step toward us when the little girl wrapped her chubby arms around her grandmother's legs and wouldn't let go. Mrs. Irving reached down and scooped her granddaughter up. "Sorry about that. My grandkids, Olivia and Owen, are staying with us this week while their parents take a last-hurrah vacation before baby number three arrives."

"Thanks for taking the time to see us, Linda." Tillie walked over to her and lightly touched the little girl's arm. She buried her face in her grandmother's neck. "Aren't you a beauty! Grandchildren are such a blessing, but they can be tiring. We won't take up much of your time. Let me introduce you to my assistant, Ms. Gosser, and a family friend of Lisette's, Will Trenton."

"It's nice to meet you, Mrs. Irving." I raised my hand in a half wave, and Will did the same.

"Please call me Linda. There's no need for formalities around here." She shifted the girl's weight then leaned toward me as if to study my face. "Aren't you the caterer?"

"My twin sister owns the company. I help out when she needs me, which seems to be a lot these days since giving birth to her little boy."

She gave me a sidelong glance. "Come on back. I'll give the kids a snack, and we can chat while they eat."

Tillie nudged my arm and pointedly looked at the cubby holding street shoes and the basket of house slippers beside it. The three of us slipped our shoes off.

"Thank you." Linda motioned at the basket of slippers and smiled. "Feel free to wear a pair. They're clean. Or you can remain barefoot."

Will remained in his black dress socks, but I assisted Tillie with putting cozy slippers on her feet before I did the same. It felt like walking on clouds, and I resisted the urge to bend back down to check the label. I wanted a pair for myself.

While the bones of the house were opulent, it still managed to have a homey, lived-in feeling, especially when we stepped into the great room. Soft gray sofas, with pink quilts thrown over the armrests, were situated in an L shape. A cushy and overly large ottoman sat in front of the sofas. A variety of toys littered the room, and a pink-and-white toy kitchen with a matching kid-sized table and chairs took up the space of one corner. Instead of the marble flooring that ran from the entryway and down the hall, plush dark-gray carpet softened the area.

Linda sat her granddaughter down onto one of the child-sized chairs and opened two bento-box-style snack trays that sat on the small kids' table. Owen ran around the room before plopping himself next to his sister. He picked up a lime-green tablet and began playing a game while absentmindedly eating apple slices.

Olivia picked the pink tablet up and handed it to her grandmother. "Elmo! Elmo! Elmo!"

"Okay, but you need to eat your apples too." Soon the familiar sound of the red puppet character sounded in the room. Linda hastily lowered the volume then propped the device in front of the child.

She gestured at the sofas. "Please have a seat and make yourself comfortable. Can I offer you something to drink or a snack?"

"No, thank you. We just came from lunch and don't want to take much of your time." Tillie lowered herself onto the sofa, closest to the joint of the L.

I sat next to her, while Will sat down next to me.

"No worries. I delayed their snack and their screen time, so we should have some uninterrupted time to chat." Linda sat on the sofa adjacent to Tillie and tucked her feet beneath her. "I believe you had some questions for me concerning the party?"

"As you're aware, the caterer's employee was arrested for the, ah, murder of Mr. Jorgensen." Tillie took the lead and kept her voice low so little ears wouldn't overhear. "We think it was a mistake. Sal would never kill someone."

Linda leaned forward and once again seemed to study my face. "There did seem something odd about Lisette's immediate reaction and the arrest of that young man. On the other hand, Arthur was insistent he'd had something to do with the death of the Jorgensen boy, so perhaps there was prior knowledge I don't know about."

"Sal insists that wasn't the case, and he'd never met or even heard of the Jorgensens until we catered the party." I tugged at the hem of my dress, wishing I were wearing yoga pants like our hostess. "Your husband sat right next to Mrs.

Jorgensen, and you were on the other side of your husband during the party, correct?"

"Yes. I was so relieved I wasn't right next to Arthur. He was hideous." She rolled her eyes and huffed out air. "Not to speak ill of the dead, but that man was a monster. I wanted to slap him across his face when he grabbed you and then throw a glass of wine at those cretins who thought it was funny."

Her anger on my behalf was touching. "Thank you. My sister wanted to quit on the spot, but with the new baby, well, she couldn't really afford a gesture like that."

"I probably would've acted on my impulse to throw the wine at least, but my husband knew me too well and kept hold of my hand." She sighed. "We wouldn't have attended the party, except Arthur promised my husband recompense that night for some of our money his company lost. We couldn't jeopardize the opportunity, although with the way things turned out, we didn't see a penny. So, you see, we didn't have any motive for seeing him dead, but I certainly don't begrudge you trying to free your employee."

I gazed around the large, airy room. The house alone was worth millions of dollars. If they were hard up, wouldn't they sell the house and move?

Linda must've read my thoughts. "I've been pushing to sell the house and get something more suitable, but my husband's a stubborn man. Mind you, we're not broke, just struggling a bit."

"How well do you know any of the other guests?" Tillie got the conversation on track.

"I'd say I'm a passing social acquaintance with about half of the attendees. I certainly don't know any of their deep, dark secrets to share." Linda's laugh tinkled. "I'm addicted to Hallmark Mystery Channel, so I know what kind of information you're looking for. I doubt I'll be much help, but you never know, right?"

"Were any others expecting to receive compensation that

night as well?" I still couldn't get over her husband's reluctance to sell the house if they were struggling. Although perhaps her definition of struggling didn't come close to my definition of struggling—such as losing your husband, your job, and your home all within the space of a few days like I'd experienced last summer.

"According to my husband, there were several others there who'd invested heavily with Seacliff. The Dewitts, the poor souls who sat next to Arthur, were one of the couples who thought they'd be receiving money back that night. Have you talked with them yet?"

"We'll be dropping in on them a bit later today," Tillie said.

"You know, I just remembered something. Ted Dewitt got into an argument with Arthur right after he arrived at the house. Lisette made them go around the side so her other guests wouldn't be disturbed, but I could tell Ted was very angry."

"How did Mr. Dewitt seem at dinner?" I didn't remember him causing a scene once everyone had sat at the long table, but neither could I remember any particulars. I'd been much too busy waiting on the guests and plating food.

"He was stinkin' drunk. He probably popped a Percocet or a Valium after the argument then guzzled down vodka tonics, but at least he didn't get into any arguments with our host during dinner."

Tillie tapped her index finger against her lips. "The police haven't released this information yet, but I think we can trust you to keep it to yourself. Am I right?"

Linda leaned forward with eagerness. Her violet eyes sparkled. "You have my word."

I didn't know what Tillie planned to share, but if Detective Tran hadn't released the information to the public, I was sure it wasn't a good idea. Unfortunately, I couldn't rein Tillie in.

"Mr. Jorgensen ingested some oleander, which contributed

to his death." Tillie leaned back. She appeared entirely too pleased after sharing such an important piece of the investigation. I just hoped the detective didn't find out and regret telling me in the first place.

"No! But that's poisonous! How? Why?" Upon her outburst, her grandchildren looked up from the tablets. She smiled at them, and when they returned their attention back to the screens, she lowered her voice. "Who would do something like that?"

"Obviously, someone put it into something he ate or drank, and it wasn't the caterers or their employee." I wanted to make it clear we were not responsible.

"I believe you. Otherwise more people would have gotten sick or died."

"Exactly." I gazed at her face, watching for a reaction to my next question. "Do you remember if anything odd happened at dinner? Or if someone would have had an opportunity to sprinkle anything onto Mr. Jorgensen's meal or into his wine?"

Linda twisted her lips to the side as she thought. "I tried chatting with Lisette early on in the dinner, but she seemed unfriendly or else distracted, probably by Arthur's antics, and barely said a word to me. Harry Renault sat on my other side and proved to be a charming conversationalist. At least he diverted me from having to pay attention to the Jorgensens for most of the evening. So, I guess I'd have to say I didn't notice anything odd happen other than Arthur spilled a glass of wine, which shouldn't surprise anyone."

"Mr. Renault is the short man with thinning gray hair who wore his shirt unbuttoned halfway down his chest?" I'd almost blurted out that he'd sported a bad comb-over but stopped myself in the nick of time.

"Yeah, that's him. Why do men think comb-overs hide their bald spots?" Linda chortled. "And seriously, no woman ever thought a hairy chest sporting gold chains was sexy."

"So true," Tillie and I answered together.

"I don't know if you noticed the young woman sitting on the other side of Harry?"

"The surgically enhanced, barely legal woman dressed in the white halter dress?" She was hard not to notice, since the front of the dress plunged practically to her navel. I'd wondered how the narrow strips of fabric covering her ample chest didn't fall off or reveal more than they already did. I was sure none of the men there could have told you the color of her hair or eyes.

"That's Giselle Renault. Harry's new wife for all of three months."

"Wow!" I couldn't think of anything else to say because saying what I'd been thinking probably wasn't wise.

"You can say that again." Linda glanced at her grandkids, who were still absorbed in their devices. "Harry barely spoke to her all evening, and she was pretty sloshed by the time the police let us leave."

"Did Harry invest with Seacliff?" Tillie asked.

Linda shrugged. "My husband probably knows more than I do. If you like, I can ask him for a list when he returns home later this week. He's in New York for a seminar or something, and with the kids here, I don't have much of an opportunity to talk on the phone for long."

"If it's convenient for him to give us some names when he gets home, that would be great." I wondered whether Detective Tran had the list of Seacliff investors or if she was even looking in that direction. "Has Detective Tran been by to talk to you?"

"No. We gave our statements before we left, along with our contact information. I spoke to a young officer." She paused as if in thought. "I think his name was Officer Parnal. No, that's not it. Maybe it's Parnell? I might have his business card around here somewhere. Do you want me to find it?"

"There's no need. I have the investigating detective's

number practically on speed dial. I'll let her know what you said, and if she has any questions, do you mind if I provide her with your phone number? Or, if you prefer, you can contact her directly yourself."

"Give her my phone number. I don't mind. In fact, this is kind of exciting."

"We've taken up enough of your time." Tillie moved to stand. "Thank you so much for being so open with us."

I dug into my purse and extracted a business card and handed it to Linda. "If you remember anything else or have any questions, please feel free to call me."

She glanced at the card and then did a double take. "Ooohhh. You're the cupcake caterer. Did you make those lemon cupcakes at the party?"

"Yes, and the champagne cupcakes too."

"I didn't have a chance to try those, but the lemon ones were scrumptious. I'll place an order with you next month for kids' cupcakes for Olivia's second birthday party. She'll probably want an Abby Cadabby flavor, so anything pink and purple will do."

"I appreciate it, although that's not why I gave you my card." I still got a bit embarrassed when I marketed my services.

She waved away my concerns. "You'll be doing me a favor, and it's one more thing I can tick off on my party list of chores to do."

After saying our goodbyes, Tillie, Will, and I made our way to our cars. Will's face was ashen, and a bead of sweat rolled down his neck.

"Are you feeling unwell?" I lightly placed my hand on Will's arm. It felt hot to my touch. "Can I get you some water or ibuprofen?"

He shook his head. "I just overdid it today. A nap will fix me up in no time."

"Do you want me to drive you home?" I worried about his

lack of energy and his apparent fever. When I had a fever, I could barely drag myself out of bed for even a drink of water. I couldn't imagine trying to drive anywhere.

"I'm fine. I probably look worse than I feel." He gave us a quick wave and climbed into his car.

I wanted to ask him what he thought about our conversations today, but it would have to wait.

"I'm worried about that young man." Tillie stood beside me as we watched him drive away. "Do you know what's wrong with him?"

"He said he'd had cancer and went through chemo but everything's fine now."

"I sure hope he's right."

Chapter 32

Andrew drove us for a couple of miles before stopping in front of another McMansion. The style was French chateau, and the circular drive wrapped around a splashing fountain of naked cherubs. Somehow, I didn't think we'd get as warm a welcome from the Goddards as we'd received from Linda Irving.

Tillie rang the doorbell. When no one answered after a long minute, I decided we should leave. Tillie, on the other hand, had other ideas. She pushed the button down, released it and waited a few seconds, then pushed again. Within moments, heels striking stone could be heard within the house, and the ornately carved door swung open.

"Mrs. Dewitt?" Tillie stuck her hand forward, toward the frowning woman.

"Yes." Mrs. Dewitt briefly touched the tips of her fingers to Tillie's offered hand, her signature ruby ring flashing in the sunlight. She placed both of her hands tightly against the sides of her A-line heather-gray skirt the second she released Tillie's fingers. Her platinum-gray hair was pulled back into a severe chignon that showcased ruby earrings, although these rubies were much smaller than the ones she'd worn to the party. A white silk blouse and knee-high black boots with low heels completed her ensemble. I assumed she wore a ruby necklace, but I couldn't see it because of the cut of her blouse.

"I'm Matilda Skyler, and this is my assistant, Ms. Gosser. We talked on the phone yesterday about us dropping by to talk to you about the Jorgensens' party."

Mrs. Dewitt sniffed. "You asked if you could drop by, but I never gave my consent."

"You implied consent, and here we are." Tillie straightened her spine. "May we come in? We'll only take a couple minutes of your time."

Mrs. Dewitt looked like she wanted to shut the door in our faces, but in the end, she opened the door a smidgen wider and stepped to the side. "If you must."

We stepped into the ornate foyer, where marble cherub statutes covered every niche and tabletop. The overhead French rococo-style chandelier featured gilded cherubs in the center. It was all over-the-top. She led us through open French doors and into a small library situated right off the foyer. Tall bookcases lined the walls, and I caught flashes of gold-embellished volumes on the shelves. The lighting was dim inside the room, and the dark brocade draperies that covered the windows kept any natural light from penetrating the gloom. Mrs. Dewitt didn't bother to turn on any of the gold cherub table lights that sat on several end tables scattered around the room. She motioned for us to sit down on the black leather sofa while she took the wingback chair, upholstered in the same fabric as the draperies. She never gave me even the barest of glances once Tillie introduced me as her assistant.

"Thank you for agreeing to see us, Mrs. Dewitt." Tillie started the conversation since Mrs. Dewitt had been silent ever since ushering us into her home.

"You can do away with the formalities. I want to know why you're barging in here to ask questions about the murder." Mrs. Dewitt exaggeratedly lifted her wrist to check her watch. "Everyone knows that catering boy poisoned poor dear Arthur, so there's nothing more to say about the matter."

"Maybe or maybe not. After all, you sat right next to Arthur. Perhaps you're an eyewitness, and your life could be in danger." Tillie paused a moment to let that sink in. "Did you actually see the young man put something onto Arthur's plate or into his drink? Or do you think someone else could have done it and blamed him?"

Color drained from Mrs. Dewitt's face. "Nonsense. They caught the murderer right after it happened. It doesn't have anything to do with me."

I wanted to jump in and give this woman a piece of my mind, but from past experience, it was best if I bit my tongue and let Tillie take the lead. Women like Mrs. Dewitt and Mrs. Jorgensen relegated the "help" to nonentities, and she wouldn't take kindly to my intrusion.

"Has the detective been by to question you yet? I have it on good authority that new evidence has come to light that could clear the young man."

It was obvious that Tillie was channeling her favorite mystery character, Miss Marple. I bit my lip to keep from smiling and turned my gaze to study Mrs. Dewitt's reaction.

"There's no need for them to question me. I told them all I knew the night of that dreadful tragedy." She pulled her lips into a grim line.

"How did Mr. Jorgensen appear during the dinner?"

"Shouldn't the police be asking these questions? It really has nothing to do with you."

Tillie steepled her fingers together. "I have a philanthropic interest in the young man. He's my grandson's protégé with an excellent future as a renowned chef. We're certain he's above reproach and incapable of the crime he's being accused of."

"That seems like a stretch. If he's a protégé, as you claim, why was he working for that two-bit caterer?"

To keep from lashing out, I bit my tongue so hard I tasted blood.

"For experience in a variety of difficult situations. My grandson owns Oceana. I'm sure you've heard of it?"

"Why yes, we've dined there several times." Mrs. Dewitt's tone changed, and her words oozed like honey. "It's garnered quite a few accolades over the last couple of months. Say, do you think you can get us a reservation for Friday night? I was told they had nothing available until mid-September, and I so want to take my husband there for his birthday."

"I'll certainly see what I can do. I have your phone number, so if my grandson can fit you in, I'll call you with the reservation time." Tillie's voice sounded warm, like she couldn't wait to do a favor for her very best friend. I, on the other hand, wanted to scream.

"Why thank you, Matilda." Mrs. Dewitt relaxed back into her seat and crossed her ankles. "Now, back to that dreadful murder. What did you want to know?"

I noticed she didn't offer Tillie to call her Ruby. I wondered why that was. Perhaps it gave her a sense of superiority.

"How did Arthur seem that night? Was there anything odd that happened at the dinner table?" Tillie didn't seem all that perturbed that Mrs. Dewitt had demanded a bribe, so to speak, in exchange for information.

Mrs. Dewitt looked my way and furrowed her brows. "I'm not sure I should divulge any information in front of your girl. Can she wait in the car for you?"

"Nonsense. Ms. Gosser has been my confidant for over a year, and not once has she betrayed my secrets. I'm getting old and just a little forgetful at times. She keeps facts straight for me, and with something this important, it's quite necessary to remember everything correctly." Tillie leaned forward and lowered her voice as if someone might overhear her. "She's also my son's confidant. You know him, right? David Skyler?"

Mrs. Dewitt's eyebrows shot up practically to her hairline, and she gazed at me with renewed interest. "David is your son? Now how did I miss the connection? Well, if you both trust your girl, far be it from me to ask her to leave."

Gee, thanks for your vote of confidence. I wanted to put this woman in her place in the worst way. Instead, I remained a "good girl" and bit my tongue, again, as I reminded myself we were doing this for Sal.

Chapter 33

"Poor Lisette. She's had such a rough time of it." Mrs. Dewitt pulled a hanky from the pocket of her skirt and dabbed her eyes. "We've been good friends since high school."

"She's lucky to have you around during this difficult time." Tillie murmured her words in a soothing tone.

"Even before their son's death broke Arthur, Lisette suspected her husband had early-onset dementia. She thinks it contributed to that atrocious business partner of his stealing everyone's investments and taking off with the money." Mrs. Dewitt shook her head from side to side. "Between the collapse of the company and the death of dear Nathan, Arthur went off the deep end. He would've drunk himself to death had he not been poisoned first."

"Is that why Mrs. Jorgensen hired the bodyguard? To keep Mr. Jorgensen out of trouble?" I ventured to ask a question I'd been wanting to know for quite some time. "I think his name is Tiny?"

"Yes, Tiny was supposed to look after Arthur. It's a ridiculous nickname if you ask me." She turned her attention toward Tillie. "He's Lisette's nephew. After the collapse of

Seacliff, they started getting death threats, so Lisette hired him. It worked out for all of them, since he'd gone through a nasty divorce and practically lost everything but the shirt on his back. The bloodsucking lawyers were the only ones who walked away with anything."

I was grateful Will had decided against joining us. While I knew some lawyers had dishonorable reputations, Will appeared to be one of the good guys.

"And did Tiny keep Arthur out of trouble? Considering how drunk he became during the party, it seems to me the man didn't properly do the job he was hired for." Tillie tried to redirect the conversation back to the murder.

"Lisette wasn't terribly happy with Tiny, but he's family, so she put up with it." Mrs. Dewitt pursed her lips together. "Now that Arthur has passed, I wonder if Tiny will stay on. I doubt she has need of a bodyguard. After all, Seacliff was Arthur's company, not hers."

Given the multimillion-dollar paintings sitting in the Jorgensens' garage, Tiny's services seemed even more valuable. But of course, I didn't mention that to Mrs. Dewitt.

"Do you mind talking about the night of the dinner?" Tillie didn't wait for her to agree. "You sat next to Arthur. Is that correct?"

"Yes. I'd rather have sat next to Lisette, but that dreadful Martin Irving had the honors. He and his pretentious wife shouldn't have even been on the guest list." Mrs. Dewitt sniffed. "If you say that catering boy is innocent, then perhaps you should look into Martin. I heard he and Arthur had a terrible row before the party."

My eyes widened. Was Mrs. Dewitt trying to point suspicion away from her own husband and implicate Mr. Irving instead? I'd found Linda Irving anything but pretentious. She seemed genuinely kind, and the love she bestowed upon her grandchildren spoke volumes. If her husband was anything like his wife, he couldn't have killed Mr. Jorgensen. Or had

Linda misled us into thinking Ted Dewitt could have been involved?

"Did anything odd happen during dinner?" Tillie once again redirected the conversation.

"Not really. Arthur was drunk, but that wasn't unusual." She gazed up at the ceiling as if in thought. "He toppled his wineglass over, and it spilled all over my silk Carolina Herrera dress. Arthur tried blotting the wine drenching my lap with his dirty napkin, except he forgot he'd been hiding the vegetables from the salad in the linen. Lisette distracted him by giving him her glass of wine, which worked. Of course, my dress is ruined from the roasted red peppers and the oily vinaigrette the caterers used in the salad. I should send them the bill for replacing my dress because who, in their right mind, would serve red food when everyone is dressed in white?"

Ugh. Again, with the blaming the caterers for everything instead of acknowledging that Mr. Jorgensen was a nuisance. And why had he hidden the vegetables in his napkin? Why not push them to the side of his plate? I also noted, with some anger, truth be told, that she didn't consider Mr. Jorgensen's manhandling of me something odd enough to comment about. Instead, she'd worried about her expensive dress. *Sal. Just think about Sal and don't say a word.*

Tillie had more patience than I did at gently prodding for answers. "And then what happened after he spilled the wine?"

"He quieted down a little bit, drank more wine, and then the catering boy brought out the fish course. That was when everything went wrong. Tiny came and took Arthur away, and Lisette was practically in tears the rest of the night."

"Did you happen to see Mr. Jorgensen's collapse during the fireworks?" I tried to make my clenched teeth relax so I'd sound just as gentle and soothing as Tillie. I didn't succeed.

"No. I'd gotten chilled sitting there all evening with the wine soaking my dress, so I went inside to get my wrap. I didn't know anything had happened until several people shouted to call 911. That was when I went outside and saw him lying there and that catering boy covered with frosting. I still have nightmares about it." She dabbed at her eyes again.

I peeked at Tillie, who gave an almost imperceptible nod. We were almost done here, but I had one more question to ask, and Mrs. Dewitt was surely not going to like it. It would be better for her to kick me out and make me persona non grata than for Tillie to take the blame. It had worked to our advantage before.

"Mrs. Dewitt, did your husband invest and lose money with Seacliff Investments?"

"Why, you impertinent busybody! How dare you ask a question like that!" Mrs. Dewitt's voice had turned screechy.

"I apologize for distressing you, and I'll let myself out." I gave a quick nod and headed for the door. Behind me, I could hear Mrs. Dewitt demanding that Tillie not only fire me but sue me for infringement of privacy. Whatever that meant.

Andrew jumped out of the car and opened the back door for me as I stomped down the steps and across the flagstone pavers. I slid into the back seat, crossed my arms, and sulked until I remembered I hadn't checked my cell phone for messages since lunchtime.

I had three texts and two missed spam calls. The first text was from Randall saying he was sorry and that we needed to talk. He'd drop by my place around nine tonight.

The second text was from Detective Tran asking if I'd scanned the garage area security footage. She'd like to have any clips of interest by first thing in the morning.

The last text, a very long one, was from my sister with HELP typed in the first line. Apparently, my nieces had been invited to a swim party, and my sister had been volunteered, without her knowledge, to provide cupcakes for ten little girls. Said cupcakes were needed by nine thirty the next morning, and she was at the doctor with my nephew—and here my heart dropped for a second—because he had an ear infection.

She also had to work a small catered dinner that evening, and could I please, please, please with a cherry on top, bake the cupcakes, pick the girls up in the morning, and drop them all off at the party. And there was a very nice P.S. reminding me that I was the best sister ever. Carrie definitely knew how to manipulate me. I responded with a heart and a thumbs-up and said I'd call her later.

Tillie was still in the house, probably letting Mrs. Dewitt commiserate over my breach of etiquette, so I took the opportunity to search Pinterest for cupcakes that captured the flavor of summer. Lemonade cupcakes popped up, and then I remembered a pink lemonade cake a friend's mom had made when I was a kid. It was exactly the flavor I needed to make, and I knew my nieces would love it. As a bonus, I already had boxed cake mix and frozen pink lemonade concentrate in the freezer, so I wouldn't even have to stop off at the store. By the time I looked through the security video footage and got home, there wouldn't be much time to bake, which made the convenience products even more needed. Besides, boxed cake mix was pretty good when extra ingredients were added to make it seem more homemade.

Next, I sent Detective Tran a text letting her know I'd do my best to scan the security footage and get back to her first thing tomorrow. And just as I sent my "ok" text to Randall, with no other words, Tillie stepped out of the house.

She had a frown—well, as much of a frown as a Botoxed face could make—and she imitated the stomping walk I'd done twenty minutes previously. She plopped into the back seat of the car and yanked the car door from Andrew's hand and slammed it shut. My dear friend Tillie lifted her index finger and shook it in my face. Then she winked.

"That harpy is sure to be watching our performance. Can you try crying or at least cover your face with your hands?"

Andrew got into the car, his movements tentative as he

looked at us, and then he snapped his head to face forward. "Where to, Mrs. Skyler?"

"Take us to David's house, please." Tillie waved her arms all around and pointed at the Dewitts' house then shook her finger back at me.

It was hard to not giggle, so I simply covered my face and rested my head on the back of Andrew's seat. It didn't take long for my shoulders to heave when my laughter escaped after snorting from the effort of trying to hold it in. By the time we'd left the circular drive and the house was out of sight, Tillie had joined my howls of laughter.

"Mrs. Skyler? Emory? Can I offer you a bottle of water or perhaps a whiskey?" Andrew had slowed the car down, and it seemed like he planned to park on the side of the road.

"We're fine, Andrew. I'll tell you all about it later." Tillie wiped her eyes with the back of her hand. "Right now, we need to meet David."

Tillie gave me a high five as Andrew pulled back onto the road and picked up speed. "It worked, kiddo. Who knew an impertinent, ill-mannered personal assistant could flush out clues from stuck-up social climbers?"

"Thanks... I guess."

"We make a great team." She high-fived me again.

"You're doing it again." I crossed my arms in front of me. "Dragging the suspense out. It's killing me. What did that harpy say besides you needed to fire me and then sue me for every penny I owned?"

"It appears that Mr. and Mrs. Dewitt were brought to the brink of bankruptcy when they lost most of their savings to Seacliff Investments. It was only through the fortuitous timing of an ancient aunt passing away and leaving them an inheritance that they've been able to hold on to their home and maintain a semblance of prosperity. Trust me, Ruby Dewitt was loath to tell me. It wasn't until I fibbed a little and said I had to rely on my son to support me thanks to Seacliff Investments." Tillie chuckled. "I told her my son even has to pay your salary, and she said he should sue you too."

"She's crazy." I rubbed my cheek as I tried to put everything we'd heard into some kind of order. "Did she mention that Mr. Jorgensen had planned on reimbursing some of the money to the investors after the party?"

"Interestingly enough, yes. She finally admitted that her husband and Arthur had a discussion about it, but it was civil. Ted wanted the check before the party. Guess he knew Arthur would get bombed and didn't want him to forget or pass out before he gave them the money. Arthur refused and said it had to wait until after the fireworks show and not one second earlier. She also said she knew, for a fact, that at least three-quarters of the people there had lost money with Seacliff Investments."

"I wonder why he held back the money?"

"Either he was afraid no one would stay at the party if they got their money early on, or the sum he'd planned on reimbursing was so paltry it would create drama resulting in everyone leaving." Tillie gazed out the window. "You have to remember it was at Lisette's insistence that they hosted the party. I think she was lonely and didn't want to face another anniversary of her son's death by herself. It's obvious Arthur wasn't any type of companion or comfort to her, and forcing people to stay at the party might have been his way of acknowledging her pain."

"Do you think it would be possible to question Mr. Dewitt?"

"I hinted about it, but Ruby said he's back east at a conference."

"Could it be the same conference as Mr. Irving?" Perhaps there was a connection between the two men and their apparent arguments with Mr. Jorgensen.

Tillie thought for a moment. "It might be. Can you do a search and see what business the two men are in?"

As Andrew drove, I logged into LinkedIn and hunted for both men. I couldn't find any results. Next, I did a Google search and scrolled through articles until I found a photo going ten years back of the two men, side by side, holding a plaque. Their commercial real estate brokerage firm had been given an award. I showed Tillie the photo.

"These two are or were partners, and neither of their wives had thought it important to even mention the fact? I thought they both acted like they didn't know each other, except in passing."

"Search for their company website and see if they're still partners."

I did, and as suspected, they were still in business together. "I'm guessing they're at the same conference. Could it be possible the two men conspired together to kill Mr. Jorgensen?"

"It certainly muddies the water and at least provides reasonable doubt in proving Sal's innocence." Tillie tapped the face of her watch. "We need to drop into their office after the weekend and question the two men. Maybe we'll be able to gather some more clues."

This was one more thing I needed to share with Detective Tran, but I'd wait until I could do it in person.

Chapter 34

T raffic on the Pacific Coast Highway was congested, so it took much longer than usual to reach Mr. Skyler's house. Andrew stopped in front of the security gate at the same time a stretch limousine pulled up alongside us. Tillie opened the car door, without waiting for Andrew to do it for her, and hurried to greet her son. I, on the other hand, dawdled. My boss looked angry and exhausted. I should have caught an Uber and avoided this family crisis that didn't concern me. But of course, Tillie and Mr. Skyler had a different view.

"Emory, tell me what you know about my missing paintings? Where are they?" He opened the security gate but didn't move. "And just where is Theodore? He hasn't answered my calls or my texts."

I worried about his blood pressure as his face turned bright red. "Matilda is the one who found the paintings, and the private investigator is tracking them to make sure they don't get sold or disappear."

"How did you get involved in this?" His voice rose an octave as he turned toward his mother, and then he shook his head. "Never mind. I truly don't want to know."

"We haven't heard back from Theodore, either, although I'm certain the investigator put a tracking device on whatever car he's currently driving." I wasn't certain that had been the case at all. I'd meant to have Tillie confirm before meeting up with Mr. Skyler, but in the course of collecting clues to exonerate Sal, I'd forgotten.

This time Mr. Skyler swung around to face me. "He drives a Jag that I paid for six months ago. Can someone please make sense and tell me what's going on?"

"David, come into the house. We have a lot to tell you." Tillie placed her hand on her son's shoulder. "We'll get through this, but we need to do so calmly, over a glass of wine."

I could tell he struggled to calm down. Anyone in his position would want to yell, stomp around, and demand answers. Instead, he gazed down at his diminutive mother, closed his eyes for a moment, then placed her hand in the crook of his elbow.

"That's probably a good idea." He turned his head. "Andrew, go ahead and take off. I'll drive them home when we're done here."

I followed them into the gated entrance and made sure the security gate locked behind me. Detective Tran would have to wait for me to view the security footage, and she wasn't going to be happy that I couldn't tell her why.

Once inside the house, Mr. Skyler stared with horror at the blank wall that used to hold his cherished Jackson Pollock. He fished inside his pocket and handed me a key ring and told me what bottle of wine he wanted from the locked wine cellar. I wasn't a wine aficionado, but I knew enough to realize that the bottle he wanted was expensive.

Hannah hurried into the hallway, wringing her hands. Shiny streaks of tears glistened on her cheeks. "Mr. Skyler, I am so sorry. It's all my fault. I believed you wanted your son to take the painting, and I didn't think to call you."

"It's not your fault, Hannah." His shoulders drooped. "I don't hold you responsible, and you're not going to lose your job."

"Oh Mr. Skyler, thank you." Her sobs made it almost impossible to understand what she was trying to say.

"Emory? You can bring the wine to the dining room." Mr. Skyler flicked his fingers my way to get me moving.

The last I heard, before descending the steps to the wine cellar, was Hannah trying to tell him what she'd planned for dinner and what time it would be ready to serve. Despite her anxiety over possibly losing her job, Hannah still exuded efficiency.

With the wine decanted just the way Mr. Skyler had shown me when I'd first started working for him, my boss poured generous goblets of deep-red Bordeaux. Once he'd handed the stems to Tillie and me, he took a deep drink from his own. I took a sip from my glass and could barely believe the flavors that danced in my mouth. It was by far the best I'd ever tasted... and probably the most expensive I'd ever had too. Hannah brought in a charcuterie board, and Mr. Skyler devoured half of it as if he hadn't eaten for days. I nibbled on a small slice of prosciutto and some jamón, in between sips of the wine, as I nervously waited for Mr. Skyler to start interrogating us. Tillie acted as calm and cool as ever, but then again, her job wasn't on the line.

Mr. Skyler didn't speak until he'd finished his first glass of wine and had poured his second. Tillie and I both shook our heads when he offered us a refill. I, for one, needed all my wits for what was sure to come.

"I'll start with you, Emory." Mr. Skyler pointed his index finger at me. "Tell me how you came to find my paintings missing."

I explained, as succinctly as possible, how Hannah had notified me about the missing Pollock. Upon searching through the security video, I spotted Theodore leaving the house with the Picasso and then immediately confirmed by checking his office. "I respect your privacy and don't enter your office unless you direct me to do so. Hannah told me she cleans in there every two weeks when you're traveling, and it was there the last time she did so."

"And you decided to call my mother instead of the police or try to reach me?"

I cleared my throat, afraid my voice would squeak. "Again, I respect your privacy and wasn't certain you wanted the authorities involved, since it is a family matter. Til—er, Matilda seemed like the best resource for figuring out the best and most private way to handle this delicate matter."

"Fair enough. So far, I agree with your decisions. What happened to the security footage?"

"The master video is still stored on the cloud for at least another three weeks, give or take a few days." I wanted a sip of wine to calm my nerves but talked myself into plowing forward. "I transferred copies of the footage onto flash sticks in case the original footage, uh, ah, disappeared."

"And where are the flash sticks now?"

"I hid them around your house, and one is in my purse." I'd meant to hide it in my house, but I'd forgotten.

"At your earliest convenience, can you hand each and every one to me? I'd like to lock them into a secure safe." Mr. Skyler gazed at the wine in his goblet as he swirled the deep-red liquid. Not once did he look up during our discussion.

I fished the flash stick from my purse and slid it over to him. "Yes, sir."

"To recap, my son stole my two paintings plus a couple other heirlooms, and then you, or I should say my mother, found the paintings hiding in my son's car, which is hiding in some random person's garage in Laguna Beach. Have I gotten the facts straight, so far?"

He'd jumped ahead of the story from what I'd told him, but perhaps Tillie had given him a few details while I'd searched for the wine in the cellar. "Yes. That's it in a nutshell."

"It's hardly a nutshell. A bomb ready to explode is more of an apt description."

He had a good point. "Yes, Mr. Skyler."

"Oh, for God's sake, Emory. Can you please dispense with the formalities and call me David? We're almost family, and I promise I won't bite or even bark at you."

"Of course, David. Thank you." His outburst surprised me. Perhaps finding out his mother and son wanted to find his birth daughter, who happened to be my half sister, had made him reevaluate life and how people perceived him. However, he still intimidated me a little bit because of his influential position in the community.

Tillie must've raised her eyebrows or given her son a "look." He relaxed into the upholstered high-backed dining room chair and made eye contact with us both. "I've had almost twenty-four hours to think of nothing but what went wrong with Theodore. While he's a grown man, I can't help but worry my overbearing, overcontrolling attitude has somehow contributed to this mess. I'm going to try to change, starting with how I treat the both of you."

To say I was surprised was an understatement. Tillie must have been as well because her mouth dropped open and not a sound came out. Her son had been the one who had hired me to spy on his mother and provide any information that might prove she belonged in an elderly care facility. Needless to say, I'd declined to participate in his subterfuge, but I'd still gotten to keep the job and had made a wonderful friend in the process.

I jumped in to smooth over any silent awkwardness. "Thank you. David. I appreciate your honesty."

He nodded at me then flashed his mother a rare smile. "Now that we have that out of the way, I hope you feel you can truthfully explain why you were at this random house in Laguna Beach and why you felt the need to go snooping."

We'd reached the moment of truth. Could we trust him with the awful knowledge that I was embroiled in yet another murder and Tillie had a penchant for investigating? Or did we spin a web of lies to cover our amateur sleuthing? David might not have known the whole story yet, but somehow, he'd find out the facts sooner rather than later, whether they came from us or not. I chose to go with the truth and spilled out the entire sordid story. To give my boss credit, not once did he interrupt, and only twice did he have to manage a thunderous frown that threatened to overtake his face. I couldn't blame him for not being happy about the situation Tillie and I had found ourselves in, but really, it wasn't our fault.

"This attorney, Will Trenton, I wonder if he's capable of handling the case should it go to trial." David tapped his manicured fingers on the tabletop. "While I'm concerned about Sal, I'm also worried about your exposure to all of this. I'll give my attorney a call in the morning and see what he suggests."

"That's very kind of you. Thank you." I couldn't afford an attorney if I needed one, and I hoped it wouldn't come to that.

"Now, Matilda, tell me how we're going to track Theodore down." He picked up his cell phone and checked his messages then put it back onto the table. "He still hasn't answered any of my calls or texts."

Tillie looked at her son over the bridge of her nose. "Did you happen to leave him accusatory voice mails, perchance?"

David looked chagrined. "Well, maybe a few. But in my defense, I was in shock and halfway around the world, where I couldn't do anything but wait for a flight home."

"You can't very well blame him for not wanting to face your wrath. Leave him a message, or better yet, an email so he can't hear the frustration in your voice. Apologize for being so harsh. He needs to know you're not going to have him arrested and thrown into prison for the rest of his life. You might have to give him some time to reply, so be patient."

I thought Tillie's advice was wise, although I still didn't know how David would be able to retrieve the paintings without causing a huge incident. We also needed to find out how Theodore was connected to the Jorgensens, aside from knowing their deceased son.

"You're right. I'll send an email after dinner." David rubbed his face. "Why would he do this to me? I've given him everything he could possibly want his entire life."

I thought that was probably the crux of the problem, but it wasn't my place to say so.

Hannah stepped into the dining room, and I noticed with shock that it was already dark outside. "Mr. Skyler, dinner will be ready in twenty minutes. Will your guests be dining with you?"

David looked expectantly at his mother and then at me. "Would you like to stay for dinner?"

Tillie smiled at Hannah. "That would be lovely. I so enjoy the meals you prepare."

I glanced at my phone and decided if I wanted a wink of sleep tonight, I'd have to leave. "Thank you for the invitation, but I have to bake cupcakes for delivery tomorrow morning and take my nieces to a swim party. If I don't get started on them soon, I'll be up all night."

"Call my car service to take you home, and you can join us for dinner another night." David turned his attention to the bottle of wine and poured more into Tillie's glass.

"Thank you, I appreciate it, but I'll call Uber. It'll be quicker, and I really do need to be on my way." I walked to where Tillie sat and gave her a hug. "I'll see you at breakfast."

"Save me a cupcake, Cupcake." She winked at me as I walked out of the dining room.

Chapter 35

I asked the Uber driver to drop me off at a car rental location around the Santa Ana airport. It didn't matter who I rented from at this point, as long as I had my own transportation before I collapsed. As the driver whisked me away from the beach community, running a few too many stop signs and almost red lights for my comfort, I sent Randall a text telling him I couldn't meet tonight.

He responded back with two words: **Lunch tomorrow?**

I agreed, and we decided to meet at our favorite fish taco stand at noon. After adding a calendar reminder to my phone, I chatted with the bored driver until he discharged me in front of a brightly lit car rental storefront.

When I finally arrived home, Piper barked, wagged her tail faster than rotating helicopter blades, and ran in circles. She rarely stayed at home, by herself, for such a long duration, but I'd made sure Piper had access to a doggie door for outside breaks and playtime, and I'd left her plenty of extra food and water. Still, when I'd left with Tillie that morning, I had no idea how long and exhausting the day would turn out to be. With cupcakes to bake and frost before I could collapse into bed, I switched the oven on to preheat.

Piper deserved some attention, so after changing into yoga pants and an oversized T-shirt, I threw a tennis ball for her to chase for several minutes then gave her a good belly rub. Once she ambled over to her food dish, still containing kibble, and looked at me with those big puppy dog eyes that begged for treats—which I indulged her with—I got to work on the cupcakes.

While the frozen pink lemonade concentrate defrosted in the microwave, I added the cake mix, water, eggs, vegetable oil, and a few drops of pink food coloring to a mixing bowl. When the lemonade concentrate was mostly liquid but still cold, I added it and switched the mixer to low speed until combined then mixed on medium speed for less than two minutes. A spring-loaded ice cream scoop made quick work filling the hot-pink-and-yellow paper cupcake liners with batter. I collected colorful and unique cupcake liners whenever I came across them. As a result, I had several hundred, if not a thousand liners stored in a plastic container and stashed in the pantry.

As the cupcakes baked, I grated cold butter into a clean mixing bowl to hasten its softening to room temperature and measured out confectioners' sugar and additional defrosted pink lemonade concentrate for the frosting. I'd wait until the cupcakes were completely cool to whip the buttercream together. Rummaging through boxes containing sprinkles and other cupcake-garnishing paraphernalia, I found pink and yellow jimmies, paper straws with pink-and-yellow stripes, and a few lemon-shaped jelly candies. I bit into a candy then spit it out. The jellies were stale, so the jimmies and straws would have to do as garnishes.

It was well after midnight before I tumbled into bed, and the sound of my buzzing alarm clock at six had me groaning. What little sleep I'd snatched had been disturbed by images of dead bodies and smashed cupcakes and dreams in which I tried to run from a faceless monster but couldn't move my legs. I wanted to snuggle deeper into the blankets and sleep another ten hours. Instead, I threw the covers back, struggled into overly tight jean shorts and an oversized T-shirt, and started a pot of coffee using the fragrant roasted beans Brian had given us the day before.

Piper danced around my feet then ran and whined at the drawer containing her leash. She'd already used her doggie door, so I assumed she'd slept too much the day before and had oodles of pent-up energy this morning. Snapping the leash onto her collar, I thought we'd take a brisk walk around the block. Piper tugged on her leash the second we left my yard, and instead of sniffing every bush, blade of grass, or lone tree trunk as usual, she pulled me into a trot. Rather than staying on our street, she had other ideas and led me toward the beach. While I wasn't a runner, I could do a little jogging if necessary, so I followed Piper as she picked up speed.

We reached a small park, and I had to rein her back in when she got carried away trying to catch the flock of seagulls who pecked at the grass, hunting for breakfast. I gazed at the breaking waves, allowing their calming influence to settle me. A few hardy surfers were already out, and a short distance from where they floated on their boards waiting for the perfect wave, the dorsal fins and sleek bodies of a pod of dolphins broke the surface of the water. Ruffling Piper's ears, I bent over and kissed the top of her head. She'd known all along what I needed.

By the time we reached the security gate, I'd broken out into a light sweat from the brisk jog Piper had insisted on. However, I felt better than I had in several days, as if stress had been physically lifted from my shoulders. All that came crashing down when I stepped into my yard and found one of the glass French doors had been shattered. Spiderwebbed cracks arced away from a round indentation in the glass where something had struck it. The glass had mostly remained intact, although a few shards littered the ground. A softball-sized object, encased with familiar yellow paper, lay on the patio. With Piper in my arms, to keep her paws from any miniscule glass shards I couldn't see, I toed the object until the paper came away from what looked to be a rock. Once again, in super-bold magazine cutout letters, someone had written:

This is your last warning. Stop nosing around.

I ran to Tillie's house and let myself in.

She stood on the bottom step of her stairway, her eyes wide. Her hair was combed, she had lipstick on, and she wore nice slacks and a soft pink tunic. "Emory! I didn't expect you here for another hour or more."

"I'm so sorry to barge in like this, but someone threw a rock and broke one of the glass doors while Piper and I were jogging." I studied her put-together early-morning appearance as I bent over at my waist and tried to catch my breath. Did she have an appointment I was unaware of, or had I simply forgotten about it with everything going on?

"Have you called the detective yet?"

"No, I ran here as fast as I could." I put Piper down and slipped my cell from the back pocket of my shorts. "I didn't know whether whoever did it was still around or not."

"Come into the kitchen, and I'll make coffee while you call." She started toward the kitchen, but I caught her glance up the stairs before she turned back and led the way.

I looked up at the second-floor landing before following her and thought I caught a glimpse of a retreating leg. Whoever Tillie was hiding from me could stay there until I'd called Detective Tran.

She answered on the third ring with a terse hello.

"I'm so sorry to bother you this early, but someone just threw a rock at my French doors, and there was another threatening note attached."

"Are they still there?" Her voice sounded even more strained. "Hang up and call 911 if you're in danger, then call me back."

"I don't think they hung around after breaking the door. Piper and I were out for a run when it happened. We're at Tillie's now."

"All right." Detective Tran lowered her voice and murmured something I couldn't make out. "I'll be there in about thirty minutes. Stay at Mrs. Skyler's house, and if you feel threatened at all, call for emergency services."

Without waiting for me to respond, she hung up on me. The smell of brewing coffee and the nudge of Piper's cold nose tore me away from envisioning the threatening note. Tillie had filled Piper's dishes—which Tillie had bought to keep at her house even though we lived right across the alleyway—with water and kibble while I'd been on the phone. Despite having food in her bowl, Piper had chosen to stick close to me. She must've sensed my distress.

"What did our detective have to say?" Tillie asked as she set three coffee cups onto the kitchen table.

I gave a double take at the three cups. Apparently, I hadn't imagined seeing someone upstairs. I wanted to pry but decided it could wait until Tillie confided in me. "She'll be here in about thirty minutes and said to stay here and call 911 if we felt threatened."

"We must be closing in on the murderer. I hope this will give the detective something to go on, like fingerprints or someone's image captured by street cameras." Tillie poured coffee and a splash of cream into one of the small bone china cups and handed the cup and saucer to me. "David has convinced me to put in security cameras here. Now I wish I would have done so earlier."

I raised my eyebrows. Tillie had been adamantly opposed to the idea, worried that her son and grandsons would use the technology to spy on her and restrict her lifestyle. Whomever was upstairs was a case in point. "I'm all for it as long as you don't feel like your privacy will be impinged upon."

"We came to an understanding last night, and he agreed to let us handle hiring whatever contractor and service I choose and keep it private from him. Furthermore, you and I will have our own login and passwords for the system, and he assured me there were ways to make it virtually impossible for anyone to hack in."

"That seems like a good solution."

"Now I know you're busy today, but maybe within the next few days, we can sit down together and research some security camera systems."

"I'd be happy to do that. Tomorrow should work." With all the drama of finding the shattered glass and calling the detective, I'd forgotten about the cupcakes and my nieces' party. I looked at the clock. I still had ninety minutes before I absolutely had to leave. Ideally, that would be enough time for Detective Tran to take a report. Otherwise, I'd be faced with two very unhappy six-year-old girls and one angry sister. Even if it meant skipping a shower and combing my hair, I wouldn't be late. "I'll make biscuits for breakfast with some scrambled eggs."

"Don't go to too much trouble." Tillie had poured herself a cup of coffee and carefully sipped it.

"The biscuits are only two ingredients and easy-peasy." I stared pointedly at the extra coffee cup sitting empty on the table. "How many eggs shall I scramble?"

Tillie's cheeks pinked, and her pale-blue eyes sparkled. "Perhaps you should cook an even dozen, and we'll share a few with Piper."

Piper, hearing her name and hoping for a treat—apparently, she was holding out for more than kibble—hopped up and leaned into Tillie. She obligingly scratched behind my dog's ears.

"All right." I gazed up at the ceiling, no longer able to contain my curiosity, before I pulled a mixing bowl from the cabinet and self-rising flour from the pantry. Tillie already had the container of cream sitting on the counter. "Who is this mystery guest?"

Chapter 36

"Good morning, ladies." A deep, male voice, featuring a posh English accent, filled the room. "I'm so happy to finally meet you, Emory."

I turned from the counter I'd been working at while mixing up biscuits, expecting to see a tall and handsome silver fox to match the swoon-worthy voice that had greeted me. Instead, a roly-poly man, just a few inches taller than Tillie's five-four frame, swept toward me with an outstretched hand. I reached out to reciprocate but pulled my hand back quickly. It was covered with sticky biscuit dough.

"Uh, sorry about that. It's nice to meet you, too"—I hesitated, hoping I remembered his name correctly—"John?"

"Quite right." He gave me a brief once-over then bent down to ruffle Piper's ears. "And who is this darling creature?"

"This is Piper." I went back to dropping spoonfuls of dough onto the cookie sheet, not quite believing I was making breakfast for a baron. "Tillie's made the coffee, and I'm ready to pop the biscuits into the oven and scramble eggs."

John glanced at the cookie sheet I held. "Those look more like drop scones."

"Ah, yes. I forget in England biscuits are actually cookies and not scone-like." I slid the tray into the hot oven and washed my hands. "How long are you visiting the US?"

"I guess I'll be around until Matilda tires of me or agrees to accompany me back to London."

Cracking eggs into a bowl, I tried to keep my face impassive. I didn't want to think Tillie was considering moving to London. What would I do without her? "I'm sure there are lots of things to keep you entertained around here for the time being."

"You can say that again. I'm thinking about chartering a deep-sea fishing trip." John poured himself a cup of coffee, kissed Tillie's cheek, and sat at the kitchen table. "I've heard you can catch some monstrous fish."

"There's nothing better than fresh fish straight off the boat." I poured the whisked eggs into the hot skillet and began stirring.

Just as the eggs had barely set, I removed them from the burner. The residual heat would continue cooking the eggs. The biscuits looked golden brown, and I placed those into a bread basket and tucked a linen napkin around them to keep them warm. Once I'd placed slices of melon, orange juice, and strawberry jam along with the biscuits on the table, I plated the eggs for Tillie and John. I set some aside to cool for Piper.

The security gate bell rang at the same time a text came through on my cell. It was Detective Tran wondering where I was. I rushed to answer her summons.

"Would you like a cup of coffee or breakfast before you take a look at the note?"

She looked at me like I'd lost my mind. "I'd like to secure the evidence and go back to finding a killer who seems to think you're a threat to him or her."

"Of course. I just thought since I'd pulled you away from

home so early you might not have had a chance to eat or get your coffee." I didn't like that I felt defensive, especially after our last encounter concerning Randall.

I stepped across the alleyway, and the detective followed me. Her face softened. "Thanks for the offer. I'd accept, but my child decided four was a perfectly acceptable time to wake this morning, so I've already had a full pot of coffee. On top of that, my mom is a firm believer that no one ever leaves her house without eating breakfast, no matter how old that person might be or what urgent circumstances might facilitate the need to leave."

"It sounds like you have a good support system with your parents."

"I lucked out, and so has my daughter." Once we arrived on the patio, she donned disposable gloves and picked up the note. "Was the note lying on the ground when you found it?"

"It was loosely wrapped around the rock, and I used my toe to nudge it off." I gestured at the yellow paper. "I recognized the color but wanted to make sure it was connected to the case before disturbing you. If I'd thought it was a random act of vandalism, I would have called the police."

"It appears someone thinks you've been meddling. Have you?" Detective Tran turned piercing black eyes toward me, and a frown line appeared between her delicate swooping eyebrows.

My lips twisted of their own accord as I thought how best to present the information we'd found the day before. I'd had good intentions of passing along the gossip yesterday, but with everything that happened with David, renting wheels, and baking cupcakes, I never found the time to call her. "Yeah, um, about that…"

She tapped her foot while I told her, haltingly, about what Tillie, Will, and I had found out. Several times I had to check the scanty notes I'd added to my phone to prompt my memory. The sleep deprivation from the night before was catching up with me, but at least I had the presence of mind to avoid mentioning a word about the stolen art and Theodore's connection to the Jorgensens.

"I'm sure I don't have to tell you how foolhardy it was or mention how you could have jeopardized this investigation?" Detective Tran clenched her jaws together, and her cheek muscles quivered. When she finally blew out a ragged breath, she gazed directly into my eyes. "When I'd heard how you've interfered in cases in the past, I worried you'd do the same to me. But then I thought you'd gotten to know me, and I thought you understood I'd pour everything I had into making sure every bit of evidence connected to the murder would be collected. The evidence might convict your friend, or maybe it will exonerate him, but either way I am and I have been all along investigating with an open mind and within the legal bounds of the law."

"I believe you have been working hard on this case, and I'm grateful. Not once did I ever think you weren't capable. It's quite the opposite." I gave her arm a light touch for a quick moment then dropped my hand. "It's just people tend to talk more freely to civilians, especially to little old ladies like Tillie. She has a way of loosening their tongues more than they plan."

"What does Mrs. Skyler's family think about you involving her in dangerous investigations?"

To be sure, they weren't pleased, but I wouldn't acknowledge it, at least to the detective. "Tillie does what Tillie wants. They've learned to live with that." Kind of.

"Do me a favor and let me do my job. It's hard enough being a female on the force without a civilian poking around."

"I'll try to stay out of it, but sometimes things pop up that I can't stand by and ignore."

"How about you call me when that happens, and I'll give it my attention."

"All right. I can live with that." I flashed a wry smile.

"Trust me, I never intended to make you look incompetent. In fact—and please don't tell Gabe this—you've been the best detective I've worked with."

Detective Tran laughed. It sounded like a musical chime. "Perhaps it's because this is the first time you haven't been a prime suspect."

I couldn't help but laugh, too, for the truth in her statement, even though being arrested wasn't a laughing matter.

She put the note into an evidence bag, and the rock was placed into a second bag. She shined her flashlight over the door and onto the concrete. "I'm not going to dust the door for fingerprints. From the impact, it looks like the perp stood fairly far from the door when they threw the rock. Had they been close to the door, the rock might have ended up in your house."

"It's doubtful there are any prints on the paper or rock, right?"

"Most likely, but I'll have it checked out." She slowly walked from the shattered door back toward my security gate, sweeping her light on the ground. She stopped at the gate and looked at the lock. "I'm not seeing any evidence the lock was forced open. Could someone have a key?"

"I didn't lock the gate when Piper and I left for our walk." I grimaced. "I'd only planned on going around the block, which only takes a few minutes, but she had other ideas."

"How long were you away from your house?"

"Maybe forty-five minutes?" I checked my watch. Carrie would be wondering where I was if I didn't get going soon.

"Did you happen to notice any cars or people hanging around who don't belong in this neighborhood?"

"No. Nothing seemed off at all."

"Go ahead and call a glass company to replace the door. I'll drop the note and rock off for processing, and maybe we'll get lucky." Detective Tran turned around and gave me one last look. "And Ms. Martinez? Can you please review the security footage at Mr. Skyler's house and get back to me today? It'll be a better use of your time than running all over Laguna Beach interrogating my witnesses."

Chapter 37

Carrie threw me an exasperated look even though I was only ten minutes late in picking up her daughters. I tried explaining, but she waved it away when my nephew started crying. She picked him up and bounced him while machine-gunning the address and directions I needed to deliver the girls to the party. Dark circles sat beneath her green eyes, and her normally sleek hair looked almost as frizzy as my own. Instead of being impeccably dressed, she still wore pajama bottoms, and her stained faded T-shirt held a collection of baby food and fluids on the shoulder.

"Do you need me to pick the girls up after the party?" I tried not to stare at my sister. She'd never looked this worn down, even when the twins were infants.

"One of the other mothers already volunteered to bring them home." Baby Tommy's howl practically drowned out her words. Her bouncing increased. "It's a triple whammy. Teething, an ear infection, and I think the antibiotics are bothering his tummy. Maybe I should take the girls, and you can stay home with him."

While I loved my nephew, I didn't have that magical touch

to soothe babies when they cried. "I think he'll be better off with his mommy."

"Come on, Auntie Em." Sophie grabbed hold of one of my hands, and Kaylee grabbed my other hand. They pulled me toward the front door.

"Have fun, girls, and behave yourselves." Carrie practically shut the door on us before we'd even cleared the doorway.

"Why are you late?" Kaylee demanded as I buckled her into the booster seat I'd transferred to the rental car. "Hey! This isn't your car. Whose is it?"

"I'm borrowing it to try it out because I want to buy a new one." I wasn't about to get into explaining vandalism to my nieces. I closed the passenger door and moved to the opposite side to buckle Sophie in.

"This car smells funny. I like your other car better." Sophie wrinkled her nose. "How come you didn't bring Piper?"

Oh, how I missed Sophie's mispronunciation of my dog's name. She used to call her "Pipuh" but within the last couple of months had mastered the *R* sound. "Dogs aren't allowed at the swim party, so Piper stayed with Tillie."

"Becca has a dog bigger than Piper, and her dog's going to swim with us," Kaylee informed me. "Pleeese can we pick Piper up and take her? She wants to swim."

"Not this time. I'm sure Becca's mom doesn't need another dog invited to the party."

"Awww, that's not fair." Sophie had to put her two cents in. "Poor Piper. She's going to be so lonely while we're at the party."

"She won't be alone for long. I'm only dropping you off, and then I'll go home." I made a mental note to not forget to return their booster seats to my sister.

"NOOOOOO!" The synchronized screeching of two little girls just about pierced my eardrums.

"What's wrong? Are you okay?" I envisioned a monster

attacking them from the shrieks they emitted. I hastily merged into the right lane and prepared to pull to the side of the road.

"You're supposed to stay with us. It's the rule." Sophie leaned forward and tapped my shoulder. "Hey! Why are you stopping? You're making us more late."

"You mean, even later." I took a deep breath to steady my frazzled nerves. No wonder my sister roped me into taking them, and no wonder she looked like she did. I was positive she was counting down the days until school started up. Carrie was also right about the girls acting out more since Tommy's arrival. Perhaps time would smooth things over, but in the meantime, I needed to spend extra time helping out. "What is this rule you're talking about?"

"Moms are supposed to stay at the party to supervise, especially when kids are in the pool." Kaylee's delivery of the rule sounded like she was parroting what she'd heard someone else say.

"I'll check with your mom. Maybe she made other arrangements since she can't go and I have to go to work."

"But we want you to stay." Sophie sounded close to tears. She was the emotional one between the pair.

"How about this? I'll stay at the party for an hour, and then maybe you can spend the weekend with me, and you can swim with Piper and even take her to the dog beach for a while one day."

"Yay!" Their joyful shrieks made me loosen the death grip I had on the steering wheel.

We arrived at the party, only ten minutes late. Although, according to my nieces, it was unacceptable and I needed to learn responsibility. I was certain they'd been hearing that phrase from their parents recently. Once the girls were happily playing with their friends, without a backward glance at me, I confirmed with Carrie I didn't need to stay. Several of the moms oohed and aahed over the cupcakes, and I assured them there were enough for both the girls and the adults in attendance. A couple of them even asked for my cupcake catering business card.

Becca's mom, who'd introduced herself as Darby when we'd arrived, caught up to me just as I headed out to leave. "I heard you and your sister catered the Jorgensens' party on the fourth. Such a tragic death, although, from what I hear, not many people will mourn Arthur."

"Uh, yes, we did." Was Darby fishing for gossip to share with the other mothers? "How did you hear about the, uh, tragedy?"

Darby smiled, her lips rosy and full, her teeth straight. "My husband's great-aunt attended the party. Zinny Lorroush? Did you meet her?"

"No. As you can imagine, we were pretty busy cooking and serving."

"Of course." She leaned in conspiratorially, lowered her voice, and flipped her wavy chestnut hair over her shoulder. "You might want to keep an eye on Mr. Dewitt. Now what was his first name? I can't quite remember, but anyway, Aunt Zinny thinks he had something to do with the murder."

"Ted?" Perhaps Tillie and I should plan a visit to this Aunt Zinny. Then I remembered my promise to Detective Tran.

"Yes." She flipped her hair over her shoulder again. "Aunt Zinny said she overheard them arguing at the beginning of the party, and Ted threatened Arthur. Told 'em he'd make him pay if it were the last thing he ever did. Then Aunt Zinny saw Ted give Arthur a drink right before the sit-down dinner started. That was probably how the poison was administered."

"Perhaps. The police are still investigating."

"Well, that Ted person has motive, according to Aunt Zinny."

Darby now had my full attention. "What motive?"

"Rumor has it not only did the Dewitts lose a lot of money when Arthur's investment company went belly-up, but Arthur was partner in Ted's business, and something went terribly wrong." Darby leaned back and crossed her arms. "You should check into it."

"Thanks for the information." I cocked my head to the side. "Does your aunt know what business Ted owns? I'm sure the detective is going to want to question her."

"She didn't say." Darby lifted her hand and mimicked drinking. "Maybe you shouldn't mention it to the police. Aunt Zinny is quite the tippler, so perhaps she got facts confused between one of her murder mystery shows and what happened at the party. Besides, it would take a really stupid person to poison someone right in front of a group of people, don'cha think?"

I didn't say it, but that person wasn't stupid. In fact, their daring might keep them from being caught while an innocent person languished in prison for a crime they didn't commit.

Chapter 38

K eeping an eye in the rearview mirror for ticket-hungry cops who would be tempted to pull me over for exceeding the speed limit, I rushed home. I took the speediest shower ever, applied a swipe of mascara and gloss, and donned clean clothes. I wasn't trying to make myself glamorous for Randall for what I assumed was a breakup lunch. But neither did I want to show up stinky from my morning jog with Piper and sticky from the cupcake I'd swiped and eaten on my way home from the party.

Collecting Piper from Tillie's house—with no John in sight —I let her know that the glass company would be there to repair my door at one and I'd be back by then to supervise. It would cut lunch short with Randall, but I didn't think that would be a bad thing. Honestly, I wasn't sure we'd get around to eating much if we even ordered.

RANDALL SAT at a weather-beaten picnic table with two plates, which held three foil-wrapped fish tacos each. A side of chips, salsa, and guacamole crowded the plates. Usually, my mouth watered, but this time my stomach roiled from nerves.

Piper, excited to see Randall, darted to his side and began nosing and pawing at his leg. Randall obliged my pup's demands for attention with scratches and even a kiss on top of her furry head. I climbed over the seat, opposite Randall, and plunked myself down.

"I'm sorry. Am I late?" While it was just one minute after twelve, I worried I'd missed a text from him asking to meet earlier.

"Naw. I got here early, so I decided to get in line. It moved a lot quicker than I thought." He picked up one of his tacos, extracted a chunk of fish, and fed it to Piper. She wolfed it down then turned her sad dog eyes toward Randall and begged for more. He gave her another chunk then squeezed a wedge of fresh lime over the remaining grilled halibut taco. "The order just came up a few minutes ago, so everything should still be warm."

"Thanks. What do I owe you?" I took a sip of the iced tea sitting next to my plate and watched the long line of beach-goers waiting their turn to order tacos. Colorful bathing suits and cover-ups, worn by men and women, young and old alike, added to the feeling of summer celebrations as patrons stood in line. A few teens had on Rollerblades, and a couple others held volleyballs tucked beneath their arms. The hot sun burned my arm that wasn't sheltered by the shade of the palm tree, so I scooted over a few inches until I was protected.

He waved away my offer. "It's the least I can do under the circumstances."

I nodded and added some crunchy shreds of cabbage and finely diced jalapeños to a taco then bit into the succulent grilled fish encased in a steamed corn tortilla. My taste buds zinged. I dipped a warm tortilla chip into the mild salsa Randall ordered for me and nibbled at the edges. Sweet roasted tomatoes, pungent garlic, and spicy peppers melded together into the perfect sauce.

Randall, true to form, finished his three tacos, sharing one more piece of fish with Piper, before I'd eaten even half of one. Piper and I watched as he walked the empty paper plate and cup to the trash. He wore jeans that fit him just right and a plain T-shirt that accentuated his broad shoulder muscles and his biceps. A group of bikini-clad young women walking past us did a double take then stared at Randall as they whispered together. As usual, Randall didn't even notice. He went to the taco shack's window and came back with a small cup of water, which he held out for Piper to drink. Once she had her fill, he placed the half-empty cup on the table. I pushed the remaining tacos toward him.

"Would you like to finish mine?" I smiled as I plucked another chip from the plate. "I took Kaylee and Sophie to a party this morning and ate too much." It wasn't the truth, but the nervous dread that filled my stomach had chased off my appetite.

"If you're sure you don't want them?" He waited for my answer then inhaled the two tacos. "I won't have a chance to eat until late tonight. I'm catching a flight for Florida in a while. I need to see my parents."

"Is your dad okay? Nothing's wrong, is there?" I worried about Randall's father and any complications his surgery might bring.

"He's doing great. I just need to see them, is all." He slurped up his soda then set the cup back onto the table. "How's the investigation going to prove Sal's innocence?"

I stiffened. This subject had been our last contentious conversation, and I wasn't sure what Randall's intentions were in bringing it back up. "He's still in jail, but Tillie and I found out some interesting gossip yesterday."

He chuckled. "Tillie is an amazing woman. She could pry secrets from a live clam if she had a mind to."

"All too true." She'd pried several secrets from me, and like most people, I didn't even resent her for that. Cognizant of the short time left to us before I needed to meet the glazier and Randall needing to catch his flight, I gave him the barest details of what we'd uncovered the day before. Before this week, I would have confided in him about the stolen artwork and Theodore's puzzling involvement with the Jorgensens. Tillie might have even sought his expertise in finding out the truth. Today, though, I kept it all a secret.

He whistled. "You're making progress. If anything, Sal's attorney can easily convince a jury of reasonable doubt."

"In the meantime, Sal sits in jail." The thought left a bitter taste in my mouth. "It can take months for trials to start, and while he's stuck there, I worry he'll give up hope and his drive to succeed."

"I'm sure more evidence will be uncovered soon that will at least prove his innocence if not solve the murder."

"Has Detective Tran told you something that I don't know? Does she have evidence to exonerate Sal?" Hope soared through me.

"I'm sorry to make it sound like she's found something new. But please believe me, she's working hard on the case. She has the drive and the brains to see it through."

My shoulders slumped along with my mood, so I ate a couple more chips and sipped the tea. Randall disposed of the trash when I indicated I'd finished. I glanced at my watch. It had only been twenty minutes since I'd arrived. When he came back to the table, Randall slid onto the bench next to me. He entwined our fingers together then turned to gaze at me with his sapphire-blue eyes. My heart might have pitter-pattered, although I reminded myself saying goodbye was for the best. I hoped Randall thought the same.

"Em." He heaved out a sigh. "I never expected it would come to this, and trust me, I never wanted to hurt you or have you ever believe I could betray you."

"You haven't. You're not like my ex." I gave his hand a squeeze then disentangled our fingers and placed my hands in my lap. It would be better to keep some distance between us.

Piper used the opportunity to wedge her snout between us and nudged me to pet her. "You came along when I needed you most. But people change and grow. I understand that."

"We were good together." He ran long fingers through his hair. "We were fine aside from my job always keeping me traveling and your job keeping you busy on weekends and evenings. Which isn't a complaint at all. I've admired you from the very first time I met you."

Our very first meeting was one I'd rather completely forget, even though the memory of it was quite hazy, thanks to my glass of wine being drugged without my knowledge. I elbowed him in the ribs. "Can we just pretend we met at that birthday party for the first time?"

"Sure. It's a much better memory." He smiled warmly, and then his expression turned serious. "This is the hard part I have to explain and apologize for because I never expected to see Nattie again. She left me without saying goodbye and didn't give me even one clue where she'd gone to. She hadn't talked much about her family, and all I knew was that her parents lived in California. I didn't even know their names. Otherwise I would have tracked them down to at least find some closure."

Silence lingered between us for a few moments, so I nudged the conversation forward. "And then you had your brother's death to contend with?"

"Yes. It consumed me, and then I met you and thought I had it all." He ran his fingers through his hair again and closed his eyes. "You were one hundred percent right saying I had unfinished business with Nattie that I needed to resolve. You see, I never knew... she never told me... her little girl is my daughter."

Chapter 39

After Randall dropped the bombshell, it didn't take long to say all we needed, to close the chapter on our time together. Truth be told, finding out there was a child in the equation made it easier for me instead of blaming myself, or even Randall, for going our separate ways. I hoped he'd be able to have a positive relationship with his daughter whether or not he worked things out with Detective Tran.

I made it home just as the glazier's van pulled up in front of my garage. After unlocking the gate and showing them the damaged door, I removed Piper from the car and took her to Tillie's house. She wasn't home, but by now I didn't feel awkward leaving Piper there on her own. Tillie had made me feel like a part of her family, like a cherished granddaughter. I would have liked to have been able to confide in her about Randall's newfound daughter and our breakup, but it could wait.

Surprisingly, it didn't take long for the glass to be repaired. The workmen assured me they'd removed all possible shards and splinters of glass so it was safe for Piper to return without putting booties on her. Not that Piper would ever consent to anything covering her paws.

I pulled out my insurance file folder and found my agent's information. It was something I should have done the day before. Once I'd provided the necessary information to file a claim on my totaled car, she quickly told me what eligible reimbursements I had coming my way. Come to find out, it wasn't much. Apparently sixteen-year-old Hondas with an astronomical amount of mileage didn't warrant enough to even purchase a toy Tonka truck after my deductible. The only not-so-bad news turned out to be that my rental car would be covered for one week, which meant I had six days to find a new vehicle. Oh, and come up with the means to purchase it.

With Piper ensconced back at my house, dozing on her favorite cushion, I knew I couldn't procrastinate any longer. I had to review the security footage and see if the threatening note delivery person was identifiable.

I sent Hannah a text just before I reached David's house—it seemed strange calling my boss by his first name after being formal for so long—so I wouldn't startle her when I entered my office via the spiraling staircase. Piper stayed at home, since I'd have to sit in the A/V room, scrolling through the video feed. I was fairly certain her fur wouldn't be the best thing for sensitive equipment.

After breezing through the short stack of mail that had collected since my last visit and fortunately not finding any more threats, I made my way to the A/V room. With trepidation, born from boredom at having to keep my eyes peeled onto the monitor where next to nothing happened, I pulled up the recordings, starting with the morning I'd found the note stashed within the pile of catalogs. Detective Tran's theory that someone had placed the note within an unaddressed catalog and then shoved it through the mail slot seemed logical. Unfortunately, that meant it could have happened day or night and even on the days when there'd been no mail delivery.

By the time I'd scanned through two days' worth of video without finding a single thing, my eyes were practically at half-mast. I got up and stretched then made my way to the kitchen, where I found Hannah washing baby lettuce. She startled as I said her name.

"Miss Emory! I didn't hear you come in." She turned the water off and dried her hands on a snow-white towel. "Can I get you something to eat or a latte?"

"A latte would be wonderful, but I can fix it myself." The last housekeeper hadn't been a live-in employee, so I, on occasion, had the house to myself and made my own lattes with their high-end barista machine.

"It's no trouble. I'll bring it to you." Hannah busied herself getting the milk out of the refrigerator and pulling the perfect latte mug, which held just the right amount of frothed milk, out of a cupboard.

"I'll wait. All that scrolling through video footage is making me delirious, and I need a break." I lowered my voice in case my boss was lurking around. "Is Mr. Skyler home?"

"No. He went to the office early this morning and hasn't come back yet."

The sound of grinding beans and frothing milk made it difficult to talk, so I wandered to the back windows of the kitchen and looked out onto the bay. An electric Duffy boat cruised by. A large family group, I guessed, given their similar shapes and coloring, blasted music and gawked at the houses they passed by. A little girl noticed me spying on them, so she waved then called her family's attention to me. They, in turn, all waved, and I reciprocated. Their friendliness made me suspect they weren't from around here.

"Here you go, Miss Emory." Hannah handed the mug to me. Frothed milk, poured into a fern pattern, decorated the top.

"Thank you." I took a sip, the temperature perfect. "Do you know when Mr. Skyler will return?"

"He hasn't said. Do you want me to let him know you're here should he arrive before you leave?"

I didn't necessarily want to draw attention to my search for the culprit who'd dropped off the threatening note, even though I'd briefly told him about it. We'd thrown so much information at jet-lagged David that I'd hoped he wouldn't remember all the facts. "That's all right. He'll be exhausted and jet-lagged, and there's really nothing I need to review with him this evening."

"Will you need anything else? A snack, perhaps?" Hannah removed a bowl of fruit salad from the refrigerator. The glistening strawberries, cantaloupe, and kiwi made me hungry.

"If you have plenty, I'd love a bowl of fruit. Otherwise a banana will be fine."

"It's not a problem. Give me a moment, and I'll dish it up for you."

Within a minute, I juggled a heaping bowl of fresh fruit along with the latte and made my way back to the monitor. I was determined to find the perpetrator. Two hours later, and with a serious headache developing, I finally found the note drop-off. I backed the video up and played it in slow motion. I tried to contain my disappointment by what I'd found.

A young kid, somewhere between eight to ten years old, riding a typical black beach cruiser with no discerning stickers or identifiers, stuffed the catalog into the mail slot. The entire exchange took all of three seconds before the kid pedaled out of sight. The kid wore a plain white T-shirt, cutoff jean shorts, and cheap rubber thongs on his feet. A plain blue ballcap had been pulled down tight over his forehead, so it was impossible to see his hair color or his facial features. Someone had paid this kid to do their dirty deed. The date stamp indicated it happened early evening on July fifth, less than twenty-four hours after Mr. Jorgensen's death.

While I copied the footage onto two flash sticks, one for Detective Tran and one for me, I puzzled over the timing of the threat. Aside from mostly listening to my mother's guests gossip about the murder and the Jorgensen family, I hadn't talked to anyone about proving Sal's innocence yet. Had the perpetrator been at my mother's party? Or had the killer attended the Jorgensens' soiree and found out about my reputation and hoped to scare me off before I could start asking questions?

I sent Detective Tran a text, letting her know there wasn't any way to identify the kid who dropped off the catalog but that I had the footage copied onto a flash stick anyway. While I collected my things to return home, she sent a reply indicating she'd touch base with me in the morning to schedule a time to retrieve it. After returning my dirty dishes to the kitchen and saying my goodbyes to Hannah, I hurried from the house, relieved I hadn't run into David and had to explain my presence.

Chapter 40

A honking horn pulled me from the text I'd been reading from Tillie, when the light turned green and I failed to notice. My face heated, knowing I was guilty of badmouthing other drivers who'd done the very same thing. With the accelerator pressed down almost as far as it would go, the rental car putt-putted forward through the intersection, barely faster than a snail would go. More horns tooted at me as drivers swerved around me at breakneck speed.

Tomorrow, I promised myself, I'd find a reasonable car to purchase and then beg my mom and Lars to cosign on a loan for me. Thanks to my ex, my credit rating was in tatters, even if I'd been diligently paying back loans he'd taken out with every spare cent I earned.

I stopped at the closest supermarket parking lot and read Tillie's text in full. John had whisked her off on a yacht and would be headed over to Catalina for a couple of days. She told me not to worry about her and *not* to tell her son about the impromptu trip.

So much for their agreement to be open and nonjudgmental with each other the previous night. I smiled and hoped

Tillie was having the time of her life and Frances Allain would soon hear of Tillie's tryst with an English baron.

Catalina was a small island twenty-six miles off the coast of Newport Beach. In the late 1800s, it became a tourist destination when William Wrigley, Jr., of the chewing gum empire, bought the controlling interest of the island after World War I. It was then that it began to flourish and attract wealthy clients and celebrities alike. Given the chartered yacht, Tillie and John would most likely sleep in a stateroom, rather than attempting to book an impossible-to-get room at the handful of hotels situated on the island. The island was hopping at this time of the year, and I wondered how John had even managed to secure a mooring for the yacht. Perhaps the company he'd used for the charter had connections, or else they had to forgo the coveted Avalon moorings and were on the far side of the island, where the buffalo roamed. Seriously. There were real buffalo on the island. They were brought over for a silent movie filmed in the 1920s and left there to graze the landscape.

I eyed the supermarket and tried to remember what I had in my refrigerator for dinner. It wasn't much, so maybe deli fried chicken was just what I needed. I also wanted to make sure I had plenty of lemon curd for the cupcakes I had to deliver to Brian the following day. Typically, I'd make my own lemon curd, but with the lack of sleep and the demanding issues that seemed to press on me from all sides, premade would work just fine. Granted, buying a convenience product from the jam and jelly aisle would cut into my profits, but right now my time was at a premium.

I lucked out with a speedy rush through the grocery store to pick up the things I needed. There was even a relatively minimal wait in line for the checker. Upon my return home, I set the colorful reusable nylon sacks down to unlock the security gate. I startled when it swung open at my touch. I tried to remember if I'd neglected to lock it when I'd left for David's house to work, but my head still pounded from staring at the screen, and I couldn't recall. Piper greeted me with yips and tail wags then sniffed the bags and tried to dig for the chicken. It was a temptation I couldn't allow her to indulge in until I could remove the bones and the breading and give her a small piece.

As I walked toward my new glass door, I found a gift basket sitting on a patio chair. A half-chewed card, typically attached to a floral arrangement, lay mangled on the ground beneath. I picked up the card. From the preprinted scrolled letters remaining, I could make out that it was a thank-you note. I could pick out the word "appreciate," just barely. "Delicious" was another word I guessed at, and the signature was anyone's guess. Between bite marks and wet smears— drool from Piper got my vote—I had no idea who'd been so thoughtful as to send the basket. Perhaps it had been Darby for bringing the cupcakes to the swim party and then listening to her gossip.

Balancing the gift basket in one hand and lugging the grocery sacks in another, I let myself into the pool house, Piper hot on my heels. She danced beneath the sack containing the chicken, but I was too exhausted to scold her. Ignoring the chicken and other groceries I'd stocked up on, I glanced at the thank-you note then tore off the cellophane that encased the gift basket.

Rich brownies were nestled onto a floral-patterned plate. An embossed sticker was affixed to the plastic wrap covering them, touting that they came from a well-known bakery in Beverly Hills. A goodie sack contained five dog biscuits. It, too, had a printed sticker indicating it came from an organic dog food company located in Los Angeles. One that I wasn't familiar with.

There was one more item in the basket. A tin of loose-leaf tea, from a well-known local establishment, had a vivid green bow tied around it. I tipped it over and saw it was English breakfast tea. Perhaps it was John who'd sent the gift basket as a thank-you for preparing breakfast for him and Tillie. Although, in my humble opinion, I could have done much better with a little warning that an overnight guest would join us.

I set the tea and brownies aside. I'd had more than enough caffeine, thanks to the latte Hannah had prepared for me. I'd have to see if she could stock some decaf coffee, should I decide to drink coffee so late in the day. I checked Piper's food bowl. Most of her kibble remained, as I'd suspected. The fish Randall had shared with her spoiled her into thinking she didn't need her nutrient-high kibble.

"No chicken or dog treats for you, yet." I shook my finger at Piper then reached out to tousle her ears. "I can't have you become so spoiled you won't eat the healthy stuff."

While I mixed up batter and filled the paper liners, Piper lay flat in front of her bowl, head on her paws, and watched me with big sad-dog eyes. I couldn't help laughing. "That look might work on Tillie and Randall, but I'm not going to fall for it. If you're hungry, eat your dinner, and then you can have..." I almost said the word "treat." That would've thrown Piper into a begging frenzy.

It didn't take long for the aroma of lemon cupcakes to fill the air, and soon after, my counters were covered with cooling cupcakes. I should have used Tillie's kitchen to bake the order, but with the hectic week I'd had, I longed for the cozy comforts of my own home. I also should have removed Piper from the kitchen, but I didn't have the heart tonight. I needed my dog close to me. While a triple batch of the lemon-y buttercream frosting whipped in my professional KitchenAid mixer—a gift from Tillie from the past Christmas—Piper finally gave up begging and ate her dinner.

Using a half-teaspoon measuring spoon, I scooped out a small portion from each cupcake and filled the hole with lemon curd. I'd place the cake pieces in a freezer-safe bag and use them later as a base for cake pops. I could already envision forming them into lemon shapes before dipping them in yellow candy melts. Sometimes I would press pieces of the cupcake back over the lemon curd filling, but this time, the idea of cake pops appealed to me. It reminded me that I needed to find something to garnish the cupcakes with before I delivered them to Brian.

Piper nudged my knee with her nose then ambled to the table where I'd placed the gift basket. It was her way of reminding me it was treat time. I opened the bag of dog treats and sniffed. It smelled meaty, so it wasn't any wonder that Piper wanted a taste or three. I broke the crunchy dog-bone-shaped treat in half and put the pieces into her food bowl. She wolfed them down in mere seconds then nudged my knee again.

"Nope. We'll save these for later." I placed the remaining treats in the freezer. The brownies were tempting, but I'd eaten more than my fair share of the scooped-out cake pieces dipped in a small bowl of frosting. Truth be told, my stomach complained about all the sugar, so I placed the plate of yumminess in the refrigerator. Perhaps it would be my breakfast in the morning, since Tillie wouldn't be here.

Nibbling on a piece of the fried chicken, I opened the Pinterest app and scrolled through pages of mouthwatering photos. Several bloggers had used fresh lemon slices or fresh raspberries as garnish for their cupcakes. It wasn't practical for my need, since the cupcakes would sit, refrigerated, for a day or two. Chances were the fresh fruit would leak juices and mar the swirls of buttercream. In the end, I decided on a simple yellow fondant flower, cupped to hold a candy pearl.

Waiting for the cupcakes to cool completely before I piped the frosting, I tinted a quarter pound of fondant a bright, cheery yellow. Rummaging in the cabinets beneath the countertop, I found my marble rolling pin. The heavy rolling pin flattened the fondant quickly, and with a clever mini-cutter that included a plunger to form the flowers into a cupped shape, it didn't take long until I had more than enough made. I piped a dab of frosting into the center of each flower and added a small edible pearl candy.

As I worked on the repetitious decorations, I had time to recall all the gossip and facts Tillie, Will, and I had gleaned. I went over who the suspects could be, what their motivation might have been, and whether their proximity might have allowed them to commit the murder. I kept coming back to Lisette Jorgensen. Her husband had planned to reimburse some of the investors for their loss. She sat next to her husband at the dinner and gave him her own glass of wine, when earlier she'd been nagging him to stop drinking. Plus, there was the puzzling question of why she ended up with Theodore's car and two stolen multimillion-dollar pieces of art.

Maybe it wasn't Mrs. Jorgensen. There were all the investors who'd lost so much at the hands of Mr. Jorgensen's business partner. Could one of them have sent him death threats necessitating the hiring of Tiny and finally found a way to follow through on their threat? Mr. Irving and Mr. Dewitt had been overheard arguing with the victim before the party. Could they have worked together to kill the man?

And as much as I didn't want to entertain the possibility, Sal had displayed anger each time Mr. Jorgensen had accosted him. Perhaps Sal did have a history concerning Nathan Jorgensen, and he wanted to cover up his involvement. He'd had the means to introduce the oleander into Mr. Jorgensen's food, as much as I didn't want to admit it. I hoped Detective Tran had more information than I had access to and solved the case soon. I pushed all thoughts of murder out of my head and turned on some soothing music to distract my meandering thoughts.

When I'd finished piping the swirled mounds of limoncello buttercream, I nestled a flower near the peak. With each cupcake completed, I added them to a stack of reusable plastic cupcake totes I kept on hand for friends and family. Typically, I would've used disposable cardboard cupcake boxes for customers, but Brian would see to it that these were returned to me.

Piper yawned and crawled into her crate, ready for bedtime. I looked at my watch. It was nearly midnight already, so no wonder my dog wanted to call it a night. The kitchen and counters were a disaster, but at least the stacks of cupcakes in the refrigerator were ready to be delivered on time. The cleanup could wait until the morning.

A bit after I'd tumbled into bed—making sure all the doors and windows and the gate were locked before I did so— a clump sounded, as if my security gate had bumped into the garage wall. I knew, without a doubt, I'd checked the lock less than twenty minutes ago. It had to have been my imagination. Besides, if someone had entered my patio, Piper would be at the door barking her head off. I closed my eyes and drifted off to sleep.

Chapter 41

What sounded like a patio chair scraping across the concrete for a second had my eyes flying wide open and my heart racing. I listened for Piper's response, but all I heard was her gentle snoring. Checking the time on my phone, I found I'd only been in bed fifteen minutes. I convinced myself that I must've been dreaming. I closed my eyes and willed my heart to return to normal.

A loud splash had me flying out of bed. It wasn't a dream. Of that I was certain. I grabbed my phone, pushed my feet into flip-flops, and rushed to Piper's crate, where I found her snoring away. Was my imagination getting the best of me? There wasn't any way a loud noise like that wouldn't have roused Piper. I reached into the crate and stroked her neck, whispering her name. Piper didn't wake up. Nor did her snoring stop. Something was seriously wrong. I edged to the French doors and peered out. The shape of a human, illuminated by the underwater pool light, floated in the water.

My first inclination was to open the door and rush to rescue whomever was in the pool, but better judgement prevailed. I backed away from the door and called 911 on my cell. Whispering, I gave my address, and as I told the dispatcher about the body, someone started beating on the glass door. It wasn't a knock-knock-are-you-home type of beat. No, it was a relentless whacking thud with something heavy to break in the glass.

The dispatcher asked if I was okay, as if the terror in my voice didn't convey the danger I felt. The sound of someone attempting to break through the glass door had to have been heard over the phone as well. I whispered that no, I wasn't okay, and that police needed to arrive now. She promised to stay on the phone until help arrived.

I backed into the kitchen, looking for a weapon. The heavy marble rolling pin, with bits of yellow fondant still clinging to the barrel, caught my eye. I snatched it up then hurried to position myself on the wall next to the glass French door that was under attack. Piper snored through the entire thing. The glass finally caved in, and a large, meaty hand reached in and unlocked the dead bolt. The door creaked open. I held my breath, not wanting to be seen or heard.

The hulking figure of a man stepped through the door, facing Piper's crate. His back was turned toward me. I stepped around the open door and raised the rolling pin up and brought it down, as hard as I could, on the back of his head. He was so tall the rolling pin glanced off, but as he turned toward me, I swung the rolling pin like a baseball bat and caught the side of his head. A sickening thud sounded, and then his knees buckled and he went down. The faint light cast from the patio's Malibu lighting told me what I already suspected from the size of the man. It was Tiny.

Checking on the facedown body in the pool, I realized he, or she, hadn't moved, and was beyond help. I decided it would be best to restrain Tiny, should he come to, instead of fishing the body out. I didn't need to face his murderous wrath a second time. Rummaging in my closet, I found several scarves. Using them as rope, I bound his hands and legs together as quickly as I could.

Once I was certain Tiny was secure, I rushed to the pool and waded in to reach the body. Grasping the sodden shirt that clung to the man's thin frame, I tugged him over to the shallow end steps. There was something familiar about the shape of his head and the cut of his hair, despite the dim lighting. With sirens sounding in the distance, I rolled the man onto his back, letting the water support his weight, and gazed upon his face. It was Will. Dear, sweet Will, who'd been so amiable and desirous of working hard to free Sal. Why had Tiny killed Will and then deposited his body in my pool?

As police officers stormed onto my patio, I clung to Will, letting my tears mingle with the chlorinated pool water. Gently yet firmly, hands tugged my arms away from Will, and I was led to a patio chair, where a kind paramedic wrapped me in a warm metallic emergency blanket. I couldn't stop shivering. "My dog. I think someone drugged her. Is she okay?"

"I'll check on her, but first I need to make sure you're not injured. Are you hurt?"

I shook my head. "Just shaken up, but he didn't have a chance to lay a hand on me."

"All right. I'll look in on your dog. What's her name?"

"Piper. Her name is Piper." I tried to keep my teeth from chattering, but it was an impossible task.

The paramedic stood and turned toward my house.

"Wait. I think I know how she was drugged." I thought back on the mysterious gift basket and how the card had been mangled so I couldn't tell who had sent it. "It had to be the dog biscuits. Someone left me a gift basket, and I fed her one."

"I'll hand them over to the police. They can have them analyzed." The paramedic waved a uniformed officer over and repeated what I'd told him.

"That's not all. A plate of brownies was included in the basket. You can find those in the refrigerator. And there's a tin of tea on the counter. They probably had some kind of drug in them too. Tiny didn't seem to think he had to be quiet about breaking in."

"Did you ingest any of the brownies or tea?" The paramedic pulled a penlight from his pocket and flashed it into my eyes.

"No." I wasn't going to admit I'd gorged on cupcake crumbs and buttercream frosting instead. But it might have saved my life, so I wasn't going to feel guilty over my poor eating choices. I shivered. I watched as the paramedic walked toward my house to check on my pup. I prayed she'd be okay.

"We'll bag everything up and have it tested." The uniformed officer knelt next to the chair I sat upon.

"Not my cupcakes! I made those last night. They're fine."

"If you're sure." He motioned another officer over and gave him a quick summary. The officer ran into my house, sure to spread the word about the drugged dog biscuits, brownies, and tea. "Detective Tran is on her way. Is there anyone we can call for you?"

My mind immediately went to Randall, but then I pushed that thought away. With Tillie at Catalina and it being the middle of the night, I didn't want to disturb my mother or my sister. Brad and Gabe wouldn't mind, but I'd think about it later. I shook my head. "I'll wait until I speak with the detective."

A howling Tiny, his hands cuffed behind him, was led away to a waiting ambulance. White bandage gauze encircled his head, and I hoped I hadn't done any permanent damage, no matter that he'd killed my new friend.

"You called him Tiny a minute ago. What's your relationship with him?" The officer was in cop mode, now that my health and safety weren't a concern. "And what about the victim in the pool? Did this happen because of a lovers' triangle argument?"

"Oh God, no. Nothing like that." I inhaled a deep lungful of air, ready to relay all the information I had on this tragic, convoluted mess. Before I could utter a word, Detective Tran strode in, looking surprisingly alert and fresh after being woken in the middle of the night.

"Thank you, Officer…" She flashed him her badge. "I'll take it from here. This incident is part of an ongoing case I've been investigating."

He gave her a respectful nod then gazed at me. "You're in good hands. I've heard she's solved every single case assigned to her."

Detective Tran's cheeks turned pink, and she smiled at him. "Thank you. I appreciate hearing that."

Once he'd left the two of us alone, the detective pulled a patio chair next to mine, grasped my freezing, trembling hand, and gave it a quick squeeze. "I'm so glad you're unharmed. Brad and Gabe are on the way, and they'll take you to their house."

"But what about Piper? I need to get her to the vet." I searched the uniformed men, along with a couple of women, milling about but didn't see the paramedic who'd said he'd check on my dog.

"They can help transport her to the vet's office, if necessary." It was Detective Tran's turn to look around, as if searching for someone. Her voice cracked, and she rushed her words. "Where's Mrs. Skyler? Have you checked on her?"

"She's safe on Catalina. I haven't called her to let her know what happened. I thought it best to wait until the morning."

Relief softened her clenched jaws. "I'll walk you in to change into dry clothes and collect a few toiletries, but please avoid touching or moving things as much as possible."

I cracked a wry smile. "You mean you're not going to interrogate me or read me the riot act while I freeze to death out here?"

"Naw. It's not my style." She tilted her head toward the

approaching paramedic. "I hope he has good news about Piper."

I jumped up from the chair and pulled the emergency blanket tight around my shoulders. "How is she? Will she be okay?"

"I think she'll be fine, although she'll be groggy for a while." He guided me to the chair and had me sit back down. "She woke up, yawned, then dozed back off. I checked her vitals. Her heart rate, respiratory rate, and temperature all seem fine."

"Thank you, thank you!" As relieved as I was, it made me curious how he knew what to look for in an animal. "Do they teach you how to treat pets in paramedic school?"

"No." He chortled. "My sister is a vet tech, so I called her, and she walked me through what I needed to look for."

"I'm sorry you had to wake her up, but I truly appreciate it."

"She's in Hawaii, so it's not so late there."

"Please tell her thank you for me." I thought about how Piper hated the vet taking her temperature. It took three of us to hold her to get the reading. "Do you carry around a doggie thermometer in your bag? I have some hydrogen peroxide if you want to disinfect it."

"My sis said to feel Piper's ears, paws, and armpits for heat. It's kind of like touching your forehead for fever. She wasn't overly hot, and like I said, her heart rate and respiratory rate were all within range." He checked his watch. "I guess if you don't need anything else, I'll collect my crew and head back to the station."

"Wait! Did you ask your sister if she thought I should take Piper to a vet right away?"

"I'm sorry, I didn't think to ask." He scratched his head. "If she were my dog, I'd monitor her and let her sleep off whatever is in her system. If any changes occur in her vitals, or if she refuses water, or can't keep it down, then I'd take her in. But you need to do what makes you most comfortable."

"Thanks." I'd have Gabe and Brad drop us off at the after-hours animal hospital. I'd never forgive myself if Piper needed medical attention and I hadn't given it to her.

When the paramedic was out of earshot, Detective Tran said, "Once I'm done here, I'll meet you at Gabe and Brad's to hear your take on what transpired tonight. It'll probably be morning before that happens, so get some rest if you can."

"I know you can't tell me much, but do you think Tiny and Mrs. Jorgensen worked together to murder Mr. Jorgensen? Every time I think back on what gossip has been shared with us, she seems to be in the center of things."

"I don't know. I'm hoping Tiny will give us the answer to that sooner than later." She winked at me. "I'll try to keep you informed as I find information out."

This could get awkward. Tillie had a private investigator watching the art, and now the police would be focusing on Mrs. Jorgensen. It seemed like it might be even harder to get the art back without the theft becoming public knowledge.

"Okay, but one last thing. Can you tell me why Will lost his life?"

"I have no idea, but I promise you, I'm going to find out." Detective Tran's face turned ashen as she slowly shook her head from side to side. "It's such a senseless tragedy."

Chapter 42

Gabe and Brad stepped onto the patio. An officer, holding his arm out stiffly, palm facing outward in the halt position, stopped them from walking farther. Gabe flashed his badge. Not that this was his crime scene, but he'd been invited at the behest of Detective Tran.

The badge had the magic touch, and Brad soon had his warm arms wrapped around me. He kissed the top of my head. "Em! You've got to stop scaring me half to death. You're giving me gray hairs, and I'm not ready to hit the bottle to hide them."

His caring jesting to lighten what had transpired made my waterworks flow. Gabe, who'd been conversing with the detective in quiet tones, pulled a hanky from his sharply creased jeans pocket and handed it to me. I wiped my eyes and nose then crumpled the hanky in my hand and looked at Brad.

"Don't you be giving that used hanky to me. Why that man refuses to carry disposable pocket tissues like most of us is beyond me." Brad wrinkled his nose. "I don't think any amount of bleach can make it reusable, in my opinion."

As he probably hoped, I couldn't help but smile. While Gabe was a fastidious clotheshorse—his pressed blue jeans and starched button-down baby-blue shirt worn to a midnight crime scene was a perfect example—it was Brad who bordered on germophobic. Okay, that was an exaggeration, but Brad had a few quirks that I didn't mind teasing him about. And he, good-naturedly, teased me in return. We'd been close high school friends, and I was grateful we'd reconnected this past year.

Detective Tran crooked her index finger to me then pointed at the house. "Go ahead and put on dry clothes and leave your wet garments in the bathtub in case they need to be collected for forensics. As soon as you do, you're free to take Piper and go with Gabe and Brad."

"Thank you." I pulled the blanket tighter around me as I slogged toward the house. "I'll see you in the morning."

I doubted she heard me, since the detective was in the process of greeting an older man and pointing toward the body of Will Trenton. My tears wanted to flow again, but I choked them back—that was, until Piper lifted her snout and whined when she saw me. I knelt beside her and stroked her fur, whispering my love for her in between sobs. Brad handed a tissue box to me, and Gabe encouraged me to hurry up and change clothes. I didn't want to leave her side, especially when Piper whined even louder as I walked away. Rushing back, I knelt by Piper's side.

"Em, how about I bring Piper to your bedroom. She can stay with you while you change, and then I'll carry her out to my car when you're ready to leave." Gabe held a reassuring hand on my arm. "Will that make you feel better?"

I nodded and scooted back a step so Gabe could scoop my dog into his muscular arms. Once on my bed, Piper snuggled into the soft comforter and seemed to heave a sigh of contentment. She wasn't allowed on my bed, so this was the ultimate spoiling. Once Gabe shut the door behind him, I changed into clean sweatpants and a T-shirt. I put another set of clothes into a tote with clean underwear then slipped comfortable sandals onto my feet.

While Gabe picked Piper back up, I threw the wad of sodden clothes into the bathtub then tucked a few necessary toiletries into the tote as well. By the time we'd reached the security gate, Brad had his car waiting for us in the alleyway. I slid into the back seat of the Tesla, and Gabe laid Piper onto my lap. She rested her snout on my shoulder then reached up and licked my ear. She seemed more alert than even ten minutes ago.

I grabbed Gabe's hand before he shut the door. "I want to take Piper to the pet emergency hospital. Can you ask Detective Tran for one of the dog biscuits I put into the freezer? Maybe the vet can use it to help determine what kind of drug Piper ingested."

He agreed and strode out of sight.

Brad turned around in his seat and reached back to stroke Piper's ears. "I have so many questions right now, and I hope you appreciate how patient I'm trying to be until you can share with both of us, at the same time."

Before I could respond, Gabe climbed into the car, holding aloft a doggie biscuit secured in a ziplock baggie. "Where to now?"

I rattled off the address, and Brad drove much faster than I thought necessary. But I kept my mouth shut, only too happy knowing Piper would receive medical attention soon. It didn't take long until we parked in front of an industrial business park single-story building that hosted multiple businesses. The emergency pet hospital had a large, colorful sign, showcasing a variety of pets, hanging above the door. A Ring doorbell sat next to the locked door with instructions on how to use it. I complied, and the sleepy voice of a young woman answered, asking what our emergency was. I had barely said the words "my dog was drugged" when a buzzer sounded, and she told me to push the door open.

Stepping inside, the brightly lit reception office made me squint my eyes against the glare. The air-conditioning was set on super-chill, and I shivered. I wished I were the one holding my snuggly dog, but instead, Gabe cradled her in his arms while Brad stroked her ears.

The vet, petite with cocoa-brown skin and striking almond-shaped emerald eyes, stepped into the reception area. She introduced herself as Dr. Cat then chuckled when my eyebrows went upward.

"My last name is Catalonia, so I've shortened it to Cat. It's easier, especially when young children come in with their sick pets. It helps put them at ease." She gestured through the doorway she'd entered from. "Bring your poor doggie into the first examination room."

Gabe carefully put Piper onto the table, and Dr. Cat handed him a clipboard with forms to fill out. "You can work on this while I examine her."

"Piper's not my dog." He pointed at me. "She's hers. We're just friends helping out."

"All righty, then." She took the clipboard from Gabe's hands and gave it to me. "Can one of you tell me what seems to be the problem with Piper? You mentioned she'd been drugged? Was it accidental or on purpose?"

How to answer that last question? Tiny had purposely given us the treats in the gift basket, but I'd accidentally allowed Piper to ingest one, not knowing it would harm her. I guessed I had remained quiet too long, because Dr. Cat interrupted my thoughts.

"Apparently there's a story behind this." She gestured toward my lethargic pup. "Let's get her examined and draw a blood test first, and then we can have a chat."

Brad pulled Gabe from the crowded room. "We'll wait out in the reception area. If you need anything, you know where to find us, preferably after the blood test."

That was another one of Brad's idiosyncrasies. Needles

were not his friend. He'd passed out getting a tetanus shot in high school, and he'd been afraid of needles ever since.

Gabe stuck his head back through the doorway and waved the baggie at me then gave it a gentle toss so that it landed perfectly in my hand. Piper's ears perked up, and she snuffled her nose and licked her lips. I yanked the baggie away from her and hid it behind my back.

"Is that to reward her for putting up with the examination?" Dr. Cat had a stethoscope hanging from her ears, with the round doohickey thing resting first on Piper's chest. Then she moved it to her sides and then her back.

"That dog biscuit is what I think drugged Piper. It's the only unknown thing I fed her tonight."

"How many did she eat, and what happened after she ate?" Dr. Cat continued her thorough examination, including the dreaded thermometer stuck where the sun didn't shine. For once, Piper didn't flinch or attempt to scoot away. She was even remarkably calm when the vet drew two small vials of blood.

I explained how I'd found the gift basket, and fortunately, Piper had only eaten one biscuit. Then I went on to relay all the horrible events of the night. Dr. Cat edged away from me when I came to the part about finding Will's body, so I immediately told her Gabe was a homicide detective and a good friend and could vouch for my trustworthiness. She seemed to relax after that.

"The good news is Piper seems to be suffering no ill effects from whatever was in the biscuit. All her vitals are healthy, and just in the short time she's been here, she's regained some of her energy."

Hearing her name, Piper thumped her tail on the examination table.

"I'll run the blood sample for the usual sedatives, which we can do here. If I don't find anything, I'll send the second sample out for further analysis." Dr. Cat shined a penlight into

Piper's eyes. "She's responsive, so I'm pretty sure you don't have to worry about anything. Although, if you want, you can leave her here overnight for observation as a precaution."

I was torn. I wanted to take Piper home, but on the other hand, if something went terribly wrong, I'd never forgive myself. Piper made the choice for me. She stood up and, before either Dr. Cat or I could react, jumped off the table, trotted out the doorway, and headed straight to the exterior door. She scratched at it with her front paw and whined.

"I think that means she's ready to go home." Dr. Cat handed me the clipboard. "Maybe one of these gentlemen can take Piper outside while you complete the paperwork."

"We don't have a leash." We'd left in such a hurry, I hadn't grabbed anything for Piper.

Dr. Cat walked behind the counter, opened a drawer, then handed a leash to me. "You're not the first."

Brad clipped it onto Piper's collar, and she trotted out, pulling him behind her.

"I guess I need a couple cans of whatever dog food you think is best for Piper. I'm not sure when I'll be able to return home." Typically, I only fed Piper dried kibble, but with this scare, she deserved a treat.

I hastily filled out the forms, which in my opinion needed far too much unnecessary information, gulped as I handed over my emergency credit card to pay the budget-blowing bill, and left the drugged dog biscuit with the vet. I hugged my dog close as Brad drove us home in the silent car.

Chapter 43

A light tap on the bedroom door caused Piper to startle and bark. Since she had been sleeping right beside me, the bark made me jump sky-high, which caused her to bark even more.

Brad cracked open the door and held out a mug of coffee. "Detective Tran is here and wants to speak with you."

"What time is it?" My voice was croaky, and given how much I'd cried the night before, my eyes were sure to be red and the size of a distressed pufferfish.

"It's six. She'd like to make this quick so she can head home and get some sleep."

I groaned. Less than four hours of sleep wasn't enough, but I couldn't imagine trying to function on zero hours. "Okay. Tell her I'll be right there."

I shuffled from the bedroom, still dressed in what I'd thrown on before fleeing my home. I downed the mug of coffee and immediately refilled it before sitting down at the kitchen table, across from Detective Tran. Gabe was nowhere to be seen, but Brad stood at the counter, whipping what looked to be eggs. I hoped he'd fry up some bacon to go with it.

"Morning, Detective Tran." I tried hard not to yawn, but one escaped anyway, before I could cover my mouth.

It was contagious. The detective yawned, and then Brad did, except he put sound into his, which brought Piper running to the kitchen. It was that or else Piper wanted to eat. After glancing at the detective's exhausted face, I decided Piper would have to wait.

She pulled her phone out and opened a recording app. "Do you mind if I record our conversation? I'm too tired to think straight, and I don't want to misinterpret facts."

"Yes. That's fine." I tried to sound a little more energetic than I felt.

The detective stated our names along with everything else she felt needed to be said before the questions started. And then she grilled me, asking the same question ten different ways, backward and forward. Brad kept our coffee mugs filled then placed slices of thick French toast topped with fresh strawberries and whipped cream in front of both of us. The questions continued while we ate.

At long last she ended the recording and stood. "If I need to clarify anything, I'll call you."

"Is it safe for me to go back home? I mean, you don't think Tiny has an accomplice that'll come after me, do you?"

"You can return home." She sighed and plopped back down onto the chair. "I might as well tell you. It'll be public knowledge sooner than I'd like."

While I waited, trying to be patient for her to share the news, I shredded the napkin Brad had placed on the table alongside my plate of French toast. He sat down, frowned, then swept the shreds of paper into his hand and threw them into the trash. Once he resettled himself, Detective Tran rolled her eyes.

"Promise me this goes no further." She closed her eyes and shook her head. "Who am I kidding. You'll both be running to tell Gabe and Tillie. Fine. Go ahead, but tell no one else. Do I make myself clear?"

We both promised and held up the Boy Scout three-finger salute.

She nodded. "Carlton Yardley, aka Tiny, is putting the blame for Arthur Jorgensen's murder all on his aunt, Lisette Jorgensen. He provided us some mighty interesting information on how she researched drug interactions on her home computer then used a quack doctor to get the digoxin and the erythromycin antibiotics, which she gave to her husband mixed into his whiskey. A search warrant should be signed this morning, and then we'll confiscate her computer and thoroughly search her home."

I practically broke out in a sweat. I'd have to call David as soon as the detective left and let him know. How was he going to be able to get the paintings out? How was he going to keep Theodore's involvement with the family secret if his car still sat in the garage? I pushed that problem out of my mind, for the time being, and thought of more questions to ask to keep Detective Tran talking about the murders. "But between the interaction of those two drugs and all the alcohol he drank, he would've been dead sooner than later. Why the oleander?"

"We think she planned to use your sister's food and the oleander as a misdirection, and as it happened, a convenient scapegoat presented itself, pointed out by the victim, to take the blame for the death. According to Carlton, she pulverized oleander leaves then put some into her wineglass at dinner, right before giving him her glass. She rightfully assumed it would be an easy task getting him to drink it." The detective rubbed her bloodshot eyes. "Carlton put a few oleander leaves into the catering van while you were busy serving."

Poor Sal. He didn't deserve any of this. "So, you've arrested Mrs. Jorgensen?"

"Unfortunately, we haven't been able to locate her yet."

"Will Sal be released soon?" It worried me that Tiny might be released on bail. Would he come after me again?

"Sal will be released later this morning." Detective Tran eyed the coffeepot, which Brad noticed. He refilled our mugs. "Carlton won't be getting out of jail anytime soon. He's confessed and is now trying to work out a plea deal by testifying against his aunt once we catch her."

"Did Tiny, er, Carlton, say why his aunt killed her husband?"

"It all came down to greed." Detective Tran's lips smooshed together in a grim line. "The bottom line is, Arthur Jorgensen had dementia, and it was getting worse. He wrote checks out to several of the guests who attended their party as token recompense for his business partner embezzling their investments. From what I've read, dementia victims perform uncharacteristic actions and have personality changes. While this was for the good of those who lost their money, unfortunately, it spelled the end for him. The Jorgensens also lost a lot of their money to the partner, and once Arthur gave out the reimbursement checks, they wouldn't have had anything to live on."

"What was Carlton's motivation for assisting his aunt?" From what I observed, he was deeply involved in whatever was happening in that house.

"Same thing. Greed. If Arthur gave all their money away, Carlton wouldn't have anything to eventually inherit, nor would his aunt have funds to support his lifestyle, which apparently was quite costly." She stood and placed her mug and empty plate in the sink. "I'm sure more will come to light after we search her house. In the meantime, I'm hoping to get a few hours' sleep before I have to get back to work."

She gave Brad a peck on his scruffy cheek and gave my shoulder a quick squeeze before she breezed out of the house and drove off.

On my way to change into clean clothes and pack my

meager belongings, I caught sight of my reflection in a mirror that hung in the powder room. I screamed. Brad and Piper came running.

"How did you... why did you let me sit there for one and a half hours looking like this?" I pointed at what looked like a frizzy red squirrel sitting on top of my head.

"I thought you were making a statement about being forced out of bed at an ungodly hour." Brad tried to finger comb a few tangles out.

"Ouch!" I slapped his hand away. "That's not going to help. The pool chlorine must've cemented the tangles together."

"I'll get Gabe's weekly conditioner mask and see if that helps." He started moving toward the master suite. "You've got to leave it in for an hour, though, and applying warm heat works even better."

"Never mind. I don't have time." I had to get out of here and call David. Otherwise, we'd have a huge disaster on our hands if his investigator couldn't retrieve the paintings. "Just bring me a baseball cap. I need to borrow your car for a while, and can you keep Piper for me? I shouldn't be gone too long."

He brought me an Angels ballcap but held the Tesla keys out of reach. "I need the scoop, sister. Then you get the keys."

"Please, don't do this to me." I tried to jump up to snatch the keys from his hands, but Brad was too tall for me to reach. "I promise I'll tell you about it soon. It just can't be today. Trust me when I say the Skylers are in a precarious position, and if I don't act now... well, I can't even think how horrible it might be for them."

"You're not exaggerating, are you?" He lowered the keys and jangled them in front of my face. "Just make sure you keep your promise."

I snatched them before he could change his mind. "Thanks, and I will."

Jamming the ballcap onto my head and gritting my teeth

as I pulled my tangled ponytail through the small opening at the back of the cap, I jumped into Brad's Tesla, which he'd left parked in the driveway. I hunted for a button or switch to start the vehicle, and even though I'd ridden with Brad several times, I'd never paid attention. A knock sounded on the driver's-side window, and I startled.

Brad opened the door and leaned over my lap. "Put your foot on the brake."

I did so, and he pushed the gear shift into *R*, for reverse.

"Don't I have to turn it on or something? I don't hear it running."

He threw me a look that I chose to ignore. "Nope. Once I'm out of the way, put your foot on the accelerator, and it'll move. You probably don't want to stomp on it like you had to do with your ancient Accord. This has a lot of giddyap to it."

Great. Just what I needed... a man telling me how to drive. But I took his suggestion and eased my foot onto the accelerator once I shut the car door in Brad's face. While I'd never admit it, Brad was right. His car did have a lot of giddyap, as he'd said, and had he not warned me, I might have had a few issues.

Once I was out of view from Brad's house, I pulled to the side of the street and parked between two houses, curbside. I used extra caution so I wouldn't give his shiny wheels curb rash, and as a result, a couple cars honked at me as they passed by. I got out and looked. The tail end of the car was halfway out in the road, so I inched forward until I wasn't more than two feet from the curb. I should've just gone for a walk and called Tillie and David instead of worrying about destroying Brad's car.

I called Tillie first, since she'd been the one who'd connected with the private investigator. The call went to voice mail. I asked her to call me when she had a chance. Next, I called David. His cell phone rang several times before it went to voice mail. I checked the time. It was eight already. How soon would a judge sign the search warrant, and how long would it take for investigators to swarm the Jorgensens' residence? I disconnected before leaving a message and called Hannah. She, at least, answered on the first ring.

"Miss Emory, how can I help you?" Hannah sounded cheerful.

"Hi, Hannah, I hate to bother you, but do you know where Mr. Skyler is?"

"He's in his office upstairs."

"Great! Whatever you do, don't let him leave. It's of the utmost urgency I speak with him right away." I bent over to push the start button on the vehicle then remembered I didn't have to. "I'm on my way now and should be there in fifteen minutes or so."

I disconnected before she could say anything, put my foot on the brake, put the shifter into drive, pressed firmly on the accelerator, and shot away from the curb. It felt like someone had put me in a slingshot, pulled back, and let go. I missed my trusty Honda as I hung on for dear life.

Chapter 44

Once I reached David's house, I parked parallel with his security gate, not daring to risk Brad's car by parking on the street. After making sure I'd left room in the alleyway for other vehicles to inch by, I let myself into my office. My desk was clutter-free with nothing that needed my attention, so I walked downstairs and called out to Hannah. She came from the kitchen wiping her hands on a towel. Her face was flushed red.

"Is everything okay? Is Mr. Skyler still here?" I worried, from her color, that something had happened.

"Mr. Skyler is in his office... I..."

"Thanks. I've got to talk to him immediately." I cut off whatever she'd planned on saying and ran from the kitchen.

After taking the stairs at a much faster pace than I normally did, I was gasping for air by the time I reached the top. I desperately wanted to stop, gulp some water, comb my ratty hair, and put on lipstick before I barged into his office. But time was of the essence, which I reminded myself again when I glanced down at the huge red stain on my T-shirt. A wayward strawberry from breakfast had resisted being captured and had taken its revenge on my shirt. In the end,

Piper was the victor when she'd gulped down the berry before it had even reached the floor.

From my stained T-shirt, to my ratty sweatpants, to the cheapie flip-flops on my feet, to the red tangles I'd stuffed beneath a baseball cap, I'd taken casual workday dress to a brand-new low. And of course, there were my pufferfish-y eyes adding to the overall picture. No matter. I was here to save the Skyler family's reputation—which they cherished most in this world—and I'd do my duty.

I burst into David's office without knocking on the closed door first and came face-to-face with not only my boss but his two sons, Tillie, and a man I'd never met before.

"Good God, Emory, what happened to you?" Tillie sprang up and tried to push me from the room.

"Leave her be, Matilda." David's tired voice sounded almost defeated. "Let her join us."

I pulled back, deciding retreat might be my best choice. Tillie was having none of it and yanked me forward, more forcefully than her diminutive stature would suggest.

"Please, have a seat." David pointed, unfortunately, at the only empty chair, which sat next to Brian.

Theodore was in the center seat, flanked by the mystery man and, on the other side, his grandmother, Tillie. Brian gave me one of those wide-eyed, smashed-lip emoji looks. I wasn't sure whether it was because of my wrecked appearance or if it was because of this family gathering. Either way, I realized I'd made a huge error in barging in.

"Emory, this is our private investigator, Hank." I nodded my acknowledgement. Presumably, I didn't need to be introduced. Hank had most likely done a background investigation on me so thorough he probably knew how often I shaved my legs… which wasn't nearly often enough.

It was time for me to alert the private investigator about the impending tragedy. "I'm so sorry to barge in like this, but I just found out a search warrant is being issued for the

Jorgensens' residence this morning. I don't know what you have planned, but if you want to get the, um, pieces removed without incident, it's got to be done right away."

"It's already been taken care of." David still seemed diminished, like the weight of the world rested on his shoulders.

"It has? How?" I slapped a hand across my mouth then spoke through my fingers. "Never mind. Forget I'm even here. In fact, I can leave now if you want."

"Stay. You should know the facts in case this comes back to haunt us, since you're a part of the family." David settled back in his chair and pointed at the investigator. "Hank, when you have a chance, please give Emory any and all the facts she wants. Even those that she probably doesn't need."

Hank twisted to study me for a moment then nodded at David.

Why did David keep saying I was part of the family? What did he know that I didn't? Granted, Tillie was like a grandmother to me, and my unknown half sister was David's daughter, so perhaps that was the connection. I pushed those thoughts aside and concentrated on the here and now.

"Where were we before Emory joined us? Ah, yes. Theodore"—David pulled his expertly groomed eyebrows together and glared at his son—"was just about to explain how my most valuable pieces of art ended up in the trunk of his car, parked in the garage of some complete stranger to me."

Silence ticked by, keeping time with the clock sitting on the mantel of the fireplace. David rat-a-tatted his fingers on the desktop, his scowl deepening. Finally, he cleared his throat. "I have it on good authority that a Detective Tran will be executing a search warrant at precisely eleven this morning on the Jorgensens' residence."

I startled in my seat. How did he know the particulars? Had Detective Tran been able to at least get a few hours' sleep? David's growl jolted me from my thoughts.

"Unless I get some answers, said detective will be given, anonymously of course, information on how to track the owner of an unlicensed Jag with the VIN number missing, sitting in said garage. Not only is there the theft of the art to consider, there are now two murders for the detective to solve and the perpetrators brought to justice."

How in the world did David already know about Will's murder… at my house? His influence and reach were greater than I'd ever imagined. It kind of scared me, truth be told. I also wasn't sure of the particulars in how it involved Theodore, but I was starting to put the pieces together. David wouldn't risk losing millions of dollars on the stolen art. Nor would he risk his son being implicated. However, the murder of Mr. Jorgensen somehow coincided with the art theft and made it much more difficult to cover Theodore's theft. The private investigator was probably making a fortune covering up the theft, breaking and entering, and destruction of property. I waited to see if Theodore caved. He did.

"I had nothin' to do with those murders. Do ya hear me? Nothing!" He glared right back at his father. "Nathan Jorgensen, their son, was a good friend. We liked to hang out and party, that kinda stuff, ya know?"

I was shocked how Theodore's vernacular had changed. Every time I'd been around him before, his speech had been stilted, overly formal. Now it sounded like I was listening to a teen boy trying to be tough and failing miserably.

Tillie's soft voice filled the room. "What happened that night, two years ago?"

Of course. Tillie and David had figured out the full story before Theodore was brought in for the interrogation. I almost felt sorry for him, but it was only an almost-but-not-quite.

"It wasn't my fault. One of his friends kept cutting lines, and I couldn't say no. Nathan was high, too, and had gotten that new ride from his dad and wanted to see how it handled against my Porsche." He covered his face with his hands. His voice broke. "It was horrible. He went over the cliff, right in front of me. I coudn' do nothin' about it, so I drove as fast as I could and ended up in Vegas."

"And what happened next?" Tillie placed a hand on Theodore's heaving shoulders.

"I went on a bender for a week then came home like nothin' ever happened." Theodore wiped his eyes and sat up straighter, as if defying their judgement. "It wasn't my fault no matter what his mom said."

I regretted my rash decision to crash into David's office with my very being. The situation was worse than I'd ever imagined. No wonder David looked like he carried the weight of the world. His firstborn could not only be charged with art theft but probably involuntary manslaughter, should his crimes come to light.

"Now that you've given us the backstory, how did your involvement in your friend's death come to light? Enough so that you were blackmailed into stealing multimillion-dollar works of art?" David's stern voice brooked no argument for throwing out excuses.

Again, the sound of the ticking clock filled the room for what seemed the longest time. Finally, Theodore slumped his shoulders, defeated. "I don't know. All's I know is that scary goon, Nathan's uncle, found me and told me they had proof I caused the accident when we raced."

"Did you?" When Theodore didn't answer, David lowered his voice to almost a whisper. "Did you have anything to do with it other than recklessly race while high?"

"I don't know." Theodore's voice held raw anguish. "I got to Vegas, half out of my mind, and there was a huge dent in the front of the Porsche. I saw red paint stuck in the grille, but I swear to God, I have no idea how it got there."

"What happened to the car?" David remained gentle as if coaxing a timid creature.

"I parked down a sketchy alley and left the keys in the ignition. It wasn't there a week later, so I caught a flight home."

"Ah, yes. And then you called me to tell me the car had been stolen and you needed a new one." David's frown was back. "And while your friend's death tore apart his family, you acted like nothing was wrong and went on partying. And I'm well aware it's all been on my dime."

Brian found my hand and gripped it tightly. All the color had drained from his face, and his lips quivered, as if he was trying hard to hold in his emotions. I squeezed his hand back and rubbed my thumb over his knuckles, trying to give comfort. I didn't dare look at Tillie. There wouldn't be any hope of containing the tears that stung my eyes.

"Back to Nathan's uncle implicating you. What happened next?" David seemed determined to pull the truth from Theodore, even though, I was certain, he already knew the facts.

"He told me that thanks to Nathan's death, the family was practically bankrupted." Theodore sniffed then started talking as if a floodgate had opened. "I'd been to their house. It's worth millions, even more than your house. I told him to sell the house and to leave me alone. Instead, he broke my finger and said worse would happen if I didn't help them out."

"How did they know which pieces to have you take?" David's voice was steely. I didn't know how he could remain so calm. I, on the other hand, was ready to break down, and Theodore wasn't even my blood relative.

Theodore waved his hand about in a languid manner. "Nathan and his buds and I talked a lot, ya know. They all tried to say their families were richer than ours, so I might have done a little braggin' myself."

Here was the pretentious Theodore I'd always known. I wasn't sure why he felt like he had to be better than everyone else, but his bragging proved it. It must've had something to do with self-esteem, but I didn't see why he would feel less worthy than anyone else. He'd grown up with wealth and privilege, and although they'd divorced, both parents had remained in his life.

"And once this uncle broke your finger, you decided to help yourself to my belongings instead of coming to me for help? Is my assumption correct?"

"Yes." Theodore's voice cracked. "I knew you'd never understand. And you still don't."

"Can you explain it so I can understand it better?" David's voice turned gentle and had a soothing timbre to it.

"If I have to explain, then it doesn't matter." Theodore crossed his arms. "Forget it. You'll never get it, Pops."

Brian and I exchanged a lightning-quick glance. I knew we were thinking the same thing. No one had ever called David "Pops." He wasn't even Father or Dad. He was just, well, David. Could Theodore be on something to make him irrational and, truth be told, reckless?

David folded his hands in front of him and rested them on the desk. "Brian, please see that Matilda and Emory make it safely home. Hank, please wait outside my office while I have a word with my son in private."

Tillie struggled to her feet and placed a hand on Theodore's shoulder. He shrugged it off and turned his back to her. The expression of grief on her face just about broke my heart. Brian rushed to her side, tucked her hand into the crook of his elbow, and led her from the room. I didn't think I would ever forgive Theodore for hurting his grandmother that way. True, they butted heads, but I knew Tillie loved him and would never, ever willingly hurt him.

Chapter 45

I met up with Tillie and Brian in the foyer, after a quick detour through my office. I wanted to give them a few moments of privacy before I intruded. When I tiptoed into the foyer, Tillie held her arms out and pulled me into a tight hug. Her eyes were dry, and I wished I could have said the same about mine, yet a great sense of grief hung over her. Brian pointed at the door then left, to bring the car to the gate, I presumed.

"Brian can drive us to my house. I think we could all use some tea with brandy." Tillie clutched my arm.

"I had to borrow Brad's car. I promised him I'd bring it back right away, and by the time I get there, it'll be close to two hours since I absconded with it." I placed my hand over the one she rested on my arm. "I'll pick up Piper and come straight over."

Tillie continued to cling to my arm as I walked her to Brian's vehicle. After getting her settled in the passenger seat, I gazed at Brian, who fiddled with the radio. "Brian, are you heading to the restaurant after you drop Tillie off at home? I have the cupcakes at my house."

He pulled his gaze from the screen displaying the satellite

radio stations. "Will they keep another day? I decided the new assistant chef could sink or swim today. I need to be with family right now after that shock."

"They're refrigerated, so they'll be fine another day or two." The added lemon curd in the center would keep the little cakes moist. If Brian served the cupcakes chilled, the fondant decorations wouldn't have a chance to get tacky, either, and with the egg-rich lemon curd, keeping them chilled would be the safest bet in preventing potential food poisoning.

"Thanks. Can you hold on to them until tomorrow to drop them off?"

"That works." I started to close the door, but Tillie stopped me.

"You're coming straight over. Right?"

"Yes. I'll be there in about forty minutes, with Piper in tow."

"Good. We have a lot to discuss." Tillie shut the door, and I stepped away from the car as Brian drove off.

Tillie wasn't kidding. I didn't even know which conversation we needed to begin with first.

BRAD AND PIPER were nowhere to be found when I returned the car, but at least Brad had left a note—for which I was grateful, since I immediately worried that Piper had taken a turn for the worse—stating they'd gone for a walk on the beach and to take his car. He and Gabe would bring Piper home later.

I didn't mind Piper hanging out with friends, but I worried Brad had ulterior motives. He'd swoop in with Piper then park himself on my sofa and would want to know what was going on with the Skylers. Given what I now knew, I had to break my promise to share with him. Besides, Brad lived with a detective. I'd never expect or even consider asking Brad to keep a secret like that from his partner. No, it was better I cover up the truth and risk my friendship with him. I truly hoped it wouldn't come to that.

On the drive back home, I called Tillie and told her I needed a quick shower, and then I promised I'd come straight over. She must've remembered my frightening appearance because she agreed but told me to not take too long. After parking in front of the fence that separated my yard from the alleyway—my garage remote control long gone when vandals hit my car—I stepped onto the patio. Before I could close the security gate, a figure stepped in behind me and shoved something cold and metal into my back.

"Move slowly, or I'll shoot you right here and now." The hissing voice of Lisette Jorgensen filled my ear.

"The police are looking for you. If you leave now, I won't say a thing, and maybe you'll get away." I started to turn my head, but she jammed the gun hard enough in my ribs to make me gasp out loud. I moved slowly toward the door that still bore the damage from Tiny pounding on it. A hole gaped wide-open where he'd managed to break through to unlock the door. Shards of broken glass littered the ground.

"This is all your fault. You were warned to not interfere." Her breath came in ragged wheezes. "Did you think you could waltz into my house posing as a personal assistant without Tiny knowing what you were up to?"

Um, yeah. I'd thought I'd gotten away with it, too, but apparently Tiny was an even better actor than I was. "Tillie had nothing to do with it. She only wanted to offer you condolences."

"I don't believe you for one second. That old biddy is almost as bad as you, sticking her nose in where it doesn't belong." She jabbed me in the ribs with the gun, hard, and for no apparent reason. "That lawyer got what was coming to him, and now it's your turn, unless you tell me where my paintings are."

"I don't know anything about that." And I didn't, except

that David's investigator had somehow managed to spirit them out of the Jorgensens' residence. Where they were now was anyone's guess.

"A pity, then. I guess I'll have to see if your Mrs. Skyler can hold up to some pain unless she tells me where they are." The maniacal glee in Mrs. Jorgensen's voice made me shiver. "Open your door and do as I say, or you'll be even sorrier."

"What do you want? I don't have the paintings to give you. Nor do I know where they're at." I started to reach into my purse to extract my keys. The door was probably unlocked, given the damage, but I hoped I could use my keys as a weapon.

She jabbed the gun into my back again. "Stop what you're doing."

"If you want me to open the door, I need my keys."

"Turn around and let me see what you're doing." She sounded like she could barely catch her breath.

I turned around, as slowly as I could so as not to startle her, and held my purse open. "See? The keys are in that side pocket."

Without lowering the gun, Mrs. Jorgensen used her other hand to extract the keys. Over her shoulder, I caught a glimpse of Brian sneaking toward us, his index finger on his lips. She must've noticed my diverted attention because she turned her head and, when she spotted Brian, swung the gun around to face him.

Without stopping to think about the implications, I shoved her to the side, hoping she'd drop the gun. Just as a loud crack went off, I tackled Mrs. Jorgensen and sent us both flying to the ground. I lay there, momentarily stunned after my fore-head connected with the back of Mrs. Jorgensen's head. I was sprawled halfway on top of the thin, elderly woman, but she didn't even wiggle beneath my weight. A trickle of blood started running on the concrete where her face had connected with the ground.

Brian was on his cell, calling for emergency services, before I could roll off the unconscious woman. At least I hoped she was only unconscious. I struggled to sit upright, and I placed two fingers on the pulse point on her arm. Her heart beat strongly.

"Are you all right? Are you hurt anywhere?" Brian knelt beside me. "She didn't shoot you, did she?"

"No. Did you get shot?" I ran my eyes over his body, looking for blood or injuries. Fortunately, he was whole. "She tried to kill you!"

"I'm fine. I think it was accidental when you shoved her." He looked amused. "Nice tackle, by the way."

"Thanks. I didn't know what else to do when I thought she was going to kill you." I tried to straighten the Angels cap that sat askew on top of the ratty squirrel that had become my hair. I glanced back down at Mrs. Jorgensen. "Do you think she's okay? She's not bleeding to death, is she?"

"I'd roll her over to check, but after slamming into the concrete that hard, I worry she's got a broken bone. We'll let the paramedics tend to her unless she regains consciousness first."

"I didn't mean to hurt her." I cringed then reminded myself she was the reason Will was dead and that Tillie and I would have been next.

The sound of sirens soon filled the alleyway, and Tillie followed close behind the uniformed paramedics and police officers as they swarmed the patio. The neighbors must've hated us for disrupting their quiet neighborhood… again.

She gave Lisette a cursory glance before rushing to hug me and then Brian. "Are you both all right? Did she hurt you?"

"We're fine. Really." I gave her another reassuring hug.

Neither Brian nor Tillie said a word about the broken glass door. I assumed they probably thought it was Lisette's doing and let them go on believing that. I'd tell them the truth later.

The same officer who had been there the night before—or was it just that morning?—took one look at me and pointed at his radio. "I called this in to Detective Tran. She's on her way."

Tillie, Brian, and I stood by while Lisette was loaded onto a stretcher. She'd regained consciousness but refused to answer any questions, even those asked by the paramedics. It was safe to say that she'd probably never go free and would spend the remainder of her life in prison. Her fingerprints were on the gun, and the bullet had been retrieved from inside Brad's car. I wasn't looking forward to explaining the smashed window of the vehicle he'd been so generous to loan me for the day.

Chapter 46

By the time Detective Tran finished with us, I was ready to collapse. Instead, Tillie made me promise that after a quick shower I'd come over to her house. She had things she needed to say. She grasped on to Brian's arm, and together they walked away. I didn't bother trying to get the tangles out of my hair after my shower and instead threw it back up into a messy bun. But hey, at least it was clean. With a couple bandages placed over my scraped knees from hitting the patio, I kept my promise to Tillie.

Letting myself into her house, I missed the presence of Piper bringing lightheartedness and comfort. The murmurs of Tillie's and Brian's voices led me to the kitchen. A bottle of chardonnay sat between them.

"Have a seat, my dear." Tillie poured wine into an empty goblet and patted the chair beside her. Once I sat down, she handed the overly full glass to me.

Brian's wineglass seemed like it hadn't even been touched, and he twirled the stem between his fingers, lost in his own thoughts.

Tillie downed the wine remaining in her glass then refilled it.

"When did you return from Catalina?" Perhaps if I changed the subject, it would be easier to find our way back to talking about the elephant in the room.

"I never made it. David called before we boarded, so I did what I had to do. Bailed out of the trip."

"But you didn't come home last night."

She shook her head. "David and I had a lot of decisions to make. We were up half the night, so I stayed there."

"What decisions are you talking about, Gram?" Brian's term of endearment warmed my heart, and I was pleased to see it brought a faint smile to Tillie's lips. But then it disappeared just as fast.

"I'd hoped your father would discuss this with you both. However, he chose to break the news to Theodore in private and left it up to me to tell you." She gulped some wine. "There are no good choices for your brother, Brian. We can't pretend any longer that he doesn't have a substance abuse problem, and we can't pretend he didn't betray your father. Then to find out he might have had a hand, however accidental, in that poor boy's death? Well, there has to be consequences."

"You mean like prison?" Brian's face turned stark white. "It'll kill Theodore. I think it's a literal possibility."

"Your father had the same concerns, so no, we're not throwing him into the American penal system, however morally wrong our decision might be." She poured more wine, and I couldn't help but notice the tremble in her hand. I had yet to take a sip of mine. My stomach roiled enough as it was.

"This morning after our meeting, Hank escorted Theodore to a private jet and flew with him to Switzerland. He'll be incarcerated at an institution for detox and psychiatric help for a full year. If the doctors determine he's overcome his demons before the year is up, he'll still remain incarcerated and will be given light duties to perform, until the time is completed. Trust me when I say this is in no way a spa treatment institution. It will feel quite grim to Theodore, yet it will also keep him safe not only from other prisoners but from himself."

"And after the year?" Brian looked as sick as I felt, although Tillie was right. There were no good choices, but something had to be done. I guessed when you had unlimited amounts of money, you could make those choices more palatable.

"Theodore has been disinherited. Your father will assist in giving him a hand in finding a job that I'm sure the Theodore we now know will feel is beneath him and a small but safe place to live for the first six months after his release." Tillie drew in a ragged breath. "After the six months, Theodore will be on his own, with no help whatsoever from the Skyler family. One more thing, he is not to step foot in California for a minimum of five years nor make contact with any Skyler family member for that time."

It was harsh, and I sensed it weighed heavily on Tillie. Perhaps a prison sentence, in which Theodore felt emotionally supported by his family, might have been the better choice. But who was I to say?

Chapter 47

I offered to prepare something to eat for the two, but Brian said he'd rather keep busy and cook for his grandmother. On the walk back to my pool house, I called the glass company and scheduled them to replace the glass in the French door again. I hadn't yet told Tillie or Brian about Tiny's attack or Will's death. There would be time for that later, although I probably shouldn't wait too long, since it would be better for them to hear it from me than the newspaper or online. Right now, though, they needed time to grieve Theodore's banishment from the family.

I called my sister and shared the good news that Sal would soon be released, if he hadn't been already. She promised to connect with him and offer any assistance she could to help him recover from the ordeal and get him back on his feet. It went without saying she wanted—no, needed—him to come back to work for her. After that, I spent a while cleaning house and catching up on laundry. The sticky cupcake batter and frosting I'd neglected to wash up the evening before added to my labor. The glazier reinstalled the glass—although he did give me a funny look as he examined the damage—but took my credit card without comment. And finally, I took a long, hot shower and worked the knots and tangles from my hair.

It was early evening when Brad and Gabe dropped a freshly groomed Piper off. "Uh, Em? What happened to my car window?"

"Long story short, Lisette Jorgensen put a bullet through it. But don't worry, I'll pay for the damage." As if my credit card hadn't suffered enough this week already.

Brad and Gabe exchanged a look, but it was Gabe who spoke for them both. "While we'd like the details, it's going to have to wait. My family is hosting a dinner to meet Brad for the first time, and it's best we're not late."

"But you're okay, right, Cupcake?" Brad started to ruffle my hair, but I stilled his hand.

"I just got the tangles out a few minutes ago." I smiled and showed him my bandaged knees. "I'm fine except for these battle wounds. I got 'em when I tackled Mrs. Jorgensen when she tried to shoot Brian."

Brad plopped down beside me on the sofa. He looked up at Gabe and pouted his lower lip. "How can we leave without hearing about this?"

Gabe turned his gaze at me and rolled his eyes. "Fine, as long as Emory can give us the *Reader's Digest* version of her saga."

I complied, and Brad promised he'd be back the following day for the unabridged version as they headed out the door.

Just before they left, Brad came back and gave me another hug. "It's the first time I'm meeting his family, so wish me luck!"

"How could they not love you?" I gave him a quick peck. "Thanks for watching Piper for me, and I can't ever thank you enough for picking us up last night and helping me get through the entire ordeal."

"You'd do the same for me."

Once they'd left, I sent Tillie a text and asked if I could

come over. I didn't want to intrude if she needed some alone time with her remaining grandson. She responded that yes, I should come immediately. Piper and I found the pair sitting on the patio with glasses of sparkling water. Given the news I needed to share, I was glad Piper was there to bring some comfort. I hated to bring even more grief to this house.

I sat down in the chair closest to Tillie while Brian poured a glass of water and added a twist of lemon for me. "I have some good news and some tragic news to share."

"Skip the tragic and give us something to be happy about." Brian glanced at his grandmother. "We don't need any more bad news."

"Sal's finally out of jail!" I tried to make my tone light and chirpy. Will's death hung heavily on my mind. I couldn't figure out why he'd been killed, and according to Detective Tran, when I'd sent her a text this evening asking, Tiny still refused to say anything about it. Lisette wouldn't talk, either, and had lawyered up.

"That's wonderful news." Tillie, normally effervescent, was subdued. I couldn't blame her.

Brian, on the other hand, must've perceived my reticence in not gushing on with the full information or any pertinent gossip related to the case. "And the bad news?"

"Besides Mrs. Jorgensen killing her husband, her nephew, Tiny, was in on it." Interest seemed to spark in Tillie's eyes, so I told them about what had happened in its entirety. When I broke the news about Will's death, Tillie excused herself and went into the house. Piper followed close on her heels.

TWO DAYS after Will's death, a letter arrived, delivered by the mail carrier. The return address was located in San Diego, although the postmark was stamped with the local Santa Ana mark, dated Tuesday, July 8th. I tore it open and smoothed out two folded sheets of stationery. My eyes stung when I noticed the signature on the second page. It was from Will. I started reading the cramped script from the beginning and had to stop twice to keep tears from blotting the page.

Dear Emory,

I hope you can find it in your heart to not hate me for betraying you and the Skylers. I know you trusted me with the knowledge of discovering the pieces of art at the Jorgensens' home, but it's proved too much of a temptation. I plan on stealing them for myself, this evening. You see, I'm dying. My cancer came back with a vengeance, and I've run out of options here in the US. I've heard there's an experimental treatment available in Germany that might prolong my life, but the downside is the exorbitant expense to gain access. That's where the paintings come in. I realize I won't be able to sell them for the amount they're worth, but I hope it will be enough to provide the treatment I so desperately need. Perhaps the Skylers will be able to find the paintings, and you can use this letter to prove their ownership. I'll leave the tracking devices in the Skyler son's car.

Please don't think I've forgotten about my promise to help free Salvador. I'm certain Lisette Jorgensen and Tiny killed Arthur over money issues. I wish I could help build a case against them, but let your detective know. I'm sure between the two of you working together, you'll find enough proof.

If the treatment works and I survive, I'll spend the rest of my life trying to make up for my betrayal. Again, I hold you and Tillie in the utmost regard, and I wish I had another option.

Fondly, Will

P.S. Please consider adopting Missy as a friend for Piper. I've left her with my aunt Pansy, but when I fail to come back for her, I fear my sweet dog will end up in a shelter.

TINY MUST'VE CAUGHT Will sneaking in to steal the art and killed him. Since neither Tiny nor Lisette were speaking about his murder, I had to assume they'd planned on making his death look like a suicide-murder scenario… with me being the second victim. Oleander was found in both the brownies and the tea leaves.

After sharing the letter with Tillie, we went together to pay a visit to Will's aunt Pansy. We both agreed we would keep the particulars of his betrayal and death to ourselves. His aunt didn't need any additional grief; his murder was more than enough for her to deal with. Somehow the Skylers had managed to keep the entire sordid affair of Theodore's involvement in Nathan's accident and subsequent theft of his father's paintings a secret. I'd never voice my suspicions, but I strongly suspected David had coerced or even threatened Mrs. Jorgensen and Tiny to keep their knowledge hidden.

Pansy Trenton was as cold as ever, until she found out who my elderly companion was. Then we were shown the royal treatment with more concrete-hard scones and tepid tea. Missy wiggled around my legs, begging for love. It was obvious she missed Will and hadn't received any comfort from his aunt, so I broached the subject of adopting Missy.

"Would you, dear?" Pansy sniffed. "If you change your mind, you can drop the mutt off at the pound. Why my nephew had to dump her off on me is beyond anyone's guess."

"I'll be happy to take her. My dog and Missy get along, so they'll be good playmates for each other when I'm at work."

She gestured at a corner piled with dog accessories. "Take it all. I can't abide the creatures."

Tillie and I exchanged glances. It was time to grab the dog and run. We quickly offered our condolences again, said good-bye, scooped up Missy and her toys, and ran for the car. Andrew had the door wide open, so we quickly piled in and told him to make haste.

"Can you believe that woman?" Tillie, never having met Pansy Trenton before, was livid. She reached over and stroked

Missy's red curly fur. "You're not a mutt, my darling. You don't ever have to see that atrocious woman again."

I felt sorry for Will having been stuck with that bitter woman so often. Perhaps it affected his outlook on life, although when faced with mortality, I don't know if I could've resisted the temptation to save myself.

Piper was just as excited to see Missy as she was to see Piper. They frolicked in the yard then lay together in the warm sunshine. Tillie and I sat on the patio watching the two dogs, and I was relieved to see a few more smiles on her face and some color in her cheeks that had been missing these last several days.

Chapter 48

Brian dropped by to have breakfast with Tillie and me most mornings, and on occasion, John joined us when he was in town. I admired Brian for his dedication to his grandmother. He wasn't nearly as flighty as I once thought him to be, and it seemed like a friendship, rather than a flirtation, had started to develop between us. Luckily Tillie no longer hinted at matchmaking a romance between her grandson and me.

A few weeks after our ordeal, Brian asked me to meet him at Tillie's house one Sunday afternoon. I arrived with Piper, and let myself in. Brian called from the interior of the house and asked me to join them in the formal dining room. I bounced into the room, expecting to only find Tillie and Brian there. Instead, my mother, Lars, David, and my sister Carrie had joined Tillie and Brian. A large flat-screen computer monitor and laptop sat at the end of the table, facing away from the floor-to-ceiling glass accordion doors.

"What's everyone doing here?" Had I spaced out on a scheduled get-together or party? I'd been busy, but I didn't think I'd forget Tillie or my mother saying anything about this.

Carrie lifted both hands, palms up, and shrugged. Apparently, she was just as much in the dark as I was.

Tillie patted the empty chair beside her, so I sat. Piper curled around my feet and gazed up at Missy, who sat in Tillie's lap. My octogenarian friend had found she didn't want to let Missy out of her sight and in the end, had adopted the sweet girl. I was happy that Tillie had found a measure of comfort in her new furry friend. Our two dogs had plenty of playtime together, so it didn't really matter whose home Missy slept in at night.

Carrie sat on the other side of me and nudged me with her elbow. She whispered beneath her breath, "What's going on?"

I whispered back, "No idea! Where are the kids?"

"Mother asked Thomas to watch them, then she and Lars drove me here."

Brian sat next to the open laptop then nodded to David, who gave him a brief nod back. I studied my boss. He was relaxed and seemed almost carefree rather than the stressed-out distraught father he'd been just a short time ago after sending his eldest son away.

Brian jiggled the mouse, and the Zoom app box popped up on the large monitor. He turned to face us. "Carrie and Emory, I'm sure you're wondering why you've been asked to join us."

I glanced at Tillie. Her gaze was fixated on the monitor, and her breathing had become rapid. Touching her hand, I found it ice-cold. She barely acknowledged me, so I returned my attention to Brian.

His voice cracked, and he struggled to maintain his composure. "A week ago, I found a match for our sister."

Carrie and I both gasped at the same time. We joined hands and held tight.

"Gram, David, and Addie have already Zoomed with her a few times since then, as have I." Brian clicked the mouse a couple times, and the Join Meeting box popped up. He typed in a few words. "She's ready to meet her sisters now."

Upon that pronouncement he clicked the join button. Within a moment, Carrie and I found ourselves looking at a young woman who could have been our triplet. She was identical to us in every way.

"Emory and Carrie, let me introduce you to Vanessa. Our sister."

RECIPES

Dîner en Blanc Menu

Hors d'oeuvres
Cheeses: Brie, Asiago, Swiss, Aged White Cheddar Crudités:
Asparagus, Sliced Radishes, Cauliflower Florets, Celery Sticks
Assorted Crackers
Herbed Artichoke White Bean Dip served with Red Bell
Pepper Slices and Pita Chips
Skewered Fresh Buffalo Mozzarella Caprese Salad

Amuse-bouche
Mini Phyllo Cup with Whipped Goat Cheese
and Cranberry Stars

Soup
White Gazpacho with Fresh Baguettes

Salad
Jicama, Apple, and Berry Salad with Citrus-Ginger Dressing

Fish Course
Swordfish with Lemon-Caper-Wine Sauce
and Roasted Cherry Tomatoes

Main Course
Garlic Rosemary Roasted Pork Tenderloin
served with
Orzo Salad with Roasted Red Pepper, Feta,
and Kalamata Olives

Palate Cleanser
Lemon Sorbet

Dessert
Lemon Drop Martini Cupcakes
Champagne Cupcakes

Mini Phyllo Cups with Whipped Goat Cheese and Cranberry Stars

Makes 15

Ingredients
    1 box Athens Mini Phyllo Shells
    3 ounces goat cheese, room temperature
    2 ounces cream cheese, room temperature
    1 tablespoon heavy cream
    1 can cranberry jelly
    Extra-small and small star cookie cutters

Instructions
Follow package instructions and bake the Athens Mini Phyllo shells for 3-5 minutes to crisp. Allow to completely cool to room temperature.

Remove the top and bottom lids of the cranberry jelly and slide the cylinder out onto a cutting board. Slice the jelly into 1/4-inch slices. Using star-shaped cookie cutters, create shapes to garnish filled phyllo cups. Refrigerate until ready to serve. Use remaining cranberry jelly as you desire.

Combine the goat cheese and cream cheese together in a medium bowl, and using an electric handheld mixer, whip on high speed for 1 minute. Add the heavy cream to the mixture, and whip for 2 minutes on high speed, until smooth and fluffy.

Using a pastry bag fitted with an extra-large star tip, pipe the mixture into the completely cooled phyllo shells.

Garnish with the chilled cranberry jelly stars and serve immediately.

Herbed Artichoke White Bean Dip

Ingredients

1 (15-ounce) can artichokes, water packed
1 (15-ounce) can white cannellini beans, rinsed and drained
1 tablespoon fresh lemon juice
2 tablespoons extra virgin olive oil
1 clove fresh minced garlic
3/4 teaspoon dried thyme
1/2 teaspoon dried oregano
1 teaspoon dried basil
Salt and freshly ground white pepper to taste
Fresh parsley for garnish

Instructions

Drain the artichokes, then coarsely chop and place in a food processor.

Add the white beans, lemon juice, olive oil, garlic, thyme, oregano, and basil to the food processor and process until smooth. Season with freshly ground white pepper and salt if desired.

Place dip in a serving bowl, cover with plastic wrap, and

refrigerate overnight. When ready to serve, if desired drizzle extra olive oil over the surface and garnish with fresh parsley.

Serve with pita chips and crudités.

White Gazpacho

Serves 4 – 6 appetizer-sized portions

Ingredients

2 cups stale baguettes, crust removed and cubed
1-1/2 cups cold water, or as needed
3 tablespoons blanched almonds
1 small garlic clove
1 tablespoon chopped sweet onion
1 large cucumber, peeled, seeded, and coarsely chopped
1 tablespoon freshly squeezed lemon juice
1 tablespoon vinegar (either white or apple cider)
Salt to taste
Freshly ground white pepper to taste
Garnish: Small pieces of cubed cucumber, fresh parsley

Instructions

Place the bread in a bowl and pour 1 cup cold water over the bread. Press the bread down to absorb the water.

Place the remaining 1/2 cup water, almonds, garlic, sweet onion, cucumber, lemon juice, and vinegar into the jar of a high-powered blender. Blend, on high speed, for 1 minute.

Add the softened bread and blend until smooth, approximately 2 minutes. If gazpacho is too thick, add an extra table-spoon of water and blend. Repeat until desired consistency is reached, but the mixture should be thick.

Add salt and pepper to taste then refrigerate for at least 1 hour.

Just before serving, garnish with small pieces of cubed cucumber and fresh parsley leaves.

Jicama, Apple, and Berry Salad with Citrus-Ginger Dressing

Ingredients

Dressing:
1/3 cup orange juice

2 tablespoons extra virgin olive oil

1 tablespoon apple cider vinegar

1/2 teaspoon fresh grated ginger (or 1/4 teaspoon ground ginger)

1/4 teaspoon sea salt, or to taste

Salad:
1 pound jicama, sliced into matchsticks

2 small apples, thinly sliced (Honeycrisp, Fuji, or Pink Lady varieties work well)

1/2 cup fresh raspberries, rinsed and patted dry

1/4 cup fresh blueberries, rinsed and patted dry

Mint leaves for garnish

Instructions

Using an immersion handheld blender stick, blend the orange juice, olive oil, apple cider vinegar, ginger, and salt together until emulsified. Set aside.

Combine the jicama and apples then toss with the orange

juice dressing. Gently fold in the raspberries and blueberries. Garnish with mint or parsley and serve immediately.

Tip

If you need to prepare a few hours ahead of serving, soak the apple slices for 5 minutes in a mixture of 1 tablespoon fresh lemon juice and 1 cup water. Rinse and pat the apples dry and proceed with the recipe through mixing the jicama and apples with the dressing. Add the raspberries and blueberries to the salad just before serving.

To easily grate fresh ginger, peel the knob of ginger and freeze in a freezer-safe ziplock bag. While still frozen, grate the ginger using a Microplane rasp grater. Store remaining knob in the freezer for another use.

Swordfish with Lemon-Caper-Wine Sauce and Roasted Cherry Tomatoes

Ingredients
2 swordfish steaks, 1 inch thick
Lemon-Caper-Wine Sauce:
2 tablespoons unsalted butter, divided
1 clove minced fresh garlic
1/2 cup dry white wine, such as sauvignon blanc
1/2 cup plus 2 tablespoons low-sodium chicken broth, divided
2 tablespoons fresh lemon juice
1 tablespoon capers
2 teaspoons cornstarch
Salt and freshly ground white pepper to taste
Roasted Cherry Tomatoes:
1 pound cherry or grape tomatoes, sliced in half
1 tablespoon olive oil
2 cloves garlic, finely minced
1/4 teaspoon kosher salt
Fresh basil for garnishing

Instructions
Roasted Cherry Tomatoes:
Preheat the oven to 400 degrees (F).

Line a baking sheet with heavy-duty foil and toss the cherry (or grape) tomato halves with the olive oil and salt. Arrange in a single layer.

Roast for 10 minutes then stir in garlic. Roast for an additional 5-10 minutes, or until skins begin to shrivel. Remove from oven and keep warm.

Swordfish:

Increase the oven temperature to 425 degrees (F).

15 minutes before cooking, remove swordfish from the refrigerator and pat dry. Lightly season with salt on each side then allow to rest for up to 15 minutes. Because of food safety concerns, do not allow fish to remain at room temperature for long.

Heat an oven-safe nonstick skillet (large enough to hold both steaks) over medium-high heat on the stovetop. When skillet is hot, brush a light coating of vegetable oil over 1 side of each swordfish steak and place, oiled side down, in the skillet. Allow to cook, undisturbed, for 2 minutes. Check to see if swordfish is browning. If not, cook an additional minute.

Flip the swordfish steaks over and immediately place the oven-safe skillet in the oven. Bake for 10 minutes.

Remove from oven and allow the fish to rest in the skillet for 5 minutes. Serve with lemon-caper-wine sauce and roasted cherry tomatoes and garnished with fresh sprigs of basil.

Lemon-Caper-Wine Sauce:

While the swordfish bakes, prepare the sauce. In a small saucepan, melt 1 tablespoon butter and sauté the garlic over medium heat until fragrant. Do not allow to brown.

Add the wine and bring to a simmer until wine is reduced by half, about 2 minutes. Add 1/2 cup chicken broth, fresh lemon juice, and the capers. Heat just until sauce reaches a simmer.

In a small bowl, whisk the remaining 2 tablespoons chicken broth into 2 teaspoons cornstarch until smooth.

While stirring the caper sauce constantly, mix the cornstarch mixture in. Bring to a simmer and cook for 1-1/2 to 2 minutes, until sauce thickens.

Remove from heat and whisk the remaining tablespoon of cold butter into the sauce. Season to taste with salt and freshly ground white pepper.

Serve warm with the swordfish.

Orzo Salad with Roasted Red Peppers, Feta Cheese, and Kalamata Olives

Ingredients

Lemon Honey Vinaigrette:

1/3 cup extra virgin olive oil

1/4 cup red wine vinegar

2 tablespoons fresh lemon juice

1 tablespoon honey

1 teaspoon salt and freshly ground pepper to taste

Orzo Salad:

8 ounces orzo pasta

4 cups low-sodium chicken broth

2 whole cloves garlic

1/2 cup jarred roasted red pepper, drained and chopped

10 kalamata olives, sliced into 6 slivers each

1/3-pound asparagus, cooked crisp-tender and cut into bite-sized pieces

1/3 cup chopped fresh basil

1/4 cup thinly sliced green onions

3 ounces feta cheese, crumbled (or more to taste)

1/3 cup slivered almonds, toasted

Instructions

Lemon Honey Vinaigrette:

Combine all the ingredients in a 2-cup glass measuring cup. Using an immersion stick blender, blend on high until emulsified. Season to taste with salt and pepper then set aside.

Orzo Salad:

Combine the broth and garlic in a large saucepan and bring to a boil. Stir in the orzo and cook according to package directions. Drain the pasta but do not rinse. Remove the garlic cloves, mince, and return to the pasta. Transfer to a large bowl and add 2 tablespoons of the vinaigrette to the pasta. Stir to coat to prevent orzo from sticking and cool slightly. Refrigerate until chilled.

Just before serving, assemble salad by stirring in the roasted red peppers, kalamata olives, asparagus, basil, green onions, and vinaigrette into the completely cooled orzo. Season to taste with salt and pepper.

Sprinkle the feta crumbles and toasted almonds over the top and lightly toss to incorporate into the salad. Serve at chilled or at room temperature and store leftovers in the refrigerator.

Tip:

To toast almonds, place them in a dry skillet over medium heat and stir frequently until they become golden. Immediately remove from heat and cool the almonds on a plate to end the cooking instantly so that they don't overbrown.

Lemon Drop Martini Cupcakes

Makes 15 - 16

Ingredients

Cupcakes:
1-1/2 cups (7.5 ounces) all-purpose flour
1 teaspoon baking powder
1/2 teaspoon baking soda
1/2 teaspoon salt
1/2 cup (4 ounces) unsalted butter, melted
1-1/4 cups (9 ounces) granulated sugar
3 eggs, room temperature
2 teaspoons lemon zest
2 tablespoons fresh lemon juice
1/2 cup limoncello
2 tablespoons triple sec
1/2 cup prepared lemon curd (your favorite recipe or store-bought)

Frosting:
4 cups (18 ounces) confectioners' sugar
1 cup unsalted butter, room temperature
1/4 teaspoon salt

303

1 tablespoon limoncello
1 tablespoon triple sec
1 tablespoon fresh lemon juice
1/4 teaspoon lemon oil (optional)

Instructions

Cupcakes:

Preheat oven to 350 degrees (F). Line cupcake tins with paper liners.

In a medium bowl, whisk together the flour, baking powder, baking soda, and salt. Set aside.

Whisk together the lemon juice, lemon zest, limoncello, and triple sec. Set aside.

Using an electric mixer, beat together the melted butter and sugar. Beat in eggs, 1 at a time, until incorporated.

Alternating, add 1/3 of the flour mixture with 1/3 of the limoncello mixture, beating after each addition just until mixed.

Fill the cupcake liners 3/4 full.

Bake 15-18 minutes until a wooden skewer inserted into the center comes out mostly clean. A few moist crumbs clinging to the skewer is fine.

Remove the cupcake tins from the oven and cool for 5 minutes, then remove the cupcakes and cool completely on a wire rack.

When completely cool, using a 1/2-teaspoon measuring spoon, scoop out the middle of the cupcakes, about the size of an olive. Fill the hole with the prepared lemon curd.

Frosting:

Whisk together in a small bowl the lemon juice, limoncello, triple sec, and lemon oil, if using. Set aside.

In the bowl of a standing mixer, cream the butter until light and smooth. On low speed, mix in half the confectioners' sugar, a little at a time, until incorporated into the butter. Beat in half the limoncello mixture and alternate with the remaining confectioners' sugar and limoncello mixture.

Increase the mixer speed to medium high and beat until light and fluffy, about 5 minutes.

Using a large star tip, generously pipe the frosting in swooping swirls over the tops of the cupcakes to cover the lemon curd. If not serving immediately, refrigerate. Allow to come to room temperature for an hour before serving.

Lemon Drop Martini Cocktails

Serves 2

Ingredients
- 1 ounce vodka
- 1-1/2 ounces limoncello
- 1 ounce triple sec
- 3 tablespoons freshly squeezed lemon juice
- 1 tablespoon agave syrup (or simple syrup)

Instructions

Fill a cocktail shaker with ice and add the vodka, limoncello, triple sec, lemon juice, and agave syrup.

Vigorously shake until thoroughly chilled, then strain into two martini glasses.

To garnish, before filling the glasses, rub the skin of a lemon over the rim of the martini glasses, then dip the rim into sugar. Finish by wedging a thin slice of lemon on the rim.

Champagne Cupcakes with Champagne Buttercream

Makes 20-22

Ingredients

Cupcakes:

1 box white cake mix

1-1/4 cup champagne or prosecco

6 ounces 2% plain Greek yogurt (or substitute sour cream for richer cupcakes)

2 egg whites

1 teaspoon vanilla extract

Frosting:

1/2 cup (4 ounces) unsalted butter, room temperature

4 cups confectioners' sugar

1 teaspoon vanilla extract

4-5 tablespoons champagne or prosecco

Garnish Suggestions:

Edible gold or silver stars, sugar pearls, colorful sprinkles, fresh strawberries

To make pink champagne cupcakes:

Substitute pink champagne for regular champagne

6-8 drops pink gel food coloring

Instructions
Cupcakes:

Preheat oven to 350 degrees (F). Line a cupcake tin with paper liners.

Add the cake mix, champagne, Greek yogurt, egg whites, and vanilla extract to a mixing bowl. Beat on low speed for 30 seconds, then increase to medium speed and beat for 1 1/2 minutes.

Fill the prepared cupcake liners 2/3 full.

Bake 15-18 minutes until a wooden skewer inserted into the center comes out mostly clean. A few moist crumbs clinging to the skewer is fine.

Allow the cupcakes to cool for 5 minutes in the cupcake tin, then remove and cool completely on a wire rack.

Frosting:

In the bowl of a standing mixer, beat the butter until light and creamy, about 3 minutes. Mix in 2 cups of the confectioners' sugar then add in 4 tablespoons champagne and vanilla extract. Add the remaining confectioners' sugar and beat until light and creamy, about 4 minutes. If the frosting is too stiff, add additional champagne, 1 teaspoon at a time, until desired consistency is reached.

With a large star tip, pipe swirls of buttercream over completely cooled cupcakes. Garnish with sprinkles, edible stars or sugar pearls, or fresh strawberries.

To make pink champagne cupcakes:

Substitute pink champagne in place of the regular champagne where called for.

Start with 6 drops of pink gel food coloring and add to the cupcake batter at the same time as the champagne. Mix for 1 minute. Add additional pink food coloring until desired shade is obtained and mix for 1 additional minute. Do not overbeat the batter.

Pink Lemonade Cupcakes

Makes 16

When Emory receives a desperate last-minute request to bake cupcakes for a little girl's birthday swim party, she uses quick convenience products to add summertime flavor to a party favorite.

Ingredients
Cupcakes:
1 box white cake mix
3/4 cup pink lemonade frozen concentrate, thawed
5 tablespoons water
2 eggs
3 tablespoons vegetable oil
Several drops of pink gel food coloring (optional)
Frosting:
1/2 cup (4 ounces) unsalted butter, room temperature
4 cups confectioners' sugar
1/4 teaspoon sea salt
5-6 tablespoons pink lemonade frozen concentrate, thawed
A few drops of pink gel food coloring (optional)
Garnish Suggestions:

Lemon jelly candy slices
Pink-and-yellow-striped paper straws
Pink and yellow jimmies, or rainbow sprinkles

Instructions

Cupcakes:

Preheat oven to 350 degrees (F). Line a cupcake tin with paper liners.

Add the cake mix, defrosted lemonade concentrate, water, eggs, and vegetable oil to a mixing bowl. If using gel food coloring, add a few drops in. Beat on low speed for 30 seconds, then increase to medium speed and beat for 1 1/2 minutes.

Fill the prepared cupcake liners 2/3 full.

Bake 15–18 minutes until a wooden skewer inserted into the center comes out mostly clean. A few moist crumbs clinging to the skewer is fine.

Allow the cupcakes to cool for 5 minutes in the cupcake tin, then remove and cool completely on a wire rack.

Frosting:

In the bowl of a standing mixer, beat the butter until light and creamy, about 3 minutes. Mix in 2 cups of the confectioners' sugar then add in 5 tablespoons of the defrosted lemonade concentrate, the salt, and pink gel food coloring if using. Add the remaining confectioners' sugar and beat until light and creamy, about 4 minutes. If the frosting is too stiff, add additional defrosted lemonade concentrate, 1 teaspoon at a time, until desired consistency is reached.

With a large star tip, pipe swirls of buttercream over completely cooled cupcakes. Garnish with lemon jelly candy slices, decorative paper straws, or pink and yellow jimmies, or rainbow sprinkles.

Dedication

For my husband, Dan, who continually gives me the support and encouragement to create and believe in myself. I'm so grateful he doesn't mind my ramblings while I work out plot ideas.

And for my granddaughters, Jaidyn, who bravely fights the Rett Syndrome monster every day, and her sister, Emory, who is tenderhearted and caring of her sister. They both inspire me to find joy and laughter in the simple things in life. And lastly, to the newest member of our family, our sweet puppy, Missy! I'm so excited to have her share the pages with our grand-doggy, Piper.

Acknowledgments

It's true that it takes a village to create a book. I'd like to thank my husband, Dan, for reading and editing my manuscript several times. Not only that, he also toted my pink cupcake carrier to his golf group on numerous occasions to collect a wide variety of comments and critiques on my cupcake recipes from his peers. And to all my taste testers, thank you for your suggestions and encouragement with each tweak I did on the recipes.

I also have to give a shout-out to Lisa Kelley of Lisa Ks Book Reviews for coming up with the title. I am in awe of her quick wit and way with puns! Thank you to Janet Clause for beta reading, and to Dan for having an engineering mind to make suggestions to keep my books (mostly) logical.

I greatly appreciate the talents of cover designer Karen Phillips. She captured the spirit of my book and made it come alive with her version of my grand-doggie: Piper Doodle Dandy!

A special thanks to all of the lovely people who follow my blog, Cinnamon, Sugar, and a Little Bit of Murder, and share in my love for delicious food and mysteries! You inspire me to create stories and recipes to share with family and friends.

About the Author

Kim Davis lives in Southern California with her husband and new puppy, Missy. When she's not spending time with her granddaughters or chasing her energetic pup, she can be found either writing stories or working on her blog, Cinnamon, Sugar, and a Little Bit of Murder or in the kitchen baking up yummy treats. She has published the suspense novel, A GAME OF DECEIT, and the Cupcake Catering cozy mystery series. She also has had several children's articles published in Cricket, Nature Friend, Skipping Stones, and the Seed of Truth magazines. Kim Davis is a member of Mystery Writers of America and Sisters in Crime.

FRAMED AND FROSTED

Cupcake Catering Mystery Series Book 3

Cinnamon & Sugar Press

ISBN 978-0-9990688-6-1

ISBN 978-0-9990688-7-8

ISBN 979-8-9853601-5-8

Cover Design by Karen Phillips

Edited by Red Adept Editing

 Created with Vellum

Also by Kim Davis

The Cupcake Catering Mystery Series

SPRINKLES OF SUSPICION

One glass of cheap California chardonnay cost Emory Gosser Martinez her husband, her job, and her best friend. Unfortunately, that was only the beginning of her troubles.

Distraught after discovering the betrayal by her husband and best friend, Tori, cupcake caterer Emory Martinez allows her temper to flare. Several people witness her very public altercation with her ex-friend. To make matters worse, Tori exacts her revenge by posting a fake photo of Emory in a compromising situation, which goes viral on social media. When Tori is found murdered, all signs point to Emory being the prime suspect.

With the police investigation focused on gathering evidence to convict her, Emory must prove her innocence while whipping up batches of cupcakes and buttercream. Delving into the past of her murdered ex-friend, she finds other people had reasons to want Tori dead, including Emory's own husband. Can she find the killer, or will the clues sprinkled around the investigation point the police back to her?

Praise for Sprinkles of Suspicion

"…there is enough action, including a few surprises—plus baking—to maintain a steady momentum. The breezy book concludes with a collection of unique recipes. An engaging cozy best enjoyed with a plate of cookies." – *Kirkus Reviews*

"The mystery, characters, and mouth-watering recipes will charm readers until the very end." – *InD'tale Magazine, Crowned Heart Review*

"You are going to love this delicious new cozy mystery! Kim Davis pens characters who come to life and a story you won't want to put down, not to mention recipes that will make your mouth water. Don't miss this scrumptious treat! – *Paige Shelton*, New York Times Bestselling author of the Farmers' Market, Country Cooking School, Dangerous Type, Scottish Bookshop mysteries, and Alaska Wild suspense series

"Sparkling prose, a deliciously twisty plot, and a colorful cast of characters make this debut cozy a surefire winner!" – *Linda Reilly*, author of the Cat Lady Mysteries, Deep Fried Mysteries, and the Grilled Cheese Mystery series.

"A delightful new cozy with a cool California setting and an imminently likable heroine." *Ellen Byron*, Best Humorous Lefty Awards winner and author of the Agatha Award winning and USA Today Bestselling Cajun Country Mysteries, The Catering Hall Mysteries, and the Vintage Cookbook Mystery series.

"This story moves along at a great pace and doesn't lag anywhere. There is always something happening, drama, twists, and yes, cupcakes. So well-plotted, I was totally taken in by the entire story and flabbergasted when the real killer was revealed." *Escape With Dollycas Into A Good Book*

CAKE POPPED OFF

Cupcake caterer Emory Martinez is hosting a Halloween bash alongside her octogenarian employer, Tillie. With guests dressed in elaborate costumes, the band is rocking, the cocktails are flowing, and tempers are flaring when the hired Bavarian Barmaid tries to hook a rich, hapless husband. Except one of her targets happens to be Emory's brother-in-law, which bodes ill for his pregnant wife. When Emory tracks down the distraught barmaid, instead of finding the young woman in tears, she finds her dead. Can she explain to the new detective on the scene why the Bavarian Barmaid was murdered in Emory's bathtub with Emory's Poison Apple Cake Pops stuffed into her mouth?

With an angry pregnant sister to contend with, she promises to clear her brother-in-law's name. As Emory starts asking questions and tracking down the identity of the costumed guests, she finds reasons to suspect her brother-in-law has been hiding a guilty secret. Her search leads her to a web of blackmail and betrayal amongst the posh setting of the local country club crowd. Can Emory sift through the lies she's being told and find the killer? She'll need to step up her investigation before another victim is sent to the great pumpkin patch in the sky.

FRAMED AND FROSTED

Framed and Frosted, the third book in the Cupcake Catering Mystery series, finds cupcake caterer, Emory Martinez, working at a Laguna Beach society Fourth of July soiree, with her sister and their new employee, Sal. With a host who seems intent on accosting both catering employees and guests alike, things go from bad to worse when he accuses Sal of murdering his long-dead son.

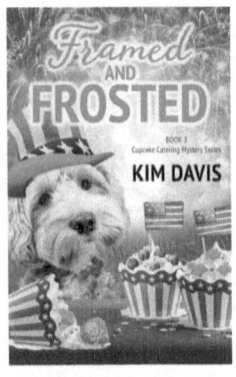

As the crescendo of exploding fireworks overhead becomes the backdrop for cupcakes and champagne, a deadly murder occurs. Can Sal and Emory explain why the cupcake the host ate, after shoving a trayful of buttercream-frosted cupcakes onto Sal, resulted in his death? Or will the detective and guests alike believe that Sal is a murderer? Emory and her octogenarian employer, Tillie, whip into action to find out who framed Sal after he was frosted by the victim.

FROSTED YULETIDE MURDER

Set against the holiday cheer of twinkling lights, costumed carolers, and a festive line of extravagantly decorated boats participating in the annual Christmas boat parade in Newport Beach, California, cupcake caterer Emory Martinez finds that the Grinch has crashed the party. Together with her sister Carrie, Emory is catering a delectable feast of holiday cupcakes and cookies aboard a luxury yacht for the new Mrs. Blair Villman and her guests.

Sparks fly when Carrie comes face-to-face with the hostess, who just happens to be Carrie's high school frenemy, and old grievances are dredged up. Adding fuel to the fire, Blair's stepson brings his mother, the former Mrs. Villman, to the party. Instead of celebrating holiday cheer, someone seems intent on channeling the Burgermeister Meisterburger and shutting down Blair's party permanently. When Emory finds a body aboard the yacht, she needs to discover who iced the victim before the Scrooge ruins not only her livelihood but her freedom as well.

BUTTERCREAM BETRAYAL

Intent on getting their two mischievous dogs under control, Emory Martinez and her half sister, Vannie, join a group dog training program led by Shawn Parker. With a graduation certificate just within grasp and a party to celebrate their hard-won achievements, what could go wrong? For starters, their two dogs have decided to wreak havoc during the party and tempers flare. It turns out not everyone is pleased with the dog trainer and his mother, the condo association president. Whispers of the mother and son's misbehavior, or worse, fly amongst the barks, whines, and growls of the canines.

When Emory finds the body of Mrs. Parker amidst an explosive situation, it becomes apparent there is more truth to the whispers instead of just gossip. Could one of the canine-loving participants be responsible? Or an outsider who hated her heavy-handed rule over the condo homeowners? Emory, Vannie, and octogenarian Tillie must sift through the clues to find out who has been betrayed and who has decided to take justice into their own hands.

MUDDLED MATRIMONIAL MURDER

With only two weeks left to finalize the arrangements for the nuptial ceremony and reception for Emory Martinez's best friend, Brad, and a Thanksgiving feast to plan, she has enough to keep her busy. But when Emory and Brad stumble across the body of his former stalker, with a wedding gift marble muddler lying next to the body, it soon becomes apparent someone is intent on framing the groom before vows can be exchanged.

How did the victim locate Brad, and how did she end up being murdered at the scene of the impending nuptials? Was someone so desperate to stop the wedding that they'd resort to murder? Or was she killed for revenge? As the countdown to the wedding speeds by, it'll take Emory and her family and friends pulling together to pick through the muddled clues to clear the groom's name.

A father's disappearance never solved, a mother's secret taken to the grave, a daughter deceived...

Kathryn Landry thinks her life is just about perfect. She is the owner of a successful interior designer business in Newport Beach, California, and she has an attentive, supportive husband. But her world comes crashing down when her husband, Neil Landry, vanishes without a trace... in a situation almost identical to the disappearance of her father twenty years before.

With her father's disappearance still a mystery, Kathryn is skeptical that the detective assigned to her case will be able to find her husband. Determined to uncover the truth, Kathryn is plunged into a world of politics, high-priced call girls and wealth. As she begins to search for her husband, a decades-old secret her mother took to the grave threatens to destroy all she holds dear. Caught up in a web of betrayals and deceit, and not knowing who to trust, Kathryn must find a way to survive as she discovers the past has a way of repeating itself.

Praise for A Game of Deceit

"...Davis deftly keeps readers as up in the air as Kathryn throughout this well-crafted tale. An impressive thriller by an author worth following." – Kirkus Reviews

"In A Game of Deceit author K. A. Davis offers up a taut, edge-of-your-seat suspense novel that will make you lock the doors, close the blinds, and wonder who you can truly trust. Don't miss this great debut from Ms. Davis." – Paige Shelton, New York Times Bestselling author of the Farmers' Market, Country Cooking School, Dangerous Type, and Scottish Bookshop mysteries.

"In A Game of Deceit, K. A. Davis has crafted an emotional suspense with a taut, satisfying ending that should delight any fan of Mary Higgins Clark." – Daryl Wood Gerber, Agatha Award-winning author of three cozy mystery series and the stand-alone suspense novels, GIRL ON THE RUN and DAY OF SECRETS.

"Sly, sexy and spellbinding, A Game of Deceit grabs you in the first chapter and doesn't let you go until its breathtaking finish. Debut author K. A. Davis creates a riveting tale of betrayal, family, suspense and murder." – Jenny Kales, author of The Callie's Kitchen Mystery series

"A Game of Deceit is a marvelous read packed with action, suspense and intrigue. I couldn't put it down!" – Catherine Bruns, USA Today Best Selling Author of the Cookies & Chance mysteries